PRAISE FOR LINDA V   VELS

It Had to Be You

"Windsor's style is fresh and pleasing.... This novel is perfect for Cl   who seek
entertainment that reflects and celebrates their value~ "
                        PUBL'

"*It Had to Be You* is a fun, rip-roa   ou
think. With likeable characters, co   quarely
in the heart, this delightful book i~
            KAREN BALL, best

"Linda Windsor sweeps you away w   memorable tropical setting and characters
who find love and God's guidance in the most unlikely places."
            ANNIE JONES, author of *The Snowbirds*

"*It Had to Be You* is a joy to read. This is the Caribbean cruise to end all. The characters
and situations are hilarious, poignant, and memorable... Linda Windsor is a real find.
Read one of her books and you're hooked!"
            THE BELLES AND BEAUX OF ROMANCE

"Linda Windsor is one of the best at writing romantic comedy and never fails to amuse.
It Had to Be You is one of her funniest yet. It's sure to refresh your spirit as well as give
you hours of pure pleasure and leave you feeling great."
            ROMANCE REVIEWS TODAY

Along Came Jones

"Every once in a while a novel comes along that's so much fun to read, it puts a smile
on readers' faces, no matter what the circumstances of their lives. *Along Came Jones* is
just such a book. Linda Windsor writes masterfully, spinning this tale with such charm
and vitality that readers can't help but be drawn into the story."
            CROSSWALK.COM

"In exquisite Linda Windsor form, *Along Came Jones* is a just-one-more-page-can't-put-
it-down fun read... Whether you are engaged by plot or characters, you won't be disappointed, because *Along Came Jones* is a rare instance where both are relevant and real."
            ROAD TO ROMANCE

"I absolutely loved this book. I hated to see it end. If DEA agents; nasty bad guys; a
sweet, vulnerable heroine; a wonderful, handsome hero; and a powerful message of
faith and encouragement are to your liking, run out and buy a copy of *Along Came
Jones*. You won't be disappointed."
            THE WORD ON ROMANCE

NOVELS BY LINDA WINDSOR

Along Came Jones
It Had to Be You
Paper Moon

THE FIRES OF GLEANNMARA SERIES:

Maire
Riona
Deirdre

It Had to be You

LINDA WINDSOR

Multnomah®Publishers *Sisters, Oregon*

IT *HAD* TO BE YOU
published by Multnomah Publishers, Inc.

© 2001 by Windsor Enterprises, Inc.
published in association with the literary agency of Ethan Ellenberg Agency
International Standard Book Number: 1-59052-565-5
Previously 1-57673-765-9

Cover images by Index Stock Imagery, Tony Stone Images and Aleta Rafton
Cover design by Christopher Gilbert/Uttley DouPonce DesignWorks

All Scripture quotations are from:
The Amplified Bible
© 1965, 1987 by Zondervan Publishing House.
The Amplified New Testament © 1958, 1987 by the Lockman Foundation.

Multnomah is a trademark of Multnomah Publishers, Inc.,
and is registered in the U.S. Patent and Trademark Office.

The colophon is a trademark of Multnomah Publishers, Inc.

Printed in the United States of America
ALL RIGHTS RESERVED

For information:
MULTNOMAH PUBLISHERS, INC.
POST OFFICE BOX 1720
SISTERS, OREGON 97759

Library of Congress Cataloging-in-Publication Data

Windsor, Linda.
    It had to be you / by Linda Windsor.
        p. cm.
    ISBN 1-59052-565-5
    ISBN 1-57673-765-9 (pbk.)
    1. Cruise ships—Fiction. 2. Cowboys—Fiction. I. Title.
    PS3573.I519 I8 2001
    813'.54—dc21

                                                2001000993

        05 06 07 08 09—10 9 8 7 6 5 4 3

To my traveling companions, who shared many of the
mishaps and mayhem in the following pages:
Mom, Jeff and Kelly, Edgar and Signe, Cynthia,
and the gals from the Hurricane Gloria cruise—
no wonder the price was so cheap.
But mostly, to the merciful Lord and Savior,
who saw each of us through the calamities
that we might live to tell the tales.

*"Love bears up under anything
and everything that comes,
is ever ready to believe the
best of every person."*

1 CORINTHIANS 13:7

One

*E*XCUSE ME, SIR, are you finished with your drink?"

Rancher Dan Jarrett handed the pretty stewardess the empty cup along with a generous tip. "Thanks, I appreciated the suggestion on the lemon."

The young woman smiled and dropped the empty cup into the trash bag. Dan could imagine she was thinking he was a hick from cattle country. It grated him to pay for water in a bottle to start with, but the tap water in these public places would gag a catfish. When the name-brand water tasted like the plastic it was bottled in to boot, he'd made the mistake of making a face. Instantly, the flight attendant had supplied him with a lemon slice to improve it.

"You're welcome, Mr. Jarrett. Enjoy your trip in the Caribbean paradise. Wish I was going."

He swallowed the better-you-than-me reply that popped into his mind and mustered a regretful smile as she moved on to the hostess station. Over the speaker, one of her coworkers announced from the open doorway that the passengers could now deplane.

Paradise… He slumped down in the seat as the plane came to life with activity. Paradise was the *last* place this cowboy wanted to be. Like the plane, the water, and his new jeans, it was going to be miserable.

He drew in his elbow as the passengers, who'd shared his flight from Houston to Miami, began threading their way off the plane through the narrow aisle next to his seat. They looked like a gaily bedecked herd of cattle. Uneasy in crowds, Dan waited, but not with the lazy patience the worn Stetson pulled down over his face implied. Unlike his clearly happy, vacation-bound fellow travelers, he felt he was on his way to one very hot place—and he didn't mean the series of Caribbean ports listed on the brochure.

The cruise his family booked was not his idea of how to spend a holiday, but then he was for skipping Thanksgiving altogether this year. As if that would change the way his life had suddenly been thrown into anarchy by his widowed mother's sudden marriage. It was bad enough his new stepfather was so desperate for a woman that he'd signed on the cruise his mother had taken with her seniors group a few months ago as a *social host,* but now…

Well, *now* he was changing tradition.

Besides, Dan's mom just hadn't been herself since this whirlwind romance. She'd moved out of the family home, dispersing the household she'd kept all those years to Dan and his sister as if it meant nothing to her. Love at first sight. Love boats. *Hah!* She was totally bamboozled, like some love-struck schoolgirl.

Dan shifted his feet beneath the plane seat in front of him, spurred by a twinge of guilt. If he'd gone on the first cruise with his mom as she'd asked him to, this wouldn't have happened. But a trip with the Sunshine Club seemed ideal for her, not him. Besides, how much trouble could a bunch of church ladies get into playing bridge on a cruise ship?

Dan clenched his teeth. How much trouble? Obviously a whole lot more than he'd imagined. And now this senior lothario was spending mom's savings right and left, and there wasn't a blessed thing Dan could do about it—at least until the investigation he'd initiated was complete.

To date, all Dan knew was that Meyers was using his mother's credit cards instead of his own. The investigators confirmed that in their first report—the one Dan had waited for, forcing him to delay his departure with the family and catch a later flight. Meyers' bad credit rating only increased the young man's certainty that his mother had made a terrible mistake and was going to pay dearly...with something far more important than her money.

With her heart.

"Oh my gosh!"

Instinctively, Daniel cringed as his hat flew to the floor, knocked askew by a giant straw bag and snapping him back to the deplaning frenzy of the present.

"I'm sorry I woke you."

"No problem, ma'am," Dan drawled. Sleep was the last thing he'd been able to do of late. He cocked his head to examine the source of the ruckus.

A slight, fair-haired young woman stared at him with wide-eyed dismay. She struggled with a hat as wide brimmed as his Stetson. Her more feminine version had a large sunflower attached to a checkered band and was perched atop a short, no muss, no fuss hairdo. Like her matching bag, it looked too big for her. Another tourist ready to part with good money.

"I need four arms." She laughed, trying to hoist the strap of her bag up to a slim shoulder with the hand carrying a cosmetic case. In the process, she nearly knocked the sunglasses off the gentleman behind her. His evasive jerk backwards had a domino effect on the line behind him.

Four arms! Daniel had to agree, but not for the reason she made the remark. For a female, traveling alone was the perfect prey for some no-good slimeball with less-than-chivalrous intentions. In addition to the woman's purse and carry-on, she was hauling a small Styrofoam cooler, which squeaked and creaked as she tried to balance it between her body and one of the seats. It was sealed with enough duct tape to finish up the air and heating system in the house he was modernizing.

No doubt about it. This woman was a perfect target for a pick-pocket or purse-snatcher.

"Here, let me help."

Carefully he raised the carry-on's strap back to her shoulder. For a moment, he was tempted to rip off a piece of duct tape and secure it, but he refrained. It would take more than tape to hold this loony bird together. His watch snagged on the material of her knit top as he drew his hand back.

"Oh, m'gosh!" The young woman's face turned scarlet as he inadvertently bared a smooth, golden-tanned shoulder.

"No problem. I can get it."

Daniel grimaced as he untangled the yarn from the pin on his watchband. Self-conscious, he smoothed the material out as he'd seen his sister do under similar circumstances.

"I don't think it'll show."

Instead of moving, the woman continued to stare at him, her lips pursed as if to speak. Daniel wondered if he should know her but quickly dismissed the notion. He'd never seen her in his life. He'd have remembered blue eyes like that. They were the color of a spring sky, the invigorating kind that made humans and animals alike want to kick up their heels and frolic after a long winter's seclusion.

"You best get going, miss, before the line runs you over." His gaze darted to the impatient passengers shuffling behind her.

"Oh yeah…sorry." With a comic grin that reminded him of Goldie Hawn, she shifted the cooler in her arms and moved to the front of the plane, squeaking like chalk on slate all the way. Fortunately for them, the passengers in the front seats had already disembarked. Shaking his head, Daniel stood and retrieved a duffel bag from the overhead compartment.

That gal needs a keeper. But Dan had his hands full of his own problems right now.

It suited him to be the last one off. He hated being rushed and was in no hurry to get in that pert walking disaster's way. As it was, he didn't even have to search for his duffel bag. It was the only one left in the overhead compartment. He hauled it down and onto shoulders broadened by hard work. The role of gentleman squire didn't suit his personality.

"Have a nice time on your cruise," the stewardess told him as he passed through the exit. "And don't forget the lemon slices."

"Sure thing. Appreciate it."

He forced a smile back, preoccupied with his quandary rather than flirtation. The thought of his mother being hurt and deceived churned in his chest till it hurt. Just let anyone mess with *his* loved ones, and he'd make a junkyard dog look like a friendly pup.

Tugging the brim of his Stetson down, he turned and strode up the long, carpeted ramp to the terminal, where he was supposed to meet a representative of the cruise line. He sure hoped his luggage made it aboard the ship like Sis said it would. It was bad enough going on this jaunt at all, but having to hold back the suspicions he had about Meyers—at least until they were confirmed—was trying his patience to the limit.

Since he did have to wait, he'd just as soon do it with a change of clothes. Unlike these flower-shirted tourists, he worked out in the sun every day—being cooped up on a ship in the middle of the tropics was the *last* place he wanted to pay hard-earned money to go.

"Aunt Sunny!"

"Hey, Jason."

Sunny Elders stood on tiptoe next to her haphazard hill of possessions and waved excitedly at her approaching nine-year-old nephew, knocking the large sunflower on her hat askew in the process. Keeping up with the hat was becoming a full-time occupation, but if she'd put it in her case it would have come out like a giant straw tortilla. As she adjusted it, she spied her niece Allison, who was a far more demure sixteen, following in her brother's wake.

"Hi, Allis—"

Before Sunny could finish her niece's name, Jason tackled her around the waist in a bear hug and tried to lift her off the floor with a macho show of strength.

"My, but you're getting to be such a man."

Rocked by her nephew's enthusiasm, Sunny reached too late to steady her hat. She barely kept her footing. "Now, don't hurt your back before we even get to the ship."

Oh yes, she was definitely going to have a good time with these two…if she survived Jason's roughhousing. He was getting too big for Sunny to handle. Not that Sunny really minded. She enjoyed his boisterous energy. In fact, her sister, Melinda, always teased that she acted like she was one of the kids, rather than their aunt.

Turning to fetch the runaway hat, Sunny came face to face with the tall and lanky cowboy she'd whacked on the head earlier. Clearly a bit wary of her, he silently picked up the hat and handed it over.

"Thank you *again*." The scorch of embarrassment fired her cheeks. "At least I have reinforcements to help me now."

Grinning like the Cheshire cat from Alice's wonderland, she motioned to Jason and Allison to move out. It wasn't as if she hadn't met handsome men before, and heaven knew, having been born and raised outside of Houston, she'd heard her share of Texas drawls. So why was she staring at the man as if he'd grown horns? Funny. She needed to think of something funny to say instead of standing on her tongue.

"Hey, *you're* going with us."

Jason's exclamation diverted the cowboy's gaze from her face. "What?"

"You're going with us." Jason repeated, fingering the tag on the man's duffel bag. "We're all going on the *Love Ahoy*." The freckled boy looked beyond Daniel with a frown. "Got any kids my age?"

"No."

Sensing more than seeing the stranger's irritation, Sunny handed Jason the cooler. "I'm sure there'll be others your age on the ship. Holiday cruises are great for whole families."

"Well, *all* my friends are staying home and having a party on Saturday, which *I* can't go to because of family," Allison complained, snatching up the cosmetic case.

Sunny pulled her niece under her arm, trying to ignore the retreating figure of the stiffly polite cowboy in the crowd ahead. "Be grateful for your family, Alli," she told the girl fiercely. "They're too precious to take for granted."

A cloud lighted briefly on Sunny's heart. She prayed Alli would not know the terrible loss Sunny and Melinda were facing. Had been facing for years. She supposed it was youth that allowed her niece to take the deaths in stride and move on so quickly. Allison was so wrapped up in figuring out who she was in the midst of puberty's changes that little else held her attention too long—unlike her mother, Melinda.

Shaking off the gloom, Sunny smiled. "I have a wonderful sister, a gorgeous brother-in-law, a beautiful niece, and an ornery nephew to spend the holidays with. What more could I ask?" Sunny squeezed her niece's slim shoulders, determined to focus on the upside of this trip, rather than the down. She hoped Melinda and Alan would do the same. "We are going to have *such* a good time."

"All passengers for the Love Ahoy, *please follow me. Stay together."*

The amplified voice of the cruise representative drew the prospective passengers together in a straggling line behind the sign he held high over his head. It was emblazoned with the name of the cruise line.

"You heard the man." Sunny glanced around. "By the way, where are your mom and dad?"

At first Melinda had said that she didn't feel like going, but finally agreed that she and Alan needed this trip. Toward the end of her parents' illness and after, Melinda had drawn into a shell, away from Alan. It was telling on their marriage. Sunny had volunteered to watch over the kids on the cruise so Melinda and Alan would have some time together without distraction to work things out.

"At the bus. They said we could meet your plane and come with you." Allison spoke with pained indifference, and Sunny grinned. Life was *such* a bore at the girl's ripe old age. At least the kids seemed to be clueless to the undercurrents between their parents.

To the unknowing eye, the entire trip was a waste of time for her niece, but Sunny knew Allison was as excited as the energetic boy who raced ahead of them through a group of seniors. According to Melinda, Allison had discussed *in detail* over the phone with all her friends every outfit she'd packed, while visions of exotic places and romance danced behind her ho-hum demeanor.

The tourist menagerie was made up of men in bright floral shirts and women in comfortable knit ensembles, some of which were a nautical red, white, and blue, and some dashed with glitter or studded with silver or gold. Sunny's hat was one among many bobbing along in the hubbub.

"This looks like it's going to be a real blast." Allison had not missed the significant show of white- and gray-haired individuals. "I'll bet the highlight of the day is bingo."

"Only if the boys who pass out the cards are cute." Sunny gave her niece a wink. "I'll bet it will be all I can do to beat the young men away with a stick when they see you."

"Aunt Sunny." Allison produced a metallic smile, forgetting her braces for a moment and blushing like the schoolgirl she was.

"Although I wouldn't mind keeping one or two for myself."

"Aunt Sunny, puh-*leeze*."

"After all, I should get something for rooming with you guys so your mom and dad can have some private time."

"You're awful."

"And I've always taught you to share."

"You're crazy."

Sunny stopped in her tracks as if shot. "I *beg* your pardon?" she said in her most offended voice.

Allison burst into giggles. "Come on, Aunt Sunny. We're going to be late."

Sunny and her charges were the last to get on the long, silver bus exhaling diesel fumes in the parking lot. Her brother-in-law, Alan, waved at her as she followed Allison through the narrow passage between the rows of double seats filled with passengers of all ages. Melinda smiled, but Sunny could tell it was a forced one.

Thank the Lord Melinda had agreed to see a doctor who

belonged to their church before she left. At least now the circles under her eyes from lack of sleep were starting to fade. Sunny had jumped at the chance to suggest Melinda see the doctor when her sister complained about them and how hard it was to sleep through the night.

He'd put her on medication to help her through this stress-related depression, but it took time to work. Sunny knew the prescription wasn't a cure all, but it would help until Melinda learned new ways to handle her depression. Of course, there was always the chance that Melinda was chemically burned out as well, that she'd need to take her medication indefinitely, much like a diabetic was forced to take insulin. But if that were the case, they'd deal with it. Together.

"Nice flight?" Melinda asked.

"Great." Unless one counted the sourpuss she'd be*hatted*. "Alan, are you keeping your wife straight?"

"Trying," her brother-in-law chuckled. "Good to see you."

Sunny stopped to hug her sister and admire a baby traveling with its parents when the driver announced that everyone had to be seated before the bus would start.

"I didn't think you were going to make it." Melinda called after her as Sunny hurried to find an empty seat.

"It's Allison's fault. She was trying to pick up guys in the terminal."

"Was not!" Allison dropped into the spare seat next to her brother. "But Aunt Sunny was flirting with a cowboy."

"Was not!" Sunny shot over her shoulder. Beneath her feet, the floor of the bus rumbled as if it were impatient to be off. "When I flirt with a cowboy, you'll *know* I'm flirting."

Contrary to what the driver said, the bus started before she sat down. She'd no more than spotted an empty place when the vehicle lurched forward, throwing Sunny into the seat. On her way down, she glimpsed a long, denim-clad leg curled in a lazy sprawl. Sunflower hat clashed with Stetson, both knocked askew. Sunny scrambled in an attempt to get out of the startled man's lap, accompanied by the echoes of concern and amusement surrounding them.

"*You* again." The disgruntled cowpoke folded his legs in front of him. He shifted and wedged his knees against the back of the next seat to make room for her. Annoyance all but erased his drawl.

"Yep, it's me…the *ma'am,*" she mimicked, venturing a toothy grimace. "Sorry I held everyone up. I had to get my things put under the bus and—"

"I shouldn't have been sprawled over two seats. My fault."

By golly, he almost smiled. A sensation akin to striking her crazy bone rushed through Sunny, the same jolt she'd felt when he'd smoothed the snag of her blouse over her shoulder. Disconcerted, Sunny forced a grin to her suddenly stiff features.

"And I *wasn't* flirting. If I was flirting, you'd know it."

"Say what?" The man clearly had no idea what she was talking about. He'd been in a world of his own—until she fell on him.

"My niece just accused me of flirting with you—" a tinge of embarrassed heat was creeping up her neck—"and I told her that if I'd been flirting with you, everyone would know it."

The more she said, the more ridiculous she sounded.

The corner of the man's mouth twitched, while the sunlight did a little dance in his eyes. They were brown…no, more than that. Flecks of amber gave them an added warmth. She supposed the color befitted the slight reddish cast of his dark brown hair.

"Oh, how's that?"

She felt like hiding beneath her seat. Instead, she volleyed back without hesitation. "I'd grab you, throw you down, and give you a kiss." After retrieving her hat from the floor, she leaned against the seat. "Yes, sir—" she tugged it John Wayne fashion over her fore-head, so that she had to look down her nose to see—"when I mean business, pardner, you'll know it."

"Hey, there, cowboy—" one of the seniors sitting behind them teased, tossing Daniel's runaway hat back into his lap—"I think you've met your match."

Buoyed by the laughter surrounding them, Sunny raised the brim of her straw bonnet and cut Daniel a sharp look. "You married?"

"Nope."

"Me, neither." She leaned over and lowered her voice. "Them younguns up there belong to my sister, but she lends 'em out every once in a while, kinda like watchdogs. They don't bite, mind you, but they do make a lot of noise."

This time he laughed, right along with the half dozen or so couples who'd been eavesdropping. Outrageous always worked when she was backed into a corner.

"Lady, you are a real piece of work."

Sunny nodded solemnly, her lips twitching with the urge to join in. "Yep, an' I aim to keep it thataway."

Looping her thumbs in the belt of her slacks, she sank against the seat in retreat. Her face was probably as red as her knit tank top, now that she'd managed to make a total fool of herself in front of a complete stranger. She couldn't help it. That's just the way she was when she was on edge—and there was something about this guy that made her feel as though she were on the brink of a very large leap...or fall.

Two

AFTER A WEAVING TRIP through Miami traffic, past tall glass buildings on streets interspersed with little concrete islands and sprouting palms, the bus maneuvered over a bridge to the harbor. Sunny idly listened to the chatter of the tourists. Everyone was caught up in the thrill of being on the way to the islands on a luxury liner. The seniors' group was from the northeast, their speech as distinguishable as that of another group from the Carolinas. For flavor there was a Hibernian tour with an unmistakable Irish lilt to their voices as they teased each other over some mischief.

Loving people-watching and, in this case, listening, Sunny remained beneath her straw-brimmed retreat until she heard Jason's excited, "Look, Mom! Dad! There's our ship. That's gotta be it."

Sunny's companion, who was still nameless of his own quiet accord, stared out the tinted window at the three large liners docked along the canal. His was the rugged jawline of one of those poster cowhands, tanned, but neatly shaven. But it was what she glimpsed in his eyes that riveted Sunny's attention. Instead of excitement, his eyes smacked of dread. No stranger to that monster, she felt a ridiculous urge to put a comforting hand on his arm, but held back. He'd made it clear he was a loner.

She slung her bag onto her shoulder. Was that by choice, or was his long, tall, lone wolf bit a charade?

You should know. Facades are your specialty...

She shrugged the inner comment away. Didn't matter. It was his business, not hers. Besides, everyone had a cloud of some sort, she supposed. Her family might be eating Thanksgiving turkey in a different setting, but her mom and dad would still be missed.

As she had time and again since losing her parents, Sunny rallied stubbornly. No point in concentrating on the pain. She needed to focus on the blessings they had, exactly as the plaque on Mom's kitchen wall suggested, how happiness was learning to be content with what one had. Their parents were not with them, but they weren't suffering. They were with God, pain free. One had not been left behind to suffer alone for very long. They were together. And those left behind had each other.

This was a time for healing, not for sorrow. Alan's idea to spend the holiday on a cruise to the Caribbean was a good prescription for all of them—and hopefully for his troubled marriage as well.

He was such a dear and so much in love with his wife that he was willing to leave his accounting business at one of its busiest times for her sake. At first, Melinda flatly refused, swearing she couldn't possibly enjoy herself, feeling as worn and torn as she did.

"It isn't healthy to dwell on the past," Sunny told Melinda, eager to help the situation in any way she could. "Remember what happened to Lot's wife."

This actually got Melinda to chuckle, for it was her sister who'd told Sunny how one of the kids in the Sunday school class had his own fractured version of the classic Scripture. "I know, a pillar of salt by day and a ball of fire by night." Melinda paused a soul-searching moment and then nodded. "Although I imagine Alan wouldn't mind the last part," she added, some of that familiar Elder humor surfacing.

The bus braked, drawing Sunny back to the present. People on both sides of the bus rose from their seats to snap pictures as the vehicle turned into a palmlined drive. Even Melinda had snagged Alan's camera, still hanging about his neck, to snap a picture of the liner commanding the entire dock area. She laughed as he feigned choking and sank back down beside him, leaning closer.

Yes, Lord! This was to be a healing cruise—just what the nurse and accountant ordered. God was opening new doors already.

Sunny glanced at her companion, slumped against his seat, hat tipped over his face. Maybe this cruise would even heal whatever boil *he* was sitting on. She resisted the urge to wedge the hat down to his ears out of sheer mischief and fished her sunglasses from the brim of her sunflower hat instead. He already thought she was from another planet. No sense in confirming it.

The bus drifted to a stop under a modern, metallic portico protruding from a large, white stone building. A pair of cruise representatives, dressed in the same crisp uniform as the person who'd fetched the passengers from the airport, waited outside for the bus to unload. One rep spoke into a walkie-talkie and laughed at a crackling reply before fastening it to his belt. The other waved the passengers off the bus like a child anxiously awaiting the arrival of loved ones. Sunny had to give the employees credit—they certainly seemed to enjoy their jobs.

After waiting for the bus to clear ahead of her, Sunny stepped into the aisle. Glancing back at her unsolicited travel partner, she asked him if this was his stop, just in case he really was asleep under that wide brim.

"I'm in no hurry." He straightened a little so that he could see what was going on. "Thanks just the same, ma'am."

With a shrug, Sunny hurried to close the gap in the line. Yep, she'd scared the living daylights out of the poor soul, she thought, not without some humor. He seemed to be one of those folks who had two speeds...slow and stop, while hers were fast and faster. Still, he was cute, in a slouch hat, cowpoke kind of way.

As she stepped into the smothering Miami heat, the bright sun overhead made her wince despite the protection of her hat and sunglasses. Thankfully, the terminal was air-conditioned, which helped keep people cool as they moved at a snail's pace through the line to get their tickets processed. Sunny managed to distract the kids while Melinda and Alan braved the long columns. After snacks and drinks, courtesy of the cruise line, and a trip to the bathroom, the family was finally cleared for boarding. They marched in order toward the canopied entrance to the boarding ramp, Alan at the lead, Sunny bringing up the rear guard with the noisy cooler.

The photographer waiting for each group embarking snapped a picture of Melinda's family before Sunny could catch up with them. Prepared to have a solo shot done, she gave her sunniest smile when the photographer's assistant pulled someone behind her into the setting and the camera flashed. Startled and blinded like a deer in someone's headlights, Sunny squeezed the cooler even tighter. To her dismay, she heard a loud *crack* and suddenly, despite her duct-tape wrap, its contents spilled everywhere.

Red, green, yellow, and orange plastic juice bottles scattered amid the half melted ice cubes crunching around her feet as she scurried to catch them. She tried to scoop them back into the two halves of the split cooler, all the while apologizing frantically to everyone within earshot. The cruise staff, apparently accustomed to such catastrophes, was quick to help her contain the mess. As she straightened, the front of her blouse and the knees of her khaki slacks soaked in ice water, she turned to those being held up behind her and found herself once again facing the stoic cowboy she'd bothered on the airplane and the bus.

"I am *so* sorry," she managed, mortified. "I always carry the kids' favorite juices and—"

"The Styrofoam burst, I know," he assured her with a scant measure of tolerance. "I saw."

"You must think I'm such a klutz."

"Oh *no*." He actually said it with a straight face.

"Excuse me, Mr. and Mrs..." A camera assistant turned the tag on the cowboy's carry-on. "Jarrett," she continued in her bounciest British accent, "but could you keep the line moving? I'll have the juices sent to your cabin."

Sunny turned, shaking her head. "Oh, you don't understand, we're not—"

Before she could finish, her unsolicited companion grabbed her arm and escorted her past the camera and onto the ramp.

"Come along, *dear,* or we're going to miss the boat."

For once, Sunny was at a loss for words.

The moment Melinda and her family gathered around her on the Biscayne deck, the nameless cowpoke was gone, belying her earlier opinion regarding his snail-like speed. Sunny couldn't say she blamed him. If someone had smacked her in the head, fallen in her lap, and spilled a cooler of drinks on her feet, she'd have run, too.

"What happened?"

"The cooler broke. Now *I'm* iced and the drinks I brought for the kids...well, the staff said they'd deliver them to the cabin." Sunny glanced at the mirrored stairwell, onto which some passengers were filtering from the ramp. Others joined flows to the right and left of the lobby down long, narrow corridors lined with cabins and little passages on both sides leading to the plusher cabins on the outside of the ship.

Alan, C.P.A. organizational instincts kicking in, pointed to a small map of the ship mounted on the stairwell wall. "You guys are one deck up on the Atlantic and to the stern, which is blue carpet for those who don't know stern from bow. Melinda and I are on the Sun deck, forward." He slipped his arm around his wife's waist. It would be easy to be jealous of the love shared between them, but Sunny was glad Melinda had a wonderful guy like Alan.

"Great," she teased. "You guys get the Sun deck while the kids and I play Ben Hur in the bilge of the ship."

"That's what we get for booking so close to the sailing," Melinda quipped, with more sauce than Sunny had seen in a long time.

"Actually, you were upgraded from the bowels. We booked you one deck lower. But look at it this way, Sun," Alan pointed out, pragmatic to the bone. The poor soul never knew how to take her jokes. "You'll have less motion to deal with than we will."

"If my life were any more motionless, I'd be a statue," Sunny answered in kind.

"This from an ER nurse!" Melinda shook her head. "You see more activity and excitement in a day than some people see in a lifetime."

"I was speaking of men." Turning, she took a playful swipe at Alan's thick, curly blond hair. "And gift horses," she added for his benefit. "But fear not, Old Paint, I was taught never to look a gift horse in the mouth." With a mischievous pinch of his chin, she turned toward her niece and nephew. "Come on, kids. This way."

"Forward or aft?" Jason questioned with a mock salute.

"Yes, I believe so," Sunny replied, straight-faced. It took a moment for Jason to register she was playing with his mind.

"Aunt Sunny," the boy responded with a grand show of

patience wearing thin. He tapped his foot.

Sunny shrugged in surrender. "Okay, I guess I have to act my age sometime. Up one, then go blue. Blue is the stern half, red the bow."

Squaring her hat, sunflower to the forward, Sunny started up the steps, leaving Alan and Melinda to head for the stern elevators. After walking through a maze of passages, they found their cabin door in an offshoot of the main corridor.

It was crowded with suitcases piled against both side walls. Upon selecting their luggage from the assortment, Jason preceded them into what was to be their quarters for the next seven days. By the time all three and their suitcases were inside, there was scarcely room to move.

"Good thing we packed light." First Sunny eyed the bunks stacked on one side of the narrow room and then the convertible sofa on the other. "I claim the sofa. Jason, you take the high road."

"Man, *I* wanted the sofa," her nephew complained.

Sunny raised a warning finger. "Don't make me act my age."

Not the least intimidated, Jason sighed. "Oh yeah, I forgot. It's hard to remember around you sometimes."

Sunny made a face. "Wiseacre."

With a toss, the boy landed his duffel bag on the top berth and climbed up the ladder at the foot. "I'm done," he announced, unzipping the bag.

That left space for Allison to put her suitcase, a large Pullman similar to Sunny's, on her bunk to unpack. Now Sunny could move. Talk about tight quarters.

"You go on and unpack, Alli. I'll do mine later in whatever drawers or closet space is left."

"I don't know how you tolerate him," Allison observed, clearly considering herself above the two of them.

"Like you're so cool, Miss Dufus," Jason derided.

Sunny intervened. "Truce. There's not enough room in here to wage even a verbal war." She opened the door at the foot of the bunks expecting a closet, but to her surprise, she found another room. It wasn't much larger than their cabin, but it contained twin beds, a dresser, and bath. Was it a part of their cabin?

"My locker at school is this big," Allison complained behind her. She held open the door of the actual closet, utter disdain on her young face.

No, this couldn't be a suite, Sunny thought, recalling the microscopic layout on the brochure Melinda had shown her. Her sister's purple-shaded rectangle had a balcony and queen bed, while the one Sunny and the kids were assigned was anemic pink for low budget and no window. Unless the upgrade Alan mentioned included an adjoining compartment big enough that one didn't have to step outside to turn around.

"I get that room if no one else takes it," Jason announced from his lofty perch.

"I don't think so, *amigo.*" Sunny stepped back into their own small cubicle and, common sense triumphing over wishful thinking, pulled the door to behind her. "It's an adjoining room, but we don't get it unless we pay for it, *comprendez?*"

"Bummer."

Jason rolled on his back and aimed a remote control at the small television mounted on the wall over Sunny's sofa bunk. He looked like his dad, with his curly blond hair and freckles, while Allison had Melinda's dark brown hair, blue eyes, and, to the girl's dismay, her father's freckles as well. Leaning against the adjoining door, Sunny picked up the shipboard announcements left by the steward on the small chest of drawers by the bathroom and scanned them hurriedly.

"There's a briefing on the cruise an hour after lunch. Anyone game to attend it with me?"

"Naw, I'm gonna watch TV."

"And miss lunch?" Sunny stared at her nephew, a dubious lift to her brow.

"Food? Yeah, right. Let's go."

"You are going to *eat* after stuffing down all those snacks?" Allison asked with the melodramatic talent natural to her age. Sometimes Sunny called her Sara Heartburn when she got off on some overdone tizzy.

"I ain't watchin' my figure to catch some poor unsuspecting guy."

"I'm *not*," Sunny corrected her nephew. *"Ain't* is a no-no."

"Neither am I," Allison shot back at Jason smugly.

"Good thing, 'cause you ain't got a figure." Her brother cackled with glee and danced beyond the sisterly swat she gave him.

Sunny grabbed the boy by a handful of hair and shook him playfully.

"Now look, Wart," she warned in a sinister tone. "Just remember, you're outnumbered two to one. You leave the seat down in the john and no more cracks about our love lives, got it?"

Jason grinned like the imp he was, revealing a gap where a tooth had been. "Got it. Now can I go see what Mom's cabin looks like?"

"Sure you know the number?"

The boy held up his palm, where both cabin numbers were written in black. "Indelible ink. No problem."

"Especially since he doesn't bathe."

"Then get outta here," Sunny growled playfully, as Jason exchanged the verbal for a physical swipe at his sister, who dodged it with practiced ease.

Sunny started for the small bathroom done in pink and black tile, reminiscent of the fifties, and paused as she heard Jason shout from the open door. "Holy smokes, look at this!"

There, literally filling the passageway, were a dozen balloons emblazoned with *Bon Voyage* and other cheerful send-offs. A rain of curling ribbons cascaded from each of the floating hearts and circles, which were anchored to a large black-and-tan trimmed Pullman similar to Sunny's.

"They're for you, Aunt Sunny."

Sunny maneuvered past Allison to take the card Jason handed to her, when she spied a pair of occupied boots standing next to the case. Pushing the wall of balloons down one at a time, she soon uncovered a Stetson-crowned face, which accompanied a long-limbed body in the boots on the other side of the buoyant latex and Mylar wall.

"I should have known," an increasingly familiar voice sighed.

It was him. No number of balloons could hide that hat.

"Well, hello," Sunny managed, knocking aside another balloon. Was this guy a harbinger of embarrassing moments or what? He was always around when she felt foolish. "Are these from you?"

"Not hardly, ma'am."

If ever a soul looked like the world was falling in on him, it was this guy. To say the least, he was less than enthused that he was to share the companionway with her. At the moment, Sunny didn't blame him. Where on earth were they going to put these balloons?

"I'm *trying* to get to my cabin," he said, glancing down at the handle of the case where the balloons were tied.

Sunny immediately started to untie the knot securing them. "Of course you are. These are from some friends."

"The ER staff, Aunt Sunny," Jason said, flipping over the card.

"ER as in *emergency* room?"

The skepticism in the stranger's voice almost made Sunny giggle. He was not the first to wonder how such a walking klutz managed in that setting. Truth was, she was a picture of professionalism there. It was everywhere else that her life ran riot.

"That's right, I'm a nurse…even have the diplomas and awards to prove it." The knot simply would not come undone. "Sunny Elders is the name. Nursing's my game."

"Daniel Jarrett," he responded. "Here, let me get that."

Sunny backed away as Daniel Jarrett grasped the balloon ribbon with strong, tanned fingers and snapped it with a macho grimace. Freed, the balloons rose to cling to the low ceiling overhead. Ducking low, he dragged a suitcase behind him and slipped through the door into his cabin. At its closing click, Allison snickered in adolescent excitement.

"Ooh, Aunt Sunny, I can't believe *he's* our neighbor!"

Sunny's attention instantly shifted from the wide expanse of balloons she was trying to gather through the narrow doorway to that of the adjoining passage. She hadn't seen a lock on the door. Not that she thought the man was an ax murderer or anything. In fact, he was probably glad the lock was on his side after all the nuisance she'd been to him in the few short hours of their acquaintance. If anything, their meeting so far had been a bust.

As though to agree, one of the balloons exploded behind her.

On the other side of the wall, Daniel Jarrett heard what could only be a bursting balloon and two ensuing shrieks. Despite himself, he chuckled. He probably should have saved that walking accident-waiting-to-happen by popping all the balloons with his knife and being done with it. A nurse. Go figure. Maybe she coped with the chaos of an emergency room better by living a life full of it.

Daniel scanned the room. He hoped his neighbors had more room in their cabin than he had in his. Slinging the Pullman on the bed next to his duffel bag, he shifted his attention to a door too wide to be a locker. It took no architectural genius to figure out whose cabin was connected to his. With a shrug of resignation, he pushed in the button lock on the knob and then wedged his duffel bag against it. Fate sure had a twisted sense of humor.

He unzipped the Pullman to unpack—*anything* to put off meeting his mother and new stepfather at the farewell party up on the sundeck. What was wrong with things the way they used to be, the way the holiday had always been? Thanksgiving at the home place, Mom cooking the turkey and trimmings and Dan's sister and her husband visiting. End of story. But no. Good ol' Charlie Meyers sweet-talked Dan's mom into taking this cruise on their monthly anniversary in lieu of gathering at the ranch for Thanksgiving. Well, confounded if Dan intended to endure the man's company any more than he had to.

So what if Dan and his sister could see the islands where his mom fell in love and "share the celebration"? He grimaced. If that wasn't a waste of good money, what was? It wasn't Dan's money, of course, but this all-expense-paid trip spelled torment to him, not paradise. Who would want to vacation in a place hotter and muggier than the Texas ranch he ran?

No, this was a pure waste of his mother's money…the money Dan's dad and Dan himself had made sacrifices for, to ensure she was provided for in her senior years. After his father's death, Dan had given up his plans to become a veterinarian, attending a local university at night for a degree in animal husbandry instead. He'd refused to use the money from the inheritance his father left for his mother's care. It was hers. The ranch was Dan's after he bought out his sister's half. His dad had taught him thriftiness, and it served

Dan well—the place was twice the size it had been when David Jarrett passed it on to his children.

This vacation couldn't possibly be his mom's idea, even though she'd begged Dan to come and charged the whole shebang on one of *her* credit accounts. This was the Big Spender's idea. Dan's mom just wasn't prone to this kind of spending—leastwise, not until love addled her brain. She was comfortable enough with the money her late husband left her, but *wealthy* wasn't a word that came to Dan's mind when he considered her finances. Before that blasted cruise a few months ago, she'd discussed all her financial decisions with Dan. Now some slick, retired, used-car salesman and ladies' man had taken over.

His sister, Gail, blamed Dan's cool reception of Charlie Meyers on Dan's having to fend for himself alone at the ranch. She'd already forewarned him that she was going to try to hook him up with someone. Just what he needed—*more* complications in his life.

Absently, Dan brushed some white cat hair off his blue jeans and genuinely smiled for a fraction of a second, probably the first time since he'd left Texas, at the reminder of Snowball. Even the cat he'd found abandoned in a frozen parking lot in midwinter acted with more sense than his mom. Snowball didn't trust every Tom, Dick, and Fluffy that came along offering affection.

His pets were enough company for anyone. He wondered how they accepted his hired hand feeding them. More than likely Snowball remained an indifferent ball of feline fur, while Hank—a half shepherd and half Heinz-of-57-varieties mongrel with a permanent grin (or snarl, depending on the circumstances)—was beside himself with glee for human companionship. Dan hoped Clive would be able to spend a little time with them apart from feeding. Despite their contrary personalities, Dan was really fond of the pets—neither of which adapted any better to change in routine than their owner.

Daniel froze. His mental picture of the two animals dolefully watching him leave from the porch vanished at the sight of the frazzled cat caricature staring up at him from the front of a folded T-shirt. In disbelief, he shook the garment out. *I don't do mornings,* it said.

What in blue blazes was going on here? He reached for the luggage tag the cruise line had provided. It had his cabin number on it, all right. The problem was, it wasn't his case. And this, he thought, deftly picking up another T-shirt as if to give the bag a second chance to get things right, was definitely not his. He stared at the one-size-fits-all garment with a voluptuous bikini-clad figure painted on it. It was big enough for two.

First finding himself next door to a loony bird and her two fledglings. Now this.

Meticulously, he folded the absurd tees, dropped them back in the case, and zipped it shut before they infected him with their twisted humor. Grumbling under his breath, he marched to the phone and dialed room service. After three rings, an accented voice answered. It was a basically one-sided conversation.

"The wrong luggage was delivered to my room…yes, the tag is mine, but the case isn't…no, I did not switch the tags, but someone obviously did. Yes, I'm *sure* these are not my clothes."

He'd grant Gail's observation that things looked pretty bleak on his romantic front, but he wasn't about to take up cross-dressing. Daniel held back his acid observation in favor of processing the broken English on the other end of the line into instructions. Take the bag to the main lobby on the Concord and search for his own there. That was where all unclaimed luggage was being taken.

Great. He slammed the receiver down on the cradle, making it jangle in protest. He should have known that if the airline didn't lose his luggage, the cruise line would. He'd never trusted these big-time operations, especially when coordinated effort was required. Right now, some ample-figured college coed was riffling through his jeans and T-shirts, probably getting just as ticked as he was.

As he grabbed the case and reached for the cabin door, an oath surfaced on Daniel's lips, only to be halted by a muted explosion from the adjoining cabin, followed by a startled shriek. *That's two.* A smile tugged at his mouth despite his dour mood. Only ten more to go, if his calculation was right. He found himself wondering if it would be a matter of days or hours. Considering what he'd seen to date, he gave his oddball neighbor fifteen minutes, tops.

No doubt about it. That woman needed a keeper.

 *Three*

$\mathcal{W}$ITH HER ROOM key and some change in her pocket, Sunny stood at the rail with Jason and Allison. They waved at the passing pleasure yachts as the *Love Ahoy* pulled out of the busy palmlined canal promptly at four o'clock. Some were big and luxurious enough to carry royalty and a full staff. Others were small boats built for racing or skiing. All were too big for Sunny's pocketbook, but for the next few days, she'd move among the ranks of their owners—or at least feel like she was floating among them.

So this is how the other half lives....

The brisk, warm breeze off the ocean toyed with her hair, its precocious fingers reflecting her mood of childlike excitement over her first cruise. Flags overhead fluttered in festive farewell to the calypso beat of the band on the open deck. Though her sandaled feet were grounded, she moved her toes to the music. All around, couples clad in island prints and nautical colors sipped before-dinner concoctions in plastic glasses embossed with *Love Ahoy* and watched Miami retreat across the sun-glazed waters astern.

"I think I'll go check out the video arcade," Jason announced.

He made a face, wrinkling his freckled nose. "Like, there's nothing *else* going on here."

Sunny pretended shock. "But there is. Just listen to the music, mon." She grabbed her nephew's hand and started an improvised conga.

"Man, Aunt Sunny. People are watching." Jason pulled away, looking around, just in case someone had seen his aunt's brief lapse of sanity.

"Some are dancing," Sunny shot back in her own defense. "What about you, Alli? Want to get into the island mood? I'll bet we could start a conga line around the pool."

"Not in this lifetime." As if she expected to be torn away from it, Allison held on to the ship's rail so tightly that Sunny had to laugh. "I think I'll go see if there are any decent books in the reading room. Catch you later, Aunt Sunny."

"Party poopers." Sunny called after her departing charges. "Don't forget, dinner is at six. That means dressed and ready to eat at six, not arrive at the cabin to change at six."

"Yeah, yeah."

"Got it."

Her charges' replies came out simultaneously, with an equally decided lack of enthusiasm. Sunny frowned. For cryin' out loud, she was starting to sound like a parent. She thought a moment. Someday, maybe. Kids were definitely a long-term investment— and then there was the problem of finding a partner in the family enterprise.

Dismissing that train of thought before it overtook her, Sunny meandered over to the bar and ordered a soda, sans the skewered fruit she'd seen poke a few tourists in the noses in all the calypso chaos. That was usually her trick with a straw, so she didn't take one of those either. She decided she'd rather just watch the embarkation festivities, so she sought out a table near the rail.

It wasn't long before she could put together group identities. The Hibernian crowd filtered out on deck, a couple or two at a time, filling the rear quarter with boisterous laughter as they sang calypso with an Irish lilt. When the music slowed, some senior couples danced with a finesse Sunny envied. Their faces, lined as they were with age, seemed to deny the old adage that they were over the hill.

A pang of regret that her parents hadn't lived to their retirement years when they could do things like this assaulted Sunny. Their small family had talked about spending a holiday aboard a cruise line, but then her dad had taken sick and the idea fell by the wayside. But that was yesterday, Sunny told herself sternly. How did the saying go about recognizing those things we cannot change and leaving them behind?

Today was for the living. She forced herself to focus on the beauty of the surrounding water canvas, painted with shades of orange, gold, and red from the rapidly descending sun. It was one of God's masterpieces and somehow, Sunny could not help but feel her parents weren't so far away after all.

"Isn't it lovely?"

Sunny turned to a vivacious older woman sitting next to her, uncertain if the remark was directed to her. The lady leaned toward her and held out a camera.

"Would you mind taking a picture of Charlie and me?" she asked. "With that beautiful horizon in the background?"

"Of course." Sunny took the camera, glad to see it was a small, purse-sized number, fully automatic. She found the shutter button with her finger. "Just press here, right?"

"If it clicks, you've got it," the gentleman sitting next to the woman told her. "We don't use those newfangled things, but if we don't bring back pictures, the neighbors'll be upset."

"They gave it to us along with six rolls of film," his wife explained. "A going-away present."

Sunny backed away, dodging a waiter with a tray full of colorful cocktails. Finally the couple fit into the frame with the sunburnished waters as a glorious backdrop. It created a halolike illusion around them, as though God were blessing them.

"Take two, in case one doesn't turn out," the man instructed through a toothy grin. "Got to use up the film somehow."

They were a cheerful, handsome pair, Sunny thought, closing the shutter once, then again, after the whirring film stopped advancing. She could picture them, with their healthy tans and gleaming white smiles, spending time on the golf greens she'd heard about that afternoon during the embarkation briefing. The lady wore a scarf to keep her hair off an attractive Grace Kelly face, while her husband had a straw cowboy hat cocked off his brow, shades of Clark Gable. Their stylish cotton knit apparel even matched. Sunny guessed them to be late middle-agers, but they acted like love-struck teens the way they'd cuddled close to pose for her.

"Thank you, Miss…"

"Everyone calls me Sunny." She offered her hand to the lady first, then the gent.

"Charlie and Esther Meyers," the man answered. "Me 'n' the missus are here with our kids for the holiday cruise."

"Me too. Except I'm here with my sister's kids so she and her husband can enjoy some privacy."

"So those two teenagers weren't yours," Esther remarked. "I told Charlie you looked too young to have kids that old."

Sunny laughed. "Don't say that in front of my sister."

"Well, it's mighty nice of you to baby-sit, even if the youngsters aren't babies. There'll be plenty for them to do. Have you ever been on a cruise before?"

"This is my first, Mrs. Meyers."

The lady placed a friendly hand on Sunny's arm. "Call me Esther and him Charlie. Don't make us feel any older than we look."

"Sorry…*Esther*." Sunny wondered how old the couple's kids were, but kept her curiosity at bay. "Is this your first cruise?"

Charlie's smile widened. "Nope, it's our second. We met on the first and got married. So I thought, what with Thanksgiving comin' up, that I didn't want my bride slavin' away over a hot stove, so we decided to take the holiday here, younguns and all." Charlie Meyers gave his wife a big hug and kiss. "It's our second honeymoon."

"Oh, Charlie," Esther chided, perfectly glowing with embarrassment—and a heavy dose of love. "We just got back from our *first* a month ago."

"It's true," Charlie told Sunny when she failed to hide her surprise. His smile was almost too broad for his face. "And we kinda thought it would be great to show the kids where we met and fell head over heels."

"That is *so* sweet," Sunny exclaimed. "So how many kids do you have?"

"A gal and a boy," Charlie told her proudly. "Well, they're Esther's technically, but never havin' had younguns of my own, I've took to 'em like a duck to water."

"A gal and *two* boys, young men actually," Esther reminded him. "We think of our daughter's husband as one of ours as well."

"Any grandchildren?"

"One on the way." Charlie reached into his pocket as if he'd been waiting for her to ask.

Esther smacked his hand as he opened his wallet. "For heaven's sake, Charlie, this girl doesn't want to see that thing. Looks like the negative of a jelly bean to me."

Ignoring his wife, Charlie Meyers produced a small black-and-white photocopy of a sonogram. "It's *our* grandchild's first picture."

Sunny couldn't help but be warmed by the couple's obvious delight in each other, in their anticipated grandchild, and in life in general. At least her mom and dad had had some good times with Melinda's children before illness incapacitated them. She studied the picture a moment and then handed it back. It wasn't in the right position to tell the gender of the infant. "I know you must be excited. Are you going to ask whether it's a girl or boy, or wait and be surprised?"

"Gail and Mike are gonna do it the old-fashioned way."

"So what about you, young lady? You married?" Charlie's eyes narrowed with a harmless, but decidedly roguish twinkle. The man must have swept the ladies off their feet when he was younger. In fact he *still* was sweeping them, judging by the way Esther looked at him.

"Not yet. My career has been rather demanding. I'm a nurse."

"Mama, there you are." An attractive young woman wearing a loose, flowing sundress walked up to the Meyers's table. "Mike is up on the sundeck looking for you."

"Well, we said we'd meet you by the outdoor bar, so here we are."

"Mama, there are *six* bars on this ship."

"Are they all outdoors?" Charlie Meyers teased.

"Gail, this is Sunny…um…"

"Elders," Sunny supplied.

"Sunny Elders," Esther Meyers went on. "She just took our pictures for us."

The woman extended her hand, her smile as friendly as her parents'. "Glad to meet you, Ms. Elders, I'm Gail Madison."

"Call me Sunny."

"Sunny," she repeated. "I didn't mean to be rude. It's just that this ship is so big and I've been walking around for the last half hour trying to find Mom and Dad. That guy you see coming down those steps over there is my husband, Mike."

"You have a beautiful baby, Gail."

Gail cut her stepfather a gentle albeit reproving look. "Now Charlie, if I'd known you were going to show that picture to everyone on board, I'd have waited till later to give it to you."

"By golly, it ain't every day a man finds out he's gonna be a granddad just a few weeks after he's become a dad." He snorted. "Like to see someone top that."

"Have you seen Dan?" Esther asked her daughter. "Charlie and I haven't seen hide nor hair of him."

Gail's bright face clouded. "Yes, I saw him. He's still trying to find his lost luggage. You'd think I personally misplaced it just because I made all the travel arrangements."

"He *is* in a tailspin," the twenty-something man who joined them admitted. Upon seeing Sunny, he extended his hand. "Hi, I'm Mike Madison."

"Sunny Elders," she answered, shaking it firmly.

His hand was soft, that of a white-collar worker, she guessed. It was a game she played at work, trying to guess what people did for a living. He wore glasses and was as pale as Alan. A fluorescent tan, she called it. Most likely he was chained to a desk somewhere behind a computer and/or pile of books. A glance at the school ring on his right hand confirmed her guess. It bore the emblem of a well-known Texas business college. Maybe he was another accountant skipping work in prime time.

"Dan isn't much of a traveler," Esther Meyers admitted. "This would have to happen to him."

"Well, I'm sure his bag will turn up and he'll start enjoyin' himself. All work and no play has made that one a dull boy. I don't think I've ever seen him smile."

Esther hugged Charlie's arm. "He's just slow to accept change. Once you get to know him and he gets to know you, you two will become best friends."

The uneasy exchange of glances between the Madison couple told Sunny the younger pair weren't as easily convinced as Charlie. It was a shame that anything or anyone should put a damper on such a lovely family's holiday. But then, as her mother always used to say, *You can't appreciate the sweet without the sour—but you do have the choice whether or not to swallow.*

"My son can't get used to the idea that his mother has a new life," Esther confided.

"Well, it's hard for him," Charlie said in the absentee's defense. "After all, he's been the man in your life since his daddy died. Then you not only take up with me, but leave him and the family ranch to gallivant all over. Like you said, it's a big change."

"He's just being selfish," Gail Madison put in with an annoyed purse of her lips. It was a typical sibling response.

Sunny felt the odd man out and was at a loss for words. How in the world had she been sucked into this little family circle? At work, she might have questioned more and given some sympathetic, if not helpful, advice based on her training and old-fashioned common sense. But she was on vacation and this was none of her affair. It wasn't her job to *fix* it.

No matter how much she itched to do so.

"Well, I'd best be checking on the kids. Good luck on the coming grandbaby. Nice to meet you all." She waved as she turned to head through one of the bulkhead doors leading to the ship's interior.

Once her eyes adjusted to the dimmer lighting in the hallway, she checked her watch. Dinner would be served in half an hour, so she had time to explore the ship. It was a casual night and she'd rather go off on an adventure and wear her traveling clothes, which had dried nicely by the time she and her little *family* settled in their cabin. All she needed to do was run a brush through her hair and make a grand entrance.

"Okay," she said to herself, trying to get her bearings. "Blue carpet means I'm in the stern of the ship." A passing couple smiled at her in understanding. They'd been studying the ship's map on the wall just inside. Sunny smacked her forehead, laughing at herself. Of *course* she was at the stern. She'd just seen Miami disappear on the horizon behind them.

Four

$\mathcal{B}$Y THE TIME HER cabin's assigned dining room doors were opened on the Atlantic deck, Sunny had a general idea of the ship's layout. She still referred to the little maps posted in the stairwells near the front, middle, and back of the ship just to confirm she was where she thought she was. Jason and Allison were nowhere to be seen in the throng of passengers who moved into the dining room. They were feeling their oats with their Aunt Sunny, no doubt. Their parents were assigned to the late sitting, despite their request for the earlier one.

As soon as the crowd dispersed to their assigned places, she spotted the kids near a saltwater-stained window overlooking the stern of the ship where Miami was just a memory on the horizon. She wove her way through beautifully dressed tables with mauve napkins folded like little birds nested on the appetizer plates. Crystal chandeliers overhead and the staff dressed in crisp black and white, like smiling penguins, added a flair of elegance to the ambience of the spacious room.

"Beat ya," Jason said in delight when Sunny reached their assigned table.

Allison cast her eyes toward the ceiling at her brother's shout. "Grow up."

"You two must have been first in line."

Sunny noticed her niece had changed into a princess-style dress of pastel floral design for the evening meal. It was hard to believe this was the same little girl Melinda had to threaten with no television to get her into something other than jeans just a few months before. Ah, the tug-of-war mind of a teen.

"My, but Dorado High's star soccer player is looking lovely. So who's the young man we intend to impress?"

"I was just dressing according to the cruise line recommendations, Aunt Sunny." The young girl gave Sunny's tank top and khaki pants a disparaging glance. "Didn't you have time to change?"

"I was waiting for you two to finish unpacking, so I'd have room to move. Besides, it's casual night. I'll do it later. Anything good on the menu?"

As Sunny took up the tasseled, pseudoleather booklet, Charlie and Esther Meyers called to her from a table on the other side of a waiter's station. She waved back and then focused on the tantalizing list of food. Her stomach rolled in anticipation. At least that's what she hoped it was, this being her first time at sea.

"Hmm…I think I'll have one of each."

"I don't even know what this stuff is." Jason's brow knit tight as his sneaker laces.

"Read it, stupid," Allison grumbled under her breath.

"I'm not eating anything I can't pronounce. Think I can get a hamburger?"

"You are so juvenile."

"I'm nine. That's how I'm supposed to be, birdbrain."

"Enough sibling repartee," Sunny intervened. "I expect you two to act as adult as you can since this is an adult setting." With that, she put her menu over her head, tent fashion, and leaned forward. "So be adventurous, Jason. What sounds the best?"

Both kids giggled, one in delight and one in mortification, but at least they'd stopped taking verbal swipes at each other. Out of the corner of her eye, Sunny caught a glimpse of western boots, a flat black against the blue-green carpet. Holding her hat in place, she glanced up and groaned inwardly. Daniel Jarrett stood at the table, scowling at the printed assignment card.

"Well, hello there, stranger," she piped up with an exaggerated drawl that seemed to come from nowhere. The menu slipped and Jarrett caught it before Sunny could.

"I was told we couldn't wear hats in here," Dan said dryly, handing it back.

His hat was gone, and his thick, dark hair was neatly combed in a rakish wave over his forehead. The brim mark was no longer visible.

"This is a dining room. In here, we wear menus, pardner," Sunny replied in an equally dry tone. If this man hadn't already labeled her a complete idiot, he certainly would now.

Thankfully, he seemed more preoccupied with his table assignment than with her.

"Need some help?"

"Something's got to be wrong," Jarrett mumbled, speaking more to the card than to Sunny. "I'm supposed to be sitting with my—"

"Hey, Dan, over here."

Sunny glanced to see Charlie Meyers standing up at his table and waving the younger man over.

Dan? Daniel Jarrett, the disgruntled cowboy in their adjoining cabin, was the Meyers-Madison family's Dan—the one who resented his mom's remarrying? She watched the cowboy's lazy retreat over to his family's table. Charlie was right. He didn't smile much. In fact, he looked positively pained.

Sunny turned her attention back to Jason's dinner decision as the maître d' joined the Meyers to discuss the seating problem. He and Sunny both settled on Surf and Turf with all the accompanying dishes. Allison, all aflutter when their young Irish waiter snapped out her napkin and laid it across her lap, chose a fish entrée. It was cute to watch her niece and nephew order for themselves after Sean, their waiter, introduced himself. He certainly knew how to make a young girl blush with his wholesome blarney and wicked grin.

"The hardest thing is going to be figuring out which of these utensils to eat with first," Sunny confided in a low voice after the waiter left them.

"Man, nobody can use all this silverware."

"I'm just glad I don't have to do their dishes," Allison chimed in.

"Cute, huh?" Sunny teased, cutting her gaze toward the waiters' station, where Sean was slicing a loaf of fresh bread on a board.

"Aunt Sunny! He'll hear you." Allison was all metallic grin, her brown eyes dancing.

"Well—"

"Pardon me, Madame."

Cut off, Sunny looked up to see the maître d' standing next to her. Beside him was Daniel Jarrett. "Yes?"

"There has been a mix-up of tables, which I am unable to rectify tonight. Would you mind if Mr. Jarrett shared your table? As you can see, there is no room at his family's table."

Not unless he sat in someone's lap, she thought, glancing over that way. "Of course not. We're already sharing a suite."

Jason snorted.

Allison caught her breath.

Sunny winced inwardly. It just slipped out before she could stop it. "I mean…that is…"

Jarrett came to her rescue. "I have a feeling we are going to know each other well before this little jaunt is over. Must be fate," he added wryly.

"Must be." Now it was Sunny's turn to color. She wrung the napkin in her lap beneath the table.

"Thank you, miss." The maître d' made a courtly bow before pivoting with drill-like precision to leave them.

"Mr. Jarrett, you remember my niece Allison and my nephew Jason, or were they behind the balloons?"

"Sure. The watchdogs, right?"

"Huh?" Jason cut a sharp look at Sunny.

"Just don't bark." She dismissed him with a playful scratch on the head.

With a crooked smile that added a whole new dimension of handsome to his features, Daniel extended his hand to Jason and shook it firmly. "Jason, you can call me Dan. You too, Allison," he added, affording her a wink that was perfectly disarming.

"We had a mix-up in seating, too," Sunny informed him. "My sister and her husband got bumped to the late seating."

"We don't need adults hanging around us anyway," Jason put in.

"Oh yeah? Well, what do you call me?"

"You don't count, Aunt Sunny. You never act your age."

Sunny leaned back against the cushioned chair, a smirk on her lips. "Leave it to a kid to tell the truth."

"Yeah," Allison chimed in. "After all, you were the one with the menu on your head."

Dan's lips twitched as the waiter appeared to take his order.

Instantly he was all business again. Steak, potatoes, salad, the basics were all he asked for, nothing fancy. Like his clothes, Sunny mused. He was what he was and didn't care what anyone thought about it.

A tap on her ankle drew Sunny's attention to her niece. Allison held up her menu, mouthing the words, *He's cute.*

There was no option but to agree. Daniel Jarrett was what the girls at work would call a hunk. It was a shame he hadn't mastered the art of laughter yet. She wondered why he wasn't as pleased as his sister to see his mother remarried. Charlie seemed like such a great guy.

"I met your family at the Bon Voyage party earlier," Sunny said, ignoring her niece's mischief. "They're delightful, especially your mom and dad."

"My mother and *step*father."

Sunny took his sharpness in stride. "Just appreciate them while you can. Life is too short." She cleared the melancholy that infected her throat.

"Kinda hard to do when he's spirited Mom off in that motor home of his. Never thought I'd see her leave the ranch."

"Change is a part of life, whether we like it or not. The trick is to make the best of it, I guess."

"You're a *real* cowboy?" Jason intervened.

Sunny breathed a sigh of relief. There she went again, sticking her nose where it didn't belong. Okay, she was just trying to make conversation. She folded her hands in her lap and listened with interest as Dan answered.

"Well, I *try* to tend to a herd of cattle, keep the home place up, and pay the bills."

Change was *definitely* good, Sunny mused. The twinkle that settled in his eyes as he spoke of his obvious love for his home was a charming plus.

"Do you have horses?" Allison ventured.

"We have a decent remuda. Do you ride?"

"No, but I've always wanted to. I signed us up for the horse-back riding on the beach in Jamaica."

Sunny was shocked from her study of their dinner guest. "Say *what?*"

"We talked about it while we were in line to get aboard, remember? I signed you, Jason, me, and Mom for the tour."

"Yeah, you said it was *romantic,*" Jason put in with a roll of eyes.

"Well, it does look like it in the commercials," she admitted.

"What're you gonna do, kiss a horse?"

That did it. Daniel Jarrett smiled. Mesmerized, Sunny stared until his dancing gaze swung to her.

"You ever been on a horse, Nurse Elders? You did say you were a nurse, didn't you?"

Something dropped in her chest, her heart, most likely—or maybe she'd just swallowed her tongue. It certainly didn't want to work. Sunny shook her head in denial. This man had the most intoxicating eyes she'd ever seen. How on earth could she have missed them before?

"Yes, I am a nurse and no, no horse experience. I'm a city gal, born and bred in Houston," she managed lamely. Although the range was starting to look more and more appealing, smile by rakish smile.

"I've done some volunteer air and ground rescue work," said Dan, "getting people out of jams so the paramedics can tend to them, but I'm not much good for more than Band-Aids and iodine when it comes to medicine."

"You ever jump out of a chopper?" Jason asked, as impressed as Sunny by their companion's versatility.

Daniel nodded. "Yep, I've crewed on a few airlifts, taking people up in a chopper from a mountain crag or water—somewhere a ground vehicle couldn't get to. Mostly I work with the local fire department on ground rescue. Haven't been able to do as much as I used to, now that I have the ranch all to myself."

"Pardon me, Mr. and Mrs. Jarrett." Yet another penguin-suited staff member stood at their table, as if a yardstick were strapped to his spine. "I am Gerard, the wine steward. As a token of thanks for your patronage, your travel agent sent this complimentary wine for your enjoyment. Shall I open it for you, or would you rather I put it aside for another night?"

Flustered by the faux pas, Sunny kicked Jason beneath the table to curtail his snickering. "I'm *Miss* Elders, and *this* is Mr. Jarrett."

"Oh, I am so sorry," the man apologized. "It is just that the maître d' said to take this to the Jarrett table and there were the children…"

"Perfectly understandable," Daniel spoke up smoothly. "But the kids belong to someone else. Just crack that thing open for us, and we'll take it from there."

"I don't think that's such a good idea for me and the kids," Sunny ventured, "but you help yourself."

Daniel paused for a moment. "Got nonalcoholic, tickly stuff?"

Sunny and her charges strained to smother amusement at the steward's startled reaction. He looked as if Dan had ordered vintage arsenic.

"But of course, sir."

"You don't have to do this," Sunny said to their dinner partner.

"Nope, but frankly, I'd rather drink fresh grape juice than the kind that's turned bad in a bottle. I was just trying not to be unappreciative."

Sunny melted inside. Handsome, considerate, great with kids…

"In that case, I'll bring something…*fresh,*" the steward said in obvious distaste.

A stern look kept the children's giggles at bay until he was out of earshot. Then Sunny joined them. Even Dan grinned, making the table unanimously incorrigible.

Gerard reappeared with a bottle of sparkling nonalcoholic wine and two additional glasses for the children. Having had time to recover from the shock to his refined senses, he made a grand show of key jingling and towel brandishing. On unscrewing the cap, he waved it under Daniel's nose, playing his role to the hilt for the wide, young eyes watching him. After all, the tips suggested at the week's end were optional, not required.

At Daniel's nod, he poured a sample. Tongue in cheek, Sunny watched as her companion swirled it in the light and then tasted it. Upon approval, the steward poured a glass for each of them and placed the rest of the bottle in ice.

"What were you smellin' it for?" Jason asked after he left.

"Busted if I know," Daniel admitted in a low voice. "Except it's what they do on TV."

Sunny laughed along with the others. Maybe Daniel Jarrett was trying to make the best of things after all. He certainly was getting in tight with the kids.

Over appetizers, Jason drilled Daniel on ranching. Sunny wondered if the boy had been drinking real wine, the way his mouth ran. Nonetheless, she found the conversation fascinating. She was a city girl, born and bred. She loved animals but was allowed no pets in her apartment building. While she knew ranching was far from glamorous, there was a part of her that found it as interesting and appealing as her nephew did. Could be the Stetson. Might be the boots and jeans. Or maybe it was just those brown eyes. Whatever it was, she felt like a wide-mouth bass about to chow down: hook, line, and sinker.

By the time dinner was over and they were trying to make

room for the scrumptious flambé dessert, she'd learned that Daniel had taken over the family ranch after his parents retired. He was twenty-nine, had a dog called Hank and cat named Snowball as live-in companions, both strays he'd taken in. It didn't bother him that he lived alone, he'd been running the family ranch since his father's death. What bothered him was his mom's sudden marriage to a man she hardly knew.

"Look at it this way. If she hasn't been impulsive in the past, maybe her decision to marry this Charlie Meyers wasn't as reckless as you think. I know you only want what's best for her," Sunny added sympathetically, "but sometimes you come across things that are just right and you know it immediately."

"If you're talking grape juice or steak, yes, but tastes of the heart take time to develop. I just don't believe in that love at first sight stuff you women are so hyped up on. It was just so blasted quick— no warning, no chance to check him out."

Sunny placed a defensive hand against her chest. "Moi? *Excusez* me, but I am not only single, but a career woman in my own right." Sure, she hoped to get married and have a family someday, but that didn't mean she was a ditz. "Stereotyping can get you into trouble, young man," she warned him good-naturedly.

Dan gave her a sheepish grin. "Sorry, present company excluded."

"*I* believe in love at first sight," Allison said to no one in particular.

"It's just that I want Mom to have the same kind of love second time round that she had with my dad, and you don't get that in a few weeks from a total stranger." Dan shook his head. "I promised Dad I'd watch out for her and I won't settle for anything less for her—kind of like God's love, unconditional, better or worse, all that stuff."

Sunny warmed inside at this unexpected confession. So Daniel Jarrett was aware of God's love. That was as endearing as his devotion to his mom's happiness, even if he was going about it the wrong way. At least in Sunny's opinion, it looked that way.

"Well, part of that kind of love involves letting us make our own choices and loving and supporting us, whether a choice is right or wrong."

"That's easy for you to say. It's not your mom's interests at stake."

Sunny wished she had her mom's interests to worry about... She rallied stubbornly from the melancholy slip to the conversation at hand. "All I can say is, if your mom hasn't had time to know the real Charlie Meyers as you claim, then you certainly haven't either. And to form an opinion this early is ill advised."

Dan digested her words, but his expression told her he didn't think much of them. With a silent groan, she took a sip of the bubbly white grape juice. *Great going, Sunny. You have a gorgeous guy at your table and you tick him off.*

He peered at her. "Are you always so blunt?"

"Comes with the job. No time to mince words in the ER. But would you rather that I just agree with you when I don't?"

"Naw, I guess not." He grinned at that, looking like a boy who'd been caught with his hand in the cookie jar.

The breath left her chest on a sigh that rendered even her littlest toe devoid of oxygen. What was it with this guy? He was opinionated and cranky, usually the type she put in his place with a degree of satisfaction. So why was she feeling as if the nonalcoholic wine was 180 proof?

"Do you have a girlfriend?" Allison ventured shyly.

"Nope, can't say that I do. Are you volunteering?"

"No, but Aunt Sunny's available."

"Allison!" Sunny's face felt as if she'd held it up against the flame of the table lamp. That she'd just thought the same thing only added to the fire into her cheeks.

"Are you going to the singles party tonight? I'm *just asking,*" her niece exclaimed at Sunny's warning glare before shifting her attention back to Dan. "Well, are you?"

Daniel shook his head slowly, glancing briefly at Sunny. "Nope, I'm still trying to find my luggage. If I do, I'm hitting the sack early. It's been a long day."

He didn't have to look like he was enjoying her embarrassment. "Allison, it's none of our business what Mr. Jarrett does."

"No, but it's mine."

Sunny looked up to find Gail Madison standing behind her brother. She leaned over with a stage whisper. "You came on the cruise to relax and enjoy yourself, Danny. Why not go to the singles bash?"

"I came because I couldn't back out without hurting Mom."

"The girl of your dreams could be at that party tonight."

"The girl of my dreams is going to be *in* my dreams, Sis. Look, just because you think being married and expecting equals deliriously happy, doesn't mean the rest of the world does, okay?"

"Are *you* going, Sunny?" Gail asked, ignoring her brother completely.

Caught off guard, Sunny shrugged. If she said yes, it would look like she was in cahoots with the other woman. "I...um..."

"See, she doesn't want to go." Daniel smirked.

Sunny was reluctant to buck his case closed statement, but she wasn't one to let someone else speak for her, especially when his feelings did not reflect her own.

"Well, actually I do. I love meeting people and plan to attend. I'm going down after my charges turn in and I change into something a little more appropriate."

She gave her niece a so-there look, but her mind was racing a mile a minute. She really did intend to go after the kids turned in.

She focused on Dan. "I'm not going to miss anything on my first cruise. But I don't want to go with you." Sunny cringed. No, that wasn't right. "I mean, I hadn't planned on going with anyone in particular. Not that I'd mind if you wanted to go with me…not as a *date,* of course. I'm just going to check it out."

"That's wonderful," Gail exclaimed. "How can you turn down an offer like that?"

Daniel shifted in his seat and stared through Sunny. "I guess I can't." He had that condemned-if-I-do, convicted-if-I-don't look.

"But I won't be staying late," he added emphatically.

"Never say never." Gail planted a big kiss on his cheek. "You just wait. You're going to have a good time in spite of yourself, Daniel Jarrett. All work and no play makes Jack a dull boy."

"So I've heard."

Daniel pushed away from the table and rose just as dessert arrived, moving as if the push to get him to go to the party had lit a fire beneath his tail. He tossed his dinner napkin aside as his parents and brother-in-law joined the group. He had to be a good six-foot-plus tall. Or maybe he just looked that way because she was sitting down.

"What's the rush?" Charlie Meyers clapped his stepson on the back.

"I'm going to see if anyone's found my luggage yet."

"Danny is going with Sunny to the singles party tonight," Gail informed the group.

Esther's face lit up. "I always say the Lord works in strange ways." She gave her husband's arm a meaningful squeeze. Cupid's wings fairly fluttered in the look she gave Sunny.

"No, Mama," Daniel corrected dryly. "My *sister* works in strange ways." He glanced back at Sunny and nodded his head shortly. "I'll see *you* later."

Sunny felt like sinking into the floor as he retreated stiffly. Nothing she'd said came out right. Now she was committed to a nondate with a man who didn't want to go out to start with. She promised herself to give Dan a chance to back out once it was just the two of them.

"Thanks for looking after him, Sunny. You're a real sport. Not that I'm trying to saddle you with Danny or anything," Gail added hastily. "It's just, well, I think it'd be great for my brother to meet someone special, and he's not going to do it stuck on that ranch, working all the time."

Next to the table, the waiter made a big show of preparing a flaming Bananas Foster, but his flair for setting ice cream and a gourmet banana sauce afire was lost on Sunny. How had she gotten into this mess?

"If Daniel wants someone to go with him, I'll be glad to go, but I don't want to shanghai him into going."

"My Dan won't be shanghaied into anything he doesn't want to do," Esther Meyers assured her. "Takes after his father in mule-headedness."

The waiter placed the flaming dessert on the table in front of them, eliciting oohs and aahs from Allison and Jason. The Meyerses and Madisons bade their farewell so Sunny and the kids could finish their meal. Sunny hardly noticed her melting ice cream. Somehow, Esther Meyers's words were not as comforting to Sunny as she wished they'd been.

Five

LATER, AS SHE walked with Daniel Jarrett into the art-deco disco lounge, Sunny still felt as if she were walking on eggs. She'd given him his chance to back out, but he seemed resigned that he was going to have to enjoy—or at least *pretend* to enjoy—the cruise, or his sister would give him no rest.

Lord, how do I get into these things?

Sitting down on a plump, cushioned bench seat in the lounge, Sunny tucked the soft, cotton knit skirt of the shirtwaist dress she'd hastily changed into after supper about her legs. Before Daniel could take a seat next to her, one of the cruise staff approached them with a clipboard.

"Hi, welcome aboard the *Love Ahoy*. You do know this party is for singles," she said tactfully.

"Oh, we're single," Sunny assured her.

"Not married," Dan chimed in with an almost insulting fervor. "Not at all."

"Oh." The staff member was thrown for a moment before her buoyant smile returned. "In that case, just sign in here."

She handed them a clipboard containing a name list. Two dozen or so singles had already signed in. Sunny glanced at the names. Most of them were women, so prospects for the single males looked good. She wasn't particularly looking, but it never hurt to notice the odds. Chalk it up to being a people watcher.

"Now, put these name tags on. We're going to play some get-acquainted games in a few minutes."

"Oh joy," Daniel groaned under his breath.

"All you have to do is say hello to someone, Dan. You don't have to propose." Sunny was shocked at the annoyance in her voice. As many charms as this guy had demonstrated, he still had a knack for drawing out the worst in her.

"Tell that to Charlie Meyers," he shot back in kind.

The cruise director looked totally puzzled. "I beg your pardon?"

"Never mind. Private joke."

Sunny breathed easier upon seeing the quick, apologetic grimace the long, tall Texan cast her way. She wondered what it was about Charlie and Esther Meyers's wedding, besides a whirlwind courtship, that put Dan on such a raw edge. There were more and more hints of a great guy beneath this current of suspicion and resentment.

"How 'bout I get us a drink. What will you have?"

"A lemon spritzer. After all, I *am* a chaperone. Oh, but with a cherry," she added with a juvenile grin.

"Humph. And I'd thought you'd been sampling the juice of the vine all along."

He was trying to make up. It was a pitiful attempt but beguiling in its awkwardness. She pulled a pixyish face and tried not to stare after him as he walked away. Instead she looked about the room.

The group was a mix of ages, but most looked to be in their twenties and thirties. Seemingly absorbed in their own conversation, a group of young women seated near the rear exit laughed noisily, all the while sizing up the men with overt glances. Fishing, Sunny called it, casting out looks and reeling in a catch. At the moment, there was considerable trawling around Dan Jarrett as he placed their order at the bar.

Maybe it was because he still wore jeans and a chambray shirt, but Sunny didn't think so. It wasn't that he didn't look good in them. Dan would draw attention whether he was dressed in fatigues or an Armani suit. It was his demeanor as much as his looks. He knew where he was going and wasn't given to side-tracks—except where his opinion of his stepfather was concerned.

As if she were an expert on men. Sunny laughed at herself. School, work, and then caring for her parents had pretty much stalled her romantic life the past year. Not that she regretted her decision to be there for Mom and Dad. Melinda had a husband and two children. There was no question in Sunny's mind as to what she would do. She stayed, she cared, she loved, she lost.

The age-old question about it being better to have loved and lost than not to have loved at all drifted into her train of thought. It was as beyond her as it was the Bard himself, so she played it safe with her heart. She preferred the date-and-run squad. ER rules all the way: no emotional commitment…at least until someone invented an anesthesia for loss. A romantic battering just might be more than her ticker could stand.

So will you run from Daniel Jarrett?

The question startled her almost as much as the man who suddenly appeared at her side.

"One lemon spritzer coming up!" Dan held the glass out to her.

Running was a moot point since he wasn't exactly chasing her.

Although he might have to run before the night was over, considering the interest lingering in his wake.

He sat down, clueless. Sunny added another notch on the charm scoreboard she'd been mentally keeping, setting off the bells and whistles of a winner.

She took a sip of her lemon and soda and decided on a no-risk, clinical demeanor. Here was a nice guy, aside from his problem with his stepdad. No foreigner to refereeing family squabbles—heaven knew she encountered enough of them at work—Nurse Fix-It rose to the occasion. It might help him to talk about it to someone uninvolved.

Maybe, just maybe, it was no coincidence that the two of them kept bumping into each other. A lightbulb came on, driving out all the earlier shadows of her introspection. Dan's family crisis wasn't terminal—it was treatable. And, just like at work, maybe God had put Sunny in a place where she could help. Okay, then. First prescription—distraction.

"Why don't you meander over to the bar? There's some decided interest in your...your boots," she finished lamely.

On the other hand, she didn't usually stumble over her tongue at work. If she had a hankie, she'd drop it, crawl under the table after it and stay there.

"What I mean is, don't worry about me. I just wanted to see what was going on tonight."

"Why, am I cramping your style?"

"No, it's just..." That Dan might actually want to remain in her company had not occurred to her. "Well, if there was a special person for you on this ship, your being with me would discourage her from coming forward. Or maybe you'd just like to talk about how fickle love and women are in general with the men at the bar—you know, guy talk."

Maybe she'd just dive under the table, hankie or not.

Daniel took a sip of root beer, then set it down on the table. Sunny noticed it, too, had a plastic sword-skewered cherry. That had to be the color of her face by now.

"First, I have no desire to talk love or women to total strangers. Second, and I already said this, I'm not interested in meeting someone new. So tell me, is this one of those 'women statements' where she's really talking about herself but pretends it's me she's worried about?"

"No!" Sunny's hair bounced with the emphasis of her denial. "I'm not looking for romance. That's the *last* thing I need. I came for fun and sun with my family."

"Why not? You're single, you're attractive in a homespun sort of way."

Had she just been insulted? "Gee, thanks."

Now it was Dan's turn to backtrack. "No, I meant…" He scrambled for the right words. "I meant you're not artificially…um…*enhanced*." He winced at his choice of words, and Sunny commiserated. No risk here. They were warming to each other like two porcupines.

"Okay, Jarrett, you're off the hook."

"Scout's honor?"

"Scout's honor." She held up three fingers, then two. "Well, whatever, I mean it. I don't do games, and like I said, romance is the last thing on my mind right now. I haven't had the time, even if I were inclined."

"And why's that? Don't tell me you're a workaholic too."

Sunny gave a little laugh. "Well, that too. But I've been too busy caring for my mom and dad. Until I lost them a few months ago."

"Both at once?"

"Within two weeks of each other. Anyway—" she had to steer

away from the bleak cloud before it engulfed her—"since then, I've been setting up in a new apartment and settling back to work." She lifted her shoulders. "I just don't know when I could work a man in, even if I met one. No offense," she added hastily.

"None taken." Dan leaned forward, his smile reflective. "I never was much for games, myself. You know, that saying-one-thing-and-meaning-another stuff? Give me my dog or cat anytime. Them, I understand."

"More of that *unconditional* love?"

Dan's scorecard was gaining by the word. Here was this gorgeous guy who could snap up any of the tanned beauties in the room, and he was missing his *pets*. It was too much for Sunny to digest. Who'd picture a poster cowboy with a kitten in his lap and dog at his feet? Maybe the dog, but—

"Exactly," he went on. "Unconditional love, fleas, hot spots, and all."

They broke into a spontaneous laugh, gazes bonding in mutual understanding. If she'd known him better, Sunny might have hugged him. She broke the disconcerting train of thought and took a sip of her lemon spritzer instead. Her mouth was so dry, her tongue stuck to its roof. She was used to being the teaser, not the teasee.

"Okay, ladies and gents, we have a lively group here this evening. How do you like the cruise so far?"

The cozy lounge erupted with cheers and foot stomping as loud as the contemporary decor of reds and purples.

"Are you ready to have some fun and meet some new faces?"

The response increased. Feedback roared over the sound system, spurring the DJ next to the small dance floor to scramble for the controls.

"All right, I need twelve volunteers."

"Look, did you mean it when you said you didn't care if we stayed for the whole thing?"

Sunny saw panic graze Daniel's face as he watched the cruise director randomly select volunteers. These weren't exactly the kind of games Sunny had referred to—she liked meeting people—but her companion, poor soul, was trying to be polite, even though he was clearly out of his element.

"Of course I did." Sunny bumped against him, nudging him to the edge of the bench seat. "C'mon, pardner. Let's see if we can find someone with fleas."

Daniel circled her waist with one arm, steering her toward the exit as if hounds were on their heels. Maybe they were, but Sunny didn't look back. She was fighting to keep coherent against the onslaught of sensation Dan's lingering hand evoked. It was just a show of gratitude of course, but shouldn't it stop, now that they were stepping out on the deck, where the moon shone in all its splendor?

The noise of the party followed them into the night until the door closed behind them. Stepping away, Daniel breathed in the ocean air as if it spelled relief. Uncertain whether she should feel relieved or disappointed, Sunny sipped the remainder of her spritzer and watched some couples gathered at the rail enjoy the hush of the starlit ocean night.

"I guess…"

"I think…"

They laughed again, her soft tones blending with his baritone.

"You first," Sunny prompted.

"I was going to say, I guess I'd better head back to the cabin to see if my case has been found yet. This ship has twelve hundred people on it, and mine is the only case still missing. Talk about luck."

"Well, let me pay you for my drink."

Sunny unzipped her waist pack and fished for some change. Better to part company before the intimate atmosphere infected her. The balmy brush of the night air, the soft blend of moonlight and lantern, the whish of waves yielding to the humming ship's engines—it was enough to make a lion and lamb cuddle up.

"After bailing me out of there and saving me from Gail's good intentions, I owe you," Daniel said. "You're a real sport, Sunny Elders."

"What can I say? I'm a lifesaver. That's my job." Sunny glanced back at the door to the lounge, trying to decide whether or not to go back. "I think I'll call it a night, too," she decided aloud. "It's been a long day and the kids will be up early. Whoa, this way."

She caught Dan's arm and pointed him to the port side of the ship as he started away under the curving wooden steps leading to an observation deck above. "We're on the left."

"Beats the tar out of me." Swinging one long leg around, he turned on his boot heel to follow Sunny. "Where I come from, we use landmarks to tell where we are, but this whole ship looks the same to me. I felt like a laboratory rat in a maze going to the dining room tonight."

"It doesn't help that we have to go up one level, across, and then down again to get to a dining room on the same deck as ours," Sunny sympathized.

"So that's how I did it."

She cut a sideways glance at her companion. There was that toe-curling grin spread from one ear to the other. He held up his hand, as if he were being sworn in as a witness.

"Honest to goodness, if I hadn't followed the crowd, I'd still be hungry."

She liked a guy who could laugh at himself. If he kept this up, she'd need another scorecard—and some good running shoes.

"Well, pardner, just follow this city gal, and I'll get you to your bunkhouse."

Sunny *thought* she had the layout of the ship figured out. Four flights of stairs and several wrong turns later, they stood in front of one of the stairwell maps, staring at the little red dot highlighting their location. She was definitely not heading forward again, where the same steward had given them directions, not once, but twice.

"That's an inconvenient place to put an engine," Dan remarked, pointing to the center of the map.

"Beats taking turns rowing in the bilge." When her companion failed to share her humor, Sunny pointed to the hall behind them. "Look. It's blue carpet. We're on the Atlantic deck. We follow the blue carpet and—"

"It's on *both* sides of the ship, Sacajawea," her companion pointed out. His patience was waning, as was hers.

Sunny started to the left, but Daniel caught her arm.

"Look, there's room numbers. We're on the right."

"Are you sure?" She hesitated, glancing back at the map of the ship.

"Sure. Come on, I'll show you."

Standing back like a gentleman, Daniel let Sunny precede him down the narrow corridor.

"Tell you what," he said, "if I'm wrong, I'll sleep in that '*I don't do mornings*' cat T-shirt and wear the bikini one tomorrow."

The comment stopped Sunny so suddenly she was nearly run over. Her mind reeled. *No. No way.*

Yet there could only be one suitcase on the ship with her sleep shirt and the bikini-clad, pinup tee her friends had given her as a bon-voyage gag gift.

"They were in the suitcase delivered in error to my room," he explained hastily, mistaking her shock for that of another kind. "I prefer that women wear such things…uh, as opposed to wearing them myself, that is."

"What did you say?" she asked again, still unsure of her ears.

"I've got some loony woman's suitcase and—" Daniel broke off, staring in equal disbelief at Sunny. She watched suspicion take root on his face. "You haven't unpacked yet, have you?"

"No, I haven't. I mean…well, this was in my hanging bag and besides my cosmetic case, there was no need to unpack the Pullman."

"Pullman." The word came out like the juror's verdict. *Guilty.*

Why didn't the floor just open up and swallow her? "Besides, when I got back to the room after dinner, the beds had been turned down and my big case was lodged under one of them."

Dan hooked his thumbs in his belt and towered over her. "Your case wouldn't be a black nylon softside with tan leather trim?"

She winced, unable to determine if her companion was going to throttle her or run. He shifted his weight from one foot to the other and finally raised a pointed finger at her.

"Lady…"

He hesitated, as though what he wanted to say wasn't exactly fit for a lady. She could hardly blame him.

"Hey, it's not *my* fault," she reminded him. But why her? Of all the suitcases the cruise line could have switched with his, why did *hers* have to be the culprit? It looked like everything that *could* go wrong and *had* gone wrong with this guy's trip had her signature on it.

Or at least her initials.

"You're right," he conceded reluctantly, "but ever since we met, it's been like traveling with the mistress of mayhem." Sunny flinched as he wrapped his fingers about her arm and firmly ushered her down the corridor. "Anyone ever tell you that you were dangerous?"

"Not in so many words," she sighed. If she told him of all the admittedly calamitous predicaments she'd been involved in, the poor guy would probably jump overboard and try swimming back to Miami.

Six

"And now may the peace of the Lord go with you until we meet again. Amen."

"Amen," echoed the small group gathered in the main salon the following morning. Through the open double doors on either side of the salon, the ocean glittered in the eastern sun, a vast testimony to the glory of the Creator.

It was the first Sunday that Sunny had ever worn a swimsuit and cover-up to church, but then the small shipboard service was geared toward vacationers. The pastor, Reverend Chuck Stuart, received a discounted fare for conducting it, which was a good thing, considering the five children seated next to his wife in the front row. Their heads looked like stairsteps graduating from the tallest of two boys to the shortest of three girls.

The Stuarts had the same adjoining room setup as Daniel and she had, except that it was on the opposite side of the ship. Sunny and her two charges breakfasted with the family at a buffet on an open deck earlier rather than attend the formal affair in the dining room. The Stuart boys had met Jason at the arcade the night before, while, to Mrs. Stuart's delight and relief, Allison took to the little girls—ages three, five, and seven—that morning. The shy teen helped the younger children with their fruit and cereal. Baby-sitting was in Allison's genes, seeing as that was how Sunny and Melinda had made extra money as kids.

"We'll see you guys up at the pool later," Melinda said as the family walked out together onto the promenade.

She'd confided to Sunny earlier that she and Alan had a wonderful evening dancing into the wee hours in the main salon. Melinda's blush was like a schoolgirl's. Alan was right. It was working.

Taken back to a time when they shared accounts of their dates, Sunny countered Melinda's story with the disastrous end to her evening with Daniel Jarrett.

"I don't know what it is about this guy," Sunny exclaimed, "but he called me a mistress of mayhem. I mean, what are the chances of *that*? Of the scillions of people traveling over the holiday, that I would be on the same plane, knock his hat off, sprawl on him on the bus, wind up in the room adjoining his, be seated at his table, *and* have his luggage?"

"Sounds like fate to me," Melinda observed, pulling a big-sister look.

Sunny ignored her. "Why is it that every time you have a romantic evening, I have a disastrous one? This princess and the clown bit is wearing thin."

It had become a family joke, one Sunny managed to laugh at, even if at her own expense. Her dad dubbed Melinda his princess and Sunny his sunshine. But as Sunny was quick to point out to her family, Sunshine was also the name of a clown.

Fortunately, Sunny had been raised with enough security in her faith and family love to realize not everyone could be everything. As children, Melinda was the perfect ballerina; Sunny was Daddy's fishing partner. In high school, Melinda was the prom queen, Sunny the valedictorian. Then, with her parents' illnesses…well, Melinda barely made it through the last few months, even though Sunny had taken on the bulk of her parents' care.

In the Elder house, each sister was loved for who she was. Still, it just figured that Sunny made an impression on a guy as a *mistress of mayhem* rather than her prettier sister's *She's so gorgeous and charming, I want to keep her.*

"Well, if he doesn't run the next time you see him," Melinda counseled, "then you've made a better impression than you think."

"He's on a ship, Sis. He can only get so far."

"It's a big boat."

It was a big world until she'd met Dan, Sunny thought. And most likely he was thinking the same thing. "I'll catch you later," she said, ending the pursuit to nowhere. Sun and fun were on her agenda, nothing else. "The kids have hooked up with friends, so I can't vouch for them."

Jason had already disappeared with the Stuart boys, and Allison was helping Mrs. Stuart round up the little ones to change into swimsuits for later.

"You are the best." Melinda hugged Sunny. When she backed away, her eyes were glazed with emotion. "I don't know what I did to deserve a sister like you. Sunny, you were right—" Her voice broke. "About everything."

Sunny switched from her silly quandary to what mattered most to her: her loved ones' happiness. A blade of relief wedged in her throat. *Yes, God. This is what I've prayed for.*

"Add me to the grateful list, too." Alan meandered back from the rail where he'd been watching some seagulls circling overhead. He bussed Sunny on the cheek and spared her the trouble of a witty reply to lighten the sudden downswing of mood. "Even if you are a mistress of mayhem."

"Just go back to bird watching, you eavesdropper."

"You have to admit, Sunny, it is rather funny…all the coincidences with you and Dan," Melinda pointed out.

"And hey, after what this family's been through," Alan inserted, "we need all the laughs we can get."

Sunny nodded in full agreement. They'd each had more than their share of burden of late. While she'd seen her parents fade away, Melinda and Alan had seen to packing up the house and settling the estate, like dismantling what remained of their childhood memories. Each of them had played a major part in the family crisis, according to their talents.

Sunny watched her sister and brother-in-law walk hand in hand down the promenade toward the gift shop and fought a pang of envy. After all, this was what they came for.

All right, already, having a guy worship the ground one walked on would be nice, especially right now. She wondered if she'd ever learn to love for keeps, instead of running a triage of the heart—just sort through them and move on. Her coworkers said she was too picky. Her sister said she was afraid of longterm commitment. Maybe Melinda was right.

The sun-sequined sea, spread beyond the rail for as far as the eye could see, held no answer. *Lord, calming the storm is your department. I'm a mistress of mayhem, no matter how hard I try for Miss Serenity.*

"Sunny!"

Gail Madison drew Sunny from her soul search. The young woman, looking decidedly pregnant in a maternity swimsuit ensemble, caught up with her. "I just wanted to thank you for taking Dan under your wing last night. Wasn't that hysterical, your suitcases getting switched?"

"Yeah, those airline gorillas are rough on luggage tags. Guess when they were torn off, the handlers just stuck them back on without checking anything. Thank goodness the cruise stickers didn't get lost."

The fact that the cabin numbers and cruise line were still identifiable was fortunate for all. Whoever found the tags simply put them on the wrong cases. It could have happened to anyone, but it had to happen to Dan and her, who by now was convinced she was fit only for a loony bin. Last night they'd switched cases in silence, lest they wake the kids, which suited Sunny fine. Everything she'd said to that point had come out wrong anyway.

Oh well, what did she care?

"I take it your brother is having a better day today, now that he has his clothes."

"Much better. I introduced him to three girls from Pennsylvania this morning. They're secretaries on vacation and *single*. The last I saw him, he was surrounded by beauties trying to talk him into entering the volleyball match this afternoon." Her expression suddenly changed from pleased to alarmed. "I mean, he said you two were just friends, so…"

Sunny cut her off with a laugh. "That's it. Sharing luggage is as far as either of us wants to go."

And what she was feeling was concern, without the slightest hint of green to it, an inner voice insisted. Her long, tall Texan had admitted his aversion to emotional game playing, and now he was surrounded by bathing beauties from the north with nothing but games on their mind. Or maybe Dan said that to make certain she wasn't entertaining romantic ideas. *As if*, Sunny thought with a snort, borrowing from Allison's vocabulary. A determined purse of her lips emphasized her assertion.

"I just wish he'd meet someone right." Gail rested her hand on her stomach, fairly beaming. "We are so blessed. And Dan loves kids. You should have seen him this morning when he felt the baby kicking. His face was priceless. He said whatever it was, it was wearing spurs."

"Ah, cowpoke to the core, eh?"

"You said it. He spends so much time on the ranch, he'll never meet Miss Right." She glanced at her watch. "I'd better catch up with the others. Just wanted to say thanks."

"No problem."

Armed with the latest medical thriller, suntan lotion, and her floppy straw hat, Sunny eventually found an empty deck chair on the less crowded level above the pool. From her vantage point, she could watch the kids below splashing and having a good time with the Stuart clan. The progress of the ship through the tropical air afforded a marvelous breeze, cooling to the rows of oiled bodies lining the rails and decks of the sun and pool levels. Judging from the clatter of dishes from a lower deck, the staff was putting out a luncheon buffet.

Good grief, her breakfast hadn't even had time to digest! She glanced at the pool deck clock.

Although Sunny had a decent base tan remaining from late-summer laps at the YMCA, she sprayed a protective layer of tanning lotion over her skin and rubbed it in before turning her body over to the penetrating rays of the tropical sun. It worked like massaging fingers on her neck and shoulder muscles, which were always tight in her line of work.

Gradually, she felt herself relaxing, letting go the coils of tension that had caused her headaches after her parents' death. God had seen her through their care and now He was answering her earlier plea with the divine sedative of the sea and sun. If she could summon up this setting for an hour each day, she could toss out the migraine medicine.

So what do you think, God? She grinned at her private jest. *Okay, just kidding.* If God didn't have a sense of humor, she was in big trouble, the way she carried on a one-sided banter with Him from time to time.

"Is this lounge taken?"

Drawn from her thoughts, Sunny squinted up at the male figure standing over her. "No, I don't think so."

As her eyes adjusted to the sunlight, her new companion stripped off a floral cotton shirt and stretched out beside her.

"This is the life, huh?"

"Sure is."

"I didn't see you at the singles party last night, but I noticed you aren't wearing a ring."

Sunny cut her gaze sideways. Now that was a direct hit, if she ever heard one.

"I checked in and left early. It was a long day yesterday. I figure by the time the cruise is over, I'll be up to flying back home."

The young man laughed, flashing picture perfect teeth. "I'm Jon Lindstrom, as in *J-O-N* not *J-O-H-N*."

"Hello, Jon, as in *J-O-N*. I'm Sunny Elders, and it's spelled just like it sounds." She shook his extended hand. He looked like a Jon, with his fair features and model tan. His muscles could sell gym products. They were slick with some coconut-scented lotion. Add salt, coconut, and sun, and "beach" immediately came to Sunny's mind. But he was just too young to her notion.

"That your real name…Sunny?"

"Sure is. Mom said she watched the sun rise through the delivery room window when I was born and *voilà!* It saved her from studying baby name books."

"Well, you look like a Sunny. You know, the light hair and that big smile. It was the first thing I noticed about you."

"Big smile or big mouth?" Now *that* was a stupid thing to say, even if it was to someone who didn't interest her. She twisted the edge of her towel and tucked it into weave of the deck chair.

"Think I'll pass on that one."

"Good call." Sunny laughed. At least he was a gentleman, a bit too young for her and too old for Allison, she thought, noting the tall daiquiri he put down by his chair. He didn't look old enough to pass the I.D. muster.

"Can I get you a drink?"

A loud squeal rose from the pool below, distracting Sunny from the conversation.

"Um, no, no thank you. I'm fine."

Her charges and the Stuart kids were all in a tangle. Suddenly a figure from underneath broke free of the group and swam underwater toward the deep end of the pool.

"Excuse me." She jumped to her feet. Why hadn't Mrs. Stuart called them down for nearly drowning some poor soul? As she opened her mouth to shout for their attention, the escapee surfaced, holding a bright pink ball over his head.

Daniel Jarrett.

"No fair going into the deep end, Dan," one of the girls complained, stretching his name to sound more like *Day-an*.

"The boys can swim out here. I'm not letting them drown me without some equalizing factor." The kids broke out in laughter at Dan's declaration.

Sunny glanced around the pool but saw no trace of the three ladies Gail had mentioned earlier.

"Don't you guys get too rough," she called out in warning. After all, she was supposed to be looking after her niece and nephew. "I'm on vacation. I don't need any emergencies."

All heads turned in her direction.

"Spoilsport!" Daniel made a face, and the kids instantly imitated him.

"Hey, it's your head," Sunny shot back. "Go ahead then, drown him."

She settled back on the lounge, grinning. *Dan with two syllables.*

"Well, I suppose that answers my next question," Jon Lindstrom remarked with a tinge of disappointment.

"Oh, what's that?"

"If you're traveling alone. Although now I suppose I should ask if any of those little tadpoles down there are yours."

"I'm watching two of them for my sister. We're on a family vacation. How about you?"

"Single, no family, thank heavens."

He was so adamant, Sunny bit back saying she was sorry. She was though.

"My mom and stepfather retired to the West Coast. We don't do holidays, what with the distance and the fact that I can't stand the man."

Oh no, not *another* one. "So you're spending Thanksgiving alone?" Not spending holidays with loved ones was unthinkable to Sunny, so unthinkable, she considered inviting the stranger to share her family's table…but a strong breeze laden with liquor breath from his direction gave her cause to think again.

"Not exactly alone. There are twelve hundred or so passengers on this boat." Jon made an encompassing wave with his arm and nearly sloshed his drink on her. Bless him, he was in his cups already and it was barely noon.

"You can be alone in a crowd."

The humorous glint in his pale blue gaze flickered. "Yeah, well, that's life. Is that your brother-in-law down there?"

Unaware that she'd continued to watch the chaos below, Sunny

felt her face grow warm. "Um, no, that's our cabin…he's a friend."
Or he was until last night, when he found she was the cause of his
day in travel purgatory.

The little kids climbed up Daniel's back and dove off his broad
shoulders as he knelt in the water. The larger ones, he simply tossed
into the deep end. At the moment the littlest Stuart girl was
perched on his back, squealing with delight as he bobbed like a
horse in the water.

"So what's keeping you from joining the chaos?"

"Got to act my age sometime," Sunny answered, not really
thinking.

"So you're footloose and fancy-free. I like that in a woman."

"What?" Sunny looked up, face blank, then she caught his
drift. "Well, I'm not that footloose and fancy-free." She stared at his
daiquiri—a facade covering loneliness.

"Tell you what. How about I watch your drink, and you go get a
burger from the bar?" Jon needed someone to talk to. She just felt it.

"Already have a fruit cocktail—" he lifted his glass—"but I'll be
glad to get you one, Sunny Sunshine."

"I'm still stuffed from brunch."

Jon leaned over Sunny's chair, white teeth gleaming. "Then
how about taking a dip with me in the hot tub and share the chemistry?"

Share the chemistry? Sunny's disposition soured. "I'm fine right
here. You go ahead without me."

Indignation flashed through the flirtation in Jon's sky blues so
suddenly that Sunny was taken back. A closer look revealed her
unsolicited admirer was not all sun and fun. "What, is Miss Sunny
Sunshine too good to hot tub with the likes of me?" His voice rose,
drawing attention from the people sunning in their deck chairs.

"No, Miss Sunshine just wants to sit in the sun and read her book, thank you." Sunny's reply was as cool as she could make it without being rude. "I have my idea of fun, and you have yours."

"What do you mean by that?"

"She means she'd rather read in the sun than stew in a tub of hot water."

Sunny jerked, as shocked by Dan Jarrett's voice as the icy droplets of water he flicked at her sun-warmed skin. But Dan wasn't looking at her. He stared Jon down. Most gals would consider it a feather in their caps to have two guys vying for their company, but not Sunny. She'd stitched up too many studly types to enjoy the charged situation.

"Actually, Jon, I'm a nurse and I was concerned that your combination of alcohol, no food, a hot tub, and the sun might cause you to pass out."

Jon looked at her in surprise, the first to give up in the eye to eye standoff. "Look, Sunshine, I came on this gig to get away from my mama." He jumped up and pointed to the vacated chaise. "And Papa," he derided at Dan.

"Well, *son,*" Dan drawled, "we only have your best interest in mind. You know that, don't you?" He clapped Jon on the shoulder and lowered his voice. "Besides, there's a whole bevy of beauties cooling their heels at the wading pool over there, if you get my drift."

"So…" Jon looked from Dan to Sunny and back. "Like, Sunshine is yours. Okay. I can dig that, man." He blew Sunny a kiss and grinned. "Alls you had to do was say so. I mean, now that I've had a chance to look, I can see you're a little too old for me anyway. No offense, ma'am."

Sunny smiled in a mingle of relief and peeve. He could have left the *little too old* part off. "None taken." Well…not much, anyway.

She watched as Jon wove his way toward the shallow pool and eased in between two bikini-clad girls who looked to be just a little older than Allison. Thankfully, her niece was not among them.

"That's just where he belongs. In the kiddie pool." Dan wise-cracked at her side.

"Poor guy," she said, turning to her knight in shining...make that *dripping* swim trunks. *Be still my heart.*

"He's a jerk."

"He's immature and doesn't have enough sense to appreciate what he has. It breaks my heart to hear how he speaks of his parents. Their generation is priceless, not just in love, but in wisdom."

Dan narrowed his gaze at her—shades of gold and umber as warm as the sun itself. "You *are* an old timer, aren't you?"

And equally as dangerous as the predator who just retreated, she thought. She cupped her hand to her ear. "Eh? What's that, sonny?"

Instead of laughing, he put his hand over hers—which quite effectively stopped her heart. "You know, just because you had two wonderful parents doesn't mean everyone does. And just because you're a nurse, doesn't mean you can fix all the family problems of the world. You're so transparent, *Sunny Sunshine.*"

Sunny hoped not. If so, Dan would see her frozen heart shivering in fear of losing another chunk—to him. Tears glazed her eyes and she looked away. *I want to help, Lord, but I don't want to get hurt.* Sunny pulled herself together. "Call me that again, buster, and I'll personally toss you off the high dive."

"Oh yeah. I forgot who I was dealing with." Chuckling, Dan took his hand back—and her heart resumed some semblance of normal beating.

Sunny busied herself taking inventory of the pool. Jason was missing.

"You didn't by chance see where Jason went, did you?"

"Nope, he's gone to the arcade with the Stuart boys...and you're welcome."

Sunny glanced sharply at him. She hadn't really *needed* rescuing, but why pop his ego? Besides, it was flattering that he wanted to rescue her. "Thank you, Sir Laugh-a-lot."

With an answering smirk, Dan rolled his wet towel and tucked it behind his head as a pillow. Like Jon, he was muscular and sun bronzed, but a pale band marked where his wristwatch usually was, and his tan was deeper on the arms and around the neck where a shirt might be rolled up or a collar opened. He obviously stripped to the waist from time to time, though, for drastic tan lines were shaded out.

Jon, on the other hand, had that gym-hound look, carefully sculpted and flawlessly tanned indoors.

"Ah, those kids nearly killed me."

Dan propped his hands behind his head, staring up at the fluttering flags overhead. A shadow of a beard told that he'd missed his morning shave. Maybe he was beginning to relax.

"Yeah, *Day-an,* I heard you shouting 'stop' all the way up here." Her sidewise look revealed he had dimples tucked at each corner of his smile, as rakish as the slight curl of his sideburns. "How come you didn't go to the arcade, too?"

He turned his head to meet her gaze. "Have to act my age sometime."

Sunny stared at him, struck by hearing her standby excuse. Could it be? Was there a kindred spirit somewhere behind those eyes? Eyes that defined warmth...

Sunny fisted her toes against the bottoms of her feet, trying to brake the sweep of awareness assaulting her. Sunblock was useless protection from those babies.

She forced words past a suddenly thick tongue. "So, you're still speaking to me, huh?"

"In self-defense." He rolled back to stare at the sky. "It helps to know one's adversary. You know, you've actually gone for twelve hours without a disaster."

"The day ain't over yet." A wry twist claimed her lips. "Least you'll be *dressed* for whatever happens next."

Daniel laughed, the ridged muscles of his stomach constricting. A six-pack abdomen, if there ever was one. Sunny had seen a belly dancer on some television show flip coins on her stomach, one at a time. She wondered if he could do the same.

Shocked at her thoughts, she looked at her book.

"So, how'd the volleyball match go?" The moment the words were out, Sunny wanted to retract them, but it was too late. Daniel raised his head and cut her a curious glance.

"It's not till later this afternoon. How'd you know about that?"

"Gail told me she'd matched you up with some girls from Pennsylvania." She winced inwardly. What else could she say, even if it looked like she was keeping tabs on him?

A waiter materialized from nowhere, carrying a tray of drinks. "Two piña coladas?"

"Yes, that's me." Daniel took two tall drinks from the tray and handed one to Sunny. "Nonalcoholic. Just a midday treat. Allison said you like coconut; Jason said strawberry with whipped cream. I took the lady's advice."

"Thank you." She watched as Daniel signed the check. He'd asked the kids what she liked? She took a sip of the delicious concoction, but it was too thick to drink without using the straw the waiter handed her.

"Do you make a habit out of reading upside down?" Dan pointed to the book she'd been studying.

Sunny blinked her eyes to focus. Sure enough, it was upside down. So much for demure. "Yeah, keeps the eye sharp. Helps when I have to do those tiny stitches in the ER."

"Ah." Dan put his drink down and folded his hands behind his head.

That one word could express so much doubt and send even more blood racing to her face was incredible. Sunny glanced at her toes, certain they were blanched white by the tidal shift within her.

"So, what's on the agenda for tomorrow in Jamaica? Do you plan to crash any planes or sink any boats?"

She stiffened. "Aw, come on, I'm not *that* bad. I'll have you know—"

Her companion reached over lazily and wiped a smidgeon of the frothy drink from the tip of her nose with his finger. If her glass hadn't been plastic, she'd have crushed it in her hand.

"I'll bet your guardian angel is in tatters, just keeping up with you."

It was an insignificant gesture, but it touched Sunny to the core. Of course, she was just an extension of the kids as far as Daniel Jarrett was concerned. He chided and treated her like one, yet the effect was not childlike at all. Sunny felt as though her lungs had been robbed of breath, while her companion waited for her reply.

For once, she was speechless.

Seven

$\mathcal{T}$HE ONLY REASON Sunny watched the volleyball match later
that afternoon was because it was on the way back from the ice
cream parlor, *not* because Daniel mentioned where and when it
would be. At least that's what she told herself. Far be it from her and
Allison, who was *not* too old to delight in such an indulgence while
the Stuart girls took their afternoon naps, to haul their sinfully delicious sundaes back to the room. The ice cream would melt by the
time she found it.

Still, she had to admit to admiring Daniel's form as he threw
himself into the game. His hair was slicked back off his face and
was curling impishly about his neck. He could have walked off the
set of one of those beach television shows, but then, so could half
the bodies on the court. Sunny had some color from her daily laps
at the Y outdoor pool, but these folks looked like they worshiped
the sun.

"Cute, huh?" Allison cast a sly glance at her aunt.

"Wipe the chocolate off your face," Sunny growled back. She
and Allison were not the only ones paying attention to the lean

physique of the tall Texan. The bikini-clad girls surrounding him never missed a chance to bump into him while going after a hit. Poor guy couldn't move without a collision.

Yeah, like he's really suffering…

"You know, Dan didn't get his table number changed after all," Allison remarked, a little too nonchalantly.

Sunny wasn't certain whether the news itself or its sly delivery from a niece growing up entirely too fast for Sunny's liking was more surprising. After a family meeting at lunch, Melinda and Alan had given into the kids' pleas to leave their seating arrangements as they were, since Thanksgiving Dinner was supposed to be an open seating in both dining rooms and the maître d' assured them it would be no problem for the whole group to eat together that one time. But Sunny had been certain Dan and his family would be united by this evening's meal. What a shame he was so stubbornly set against accepting his new stepfather. Both Charlie and Dan's mother were good people, so far as she could discern. But that was not her problem…

Sunny shook herself, resuming the role of chaperone. "Shouldn't that be *Mr.* Jarrett, young lady?"

"You know he told us to call him Dan. What do *you* call him?" The younger girl gave her a surreptitious side glance.

"None of your beeswax…although I've thought of a few names aside from *Dan*," she added with a devilish grin. "And a man like him is handsome, not cute. Marshall Stuart is cute."

"Like I noticed." It was Allison's turn to burn at the cheeks. Just as Sunny thought. All her niece's interest in the Stuart girls wasn't totally unselfish. "But he's so immature. Like, he hangs out with Jason. I'd take Sean any day."

"Sean? The waiter?"

"He is *so* awesome. I like a man with polish."

"That's not *polish*, Allison, that's an accent and impeccable manners. He's Irish, I think. Born to charm, not to mention too old for you." Come to think of it, Sean certainly seemed dedicated to sweeping crumbs off their table, especially around her niece. She studied Allison in a new light, a protective instinct surging to the fore.

"You always said I acted older than my age. Besides, I just love to hear him talk. He—" Allison had this sudden look of horror on her face. "Aunt Sunny, look out!"

Her niece's warning came too late. All Sunny saw was an incoming white ball. Then she was wearing what was left of her banana split. She couldn't blame the onlookers, who didn't have the decency not to laugh. It was just one of those funny things, provided none of them was the one sporting ice cream on her face and chest, not to mention a splattered whipped cream goatee.

"Sorry, ma'am. Are you okay?" The recreation director, a perky, ponytailed blond, bounded up the steps to Sunny's level.

"Always wanted to try a milk bath. Why not an ice cream shower?" she answered with a halfhearted chuckle.

"Let me get you a towel—"

"Got one right here." Sunny dug one out of her beach bag. "I'm fine, really." *Just go back to the game and let the dope mop the splattered split off without an audience.*

But her wish was not to be. The perky blond stood there ready to help until Sunny was finished. Which she did, with a flourish and a wave of the towel. "Let the games continue."

Had she worn an olive wreath in lieu of a sundae, a *Hail Sunny* might have been in order instead of the general round of applause her sporting attitude evoked. She offered a hapless shrug to the spectators below, where Dan stood, hands on hips, shaking his head at her. Something told her she hadn't heard the last of this.

"Guess you'll want the shower first, huh?"

Sunny gave Allison a fierce look and then burst out laughing.

"You got that right. I'd better go now, before this sticky mess dries." She dropped the remains of her plastic banana boat into the trash container next to the inner passage door. "Come on. You can tell me all about Sean and Marshall." After this, discussing men with her sixteen-year-old niece should be a piece of cake.

A shower and a catnap later, Sunny felt human again. It never ceased to amaze her how tiring lazing in the sun and eating—no, *wearing*—ice cream could be. She'd worked double shifts and had more energy. Since it was a formal night, she helped Allison roll her shoulder-length, golden brown hair into a cascade of ribboned ringlets accented with artificial baby's breath. It seemed only a few years ago that she'd been trying to work those little Velcro barrettes into what there was of her niece's hair. Allison grew prettier and prettier, a good blend of her mother and father. Tonight, she looked older than her sixteen years, at least to Sunny.

Jason blitzed through the shower while Sunny was letting her own dress steam to get out the wrinkles. There was a party for the adolescents in the disco during the captain's pregala cocktail party, including games and dancing. Jason and the guys, however, were killing the time till dinner in the arcade. Left to her nephew, he'd have a bunk between the machines.

"He is *so* juvenile." Allison commented predictably as he bolted out the door, letting it slam behind him. *Juvenile* had become her favorite word for her brother. She bent over and picked up a wadded pair of briefs. "He sheds like a snake. Wherever his clothes come off is where they stay."

"That's why we call them *juveniles*," Sunny teased. "I hear some men never outgrow it. As for the briefs, put them in his pillow. The dirty socks, too. We'll break him of snaky habits, at least in this little cabin."

Allison giggled. "Aunt Sunny, you are *so* devious."

Alli looked like a princess as they walked down the steps winding around the sparkling chandelier in the grand entrance into the dining room. They'd already posed for pictures, per Melinda and Alan's request. The couple had been just coming in from the pool as Sunny and Alli headed for the captain's receiving line. A waitress paused with a tray of glasses containing the captain's complimentary champagne, but Sunny ordered sodas instead.

"Trust me, there's not enough sugar on the ship to make it taste right," she explained, when her niece pulled a long face over being treated like the minor she was. "Not to mention not enough room for me to escape the wrath of your mom and dad if I let you sip the bubbly."

"Coward," Allison pouted.

"I prefer to think of myself as supremely intelligent with a penchant for keeping my hide *and* yours intact." Sunny gave Allison a gentle push on the tush.

"Oh, Aunt Sunny!" Her niece's giggle evoked an equally girlish one in her as well. "When are you going to grow up?"

"When Peter Pan does."

"You are *so* hopeless."

As they walked down the winding stairwell into the dining salon, Sunny held back and took notice of the admiring glances cast her niece's way with a mixture of pride, wonder, and concern. Allison was growing up so fast it made Sunny's head spin. Braces and the underwire support of the young girl's spaghetti-strapped dress just didn't seem to go together.

Jason, who would even give up a video game to eat on time, and Daniel were waiting for them at the table. Daniel stood up and nudged the boy to his feet.

"It's just Aunt Sunny and my sister," Jason remarked, as if his mentor had lost his mind.

"Ladies, nonetheless," Dan said through a winning smile. "My, but you two look ravishing."

"So do you," Sunny quipped as the table steward pulled back a chair for her. If Daniel kept looking at her like that, she might as well stick a roll in her mouth so she wouldn't have to answer. Electricity ran beneath her skin, pricking the fine hair at the nape of her neck.

"I don't know how they think a man can eat with a rope knotted at his throat," Jason complained, tugging at his clip-on tie. "I'm changing back into my cargo shorts as soon as the grub's served."

"You'll get used to it, sport," Daniel assured him. "It's one of those necessities of life. Ladies don't doll up for guys in jeans."

"Who wants 'em to?"

Dan cuffed Jason on the back of his head good-naturedly. "*You* will in a few years, Jase, trust me." He winked at Sunny and chuckled.

It was just a joke, Sunny told herself sternly. He was more at ease with her than with his family, given his circumstances. That was likely the reason he'd left the table arrangements as they stood.

But he *was* ravishing, she admitted, noting how his dark suit was tailored to define his wide shoulders and narrow waist. The dark blue silk weave was shot with threads of black to match the western tie leisurely cinching a crisp collar. And his dimples could hold sugar, Sunny thought, watching as he settled Allison in her chair before resuming his seat. Never mind hold…they could *melt* it.

"Oh, I almost forgot." Seemingly startled, Daniel rose and plucked a spare napkin from the serving station. Snapping it with a brandish, he leaned over and gingerly tucked it into the modest neckline of Sunny's dark apricot dress. "Will this do, or should I get a tablecloth?"

She'd known she hadn't heard the last of the spilled sundae. Allison giggled hysterically, but Sunny merely gave him an indulgent smile. "Ha, ha. I think I'm safe as long as they don't allow volleyballs in here."

"Yeah," Jason snickered. "Dan said you looked good in a banana split."

"That's based on my limited knowledge of women who wear ice cream," Daniel stipulated with a devilish wink.

"It was probably you who knocked the ball up there."

He threw up his hands. "Not guilty. It was Michelle something-or-other from Pennsylvania. The one who wore a pink swimsuit?"

Sunny was tempted to say that he meant the one who *almost* wore a pink swimsuit, but she retracted her claws. How women wore thongs was beyond her. The risk of sunburn alone was enough to give her the heebie-jeebies, although the girl in question had certainly tanned nicely. Sunny waylaid another catty thought and picked up the menu. If she kept on, she'd have to settle for a saucer of cream and some catnip.

"That was one clumsy group of girls," Daniel said, oblivious to her wicked thoughts. "You'd fit in perfectly."

She put her menu down. "What is this? Pick-on-Sunny day?"

"Hey, you gotta admit, you are pickable."

Jason wrinkled up his freckled brow. "Is that a word?"

"No," Sunny answered, "It's a lame excuse."

"Oooo, *busted*," Allison cheered. She held up her hand for Sunny to give her five.

"Watch yourself, young lady," Dan warned, "I have a long memory."

"You don't scare me, Dan. You're a softie. You should have seen him with Bethie Stuart. She had her *Day-an* wrapped around her little finger."

Daniel pulled a despairing look. "Well, I'll be a blue-nosed gopher, she's found me out."

Dinner came and went with continued banter. Daniel stuck to beef and potatoes, at least as near to that as the French cuisine of the evening would allow. Jason followed Daniel's lead with an equally adventurous spirit—or lack thereof—while Allison tried the mahi-mahi and Sunny ordered a scrumptious and rich duckling dish she couldn't pronounce. When Jason told the waiter not to set fire to his ice cream, appalling his sister, it was impossible for Sunny and Daniel to keep straight faces.

"Remind me to thank your sister and brother-in-law for the loan of the kids," he said, the tan lines around his eyes crinkling with humor. "A man could get used to this."

Sunny nearly choked before reason prevailed. He was talking about the kids, not her company. She couldn't blame him. She loved spending time with Jason and Allison. Someday she hoped to have a family of her own, although when she'd work it in was problematic, not to mention *with whom*. She avoided looking at Dan, afraid her rambling ideas might carry her over the line drawn by common sense.

It seemed that no sooner had the appetizers been served than the dessert was being cleared. Jason pulled back Allison's chair, as Daniel did with Sunny's—although Sunny held her breath, just waiting for her nephew to find a way to dump his sister on the floor. What had they talked about that made the time fly so? Water frolicking and ice cream? Sunny had to hand it to Dan. He hadn't forgotten how to be a kid. Just another of his growing list of admirable qualities.

"Well, you all certainly seemed to be enjoying your dinner. I never heard such giggling." Gail Madison grinned at them as they walked out of the dining room together.

"It's *their* fault—" Daniel pointed to Jason and Allison—"they made us act like kids. We tried not to, but—"

"Yeah, right, *dude*. You should have grown up with this long-limbed lunk." His sister poked Dan in the arm. "He had this incredible knack for making me laugh when I wasn't supposed to. So are you two big kids going to join us later?"

Sunny's face went blank at the unexpected turn of conversation. Had she heard right?

"After we're through chaperoning." Daniel gave Sunny a conspiratorial wink to head off the question on the tip of her tongue. "I've been noticing the way these young men have been eyeing Allison, so I figure she'll need a bodyguard."

"Not!" Allison's face was as red as her denial was adamant. "Besides, Marshall Stuart asked me if I wanted to go see the movie with them." At the surprised lift of Sunny's brow, she explained. "He called while you were in the shower."

"Well, we'll save you two a seat at the ten o'clock show," Gail told Dan and Sunny.

You *two*? Now, how had *that* happened? Part of her wanted to squeal like someone Allison's age, while another urged her to swallow both heart and tongue.

Before Sunny could work it out, Allison thumped her brother on the head. "Come on, squirt. Guess it's shorts for the evening after all."

"Excuse me, miss. You forgot your lipstick."

Sean, the Irish waiter, impeccably dressed in a short dinner jacket complete with cummerbund, caught up with them and handed a chapstick over to Allison. "Mustn't let the sun burn such pretty lips," he teased, intense blue eyes peering through a thick black fringe of lashes.

Women would pay a fortune for lashes like that, Sunny mused, watching her niece become as disconcerted as she felt.

"Enjoy your evening." Brandishing a wide, impish smile, Sean pivoted sharply to return to his duty, back straight, head up, with the fine-tuned poise of good training.

"See what I mean?" Daniel said, once the young man was out of earshot. He shooed the kids ahead of them. "Go on, get into some baggy shorts and a sloppy shirt before I have to duke it out with some smitten swain."

"A bird?" Jason queried, freckled nose wrinkled in confusion.

"Not *swan*," Sunny told him, falling in step beside Dan. It just seemed the thing to do. "A *swain* is a sweetheart, a boyfriend…"

It was all the ammunition a younger brother needed. "Wait'll I call Marshall a *swain*."

"Wait'll I bash your head in," Allison retaliated, giving him a thump for good measure. She barely made contact, for Jason was already darting down the hall ahead of her toward a flight of steps. Suddenly, Alli turned to Sunny.

"Charming, huh?" Her face sparkled from the waiter's attention.

Sunny gave her niece a not-so-heartfelt thumbs-up, sending her bolting after her brother. "I guess she's gotten over the fact that she's going to miss the Thanksgiving home game and dance."

"I'd say that's the farthest thing from her mind," Daniel agreed heartily.

"So what—"

"About later—"

Sunny recovered first from the simultaneous start. "What about later?"

"Feel like walking off a course or two of dinner?"

The way Daniel smiled and curved his arm around her, she would have walked off a plank right then if he went with the trip. It wasn't fair. He saw her as a friend, not a *girl*friend. And even if he didn't… Well, she wouldn't entertain that thought. Gathering up the fullness of her skirt as neatly as her runaway musings, she stepped over the sill of the passage leading to the deck. Her heel caught, but Daniel steadied her before she stumbled headlong on to the carpeted deck of the promenade.

"The door to our bathroom gets me every time," she admitted with a nervous laugh.

His aftershave blended perfectly with the salt sea air. It filled her nostrils and bowled a strike to her knees before he released her.

"I gambled on your good nature that you would accompany me and my family tonight."

"Sure it's worth the risk?" Sunny cut him a wry look. "After all, I am a mistress of mayhem."

"Just the lesser of two risks." The humor disappeared from Daniel's face with the gentle brush of the sea breeze. Suddenly he corrected his blunder. "Wait, that didn't come out right."

"Well, I could say I understand what you meant, but I'd rather watch you squirm."

Sunny gave him an evil grin, relieving him of the concern that she'd taken offense. If ever a soul needed to talk, Daniel Jarrett did. Chalk it up to experience in calming and consoling distraught family members, as well as patients, but she knew it.

Regardless, she didn't mind. Maybe this vacation was intended to mend more than one family. Maybe all the mix-ups weren't mistakes after all, but part of God's greater plan. She'd seen a lesser number of coincidences work wonders in the lives of people she'd met along the way. Humor expired, she walked straight ahead and waited for her companion to speak.

"You've got a great niece and nephew."

"I'm kinda fond of them."

"And vice versa."

Sunny cocked her head.

"Jason gave me the lowdown on Crazy Aunt Sunny," Daniel explained. "And Allison watches you as if she's not really sure what you're going to do next."

"Well, that makes two of us." She shrugged, wondering where this conversation was going. She certainly hadn't expected to be the topic of discussion. "The kids aren't giving you a hard time are they? I mean, they're not matchmaking or anything…"

"No, no." Daniel put up his hands. "Jason was just telling me about some of your escapades while he beat the tar out of me at some Kung Fu video game. I think it was a tactical effort on his part. Loser pays for the next game."

"That little devil." Sunny didn't know whether to run her nephew down right away and throttle him or wait till she caught him sleeping.

"I wasn't surprised by anything he told me."

"Do tell." She held her breath, mind racing over the past. What on earth could that child have said?

"Falling out a window headfirst into the Christmas pies was interesting."

"Oh, *that*." She laughed. "That could have happened to anyone. I mean, I had to climb through the window because a seven-foot Christmas tree was blocking the door to the porch of my little apartment. See, I needed the porch for extra-cold storage because my refrigerator was full, so…"

"Perfectly reasonable."

"And as I leaned out, I lost my balance and slid up to my elbows in strawberries and whipped cream."

"Perils of homemaking?"

"Or home wrecking." Laughing at herself, Sunny stepped over to the rail to avoid two joggers making their way around the deck. The breeze playfully whipped her skirts around her knees.

"Did you really volunteer to participate in a circus act with horses when you'd never been on one before?"

Sunny blushed. "Well, I had a belt on. Actually, I just wanted to fly around on the end of a rope in front of a few thousand people in a tent."

Dan laughed out loud. "I just can't picture you as an emergency room nurse. You're so—" Apparently at a loss for the right word, he settled for, "unpredictable."

Unpredictable wasn't bad, she thought. It could go with *mysterious* or *enigmatic*. Her answer tumbled out as scrambled as her thoughts. "Just say I enjoy life to the fullest outside the ER where it's just too short too often. Some days I wonder if I make a difference. Others, I'm on top of the world. Anyway, it's how I unwind. I guess. After all, a body can only stay straight and responsible for so long."

"I would say comedy is your forte."

"Hey, laughter is good medicine. Haven't you heard?"

The way he pondered her words, one would think she'd said something earthshaking instead of dancing a little sidestep around the part of her life she took most seriously: helping others in need, many who suffered in their last hours. Instinct reeled her in from the sober tangent before its cloud claimed her.

"So is this leading up to the reason why you told your sister we'd meet her later?" she asked, shifting to another tack. "Let me guess. If the comedian flops, you can always tell Crazy Aunt Sunny stories."

Head down, Daniel exhaled and shoved his hands into his pockets. His jaw squared, he whispered through his teeth. "Busted. Sorry, I'm just treading water here."

The apology in his upturned gaze knocked the starch out of Sunny's peeve. Whatever he wanted to say, it wasn't coming easy.

"I know. You took one look at me swathed in chocolate, vanilla, and strawberry and knew you had to spend the evening in my company."

His mouth slanted in a crooked grin, and Sunny's toes curled in response.

"You're okay, pardner…but that's not the reason. The reason is my sister and her matchmaking. Michelle, the girl in the pink—"

"Bikini, yeah, I remember."

"Well, she and her cronies wanted to meet me at the show and party afterward, but I told them I'd already made plans."

"With me." Sunny finished in an I-don't-believe-this tone. A faint glimmer of a hope she wouldn't even acknowledge faded like the remnant of an expired sparkler.

Daniel grimaced. "Yeah. I meant to say something before Gail cornered us. I mean, it worked great last night…for the most part, that is," He grinned. "I still haven't gotten over thinking I'd have to wear one of those weird T-shirts."

"I had a perfectly good reason for not unpacking," Sunny pointed out in self-defense.

"Just like you did to crawl out the window with a tray of pies?"

"Listen, *pardner*, I'm not the one with the problem here." Sunny crossed her arms in her most professional, charge-nurse pose. "Sure, I'll bail you out…or you could just tell Michelle and her friends the truth. You're—" She broke off suddenly, realizing she wasn't even sure why Dan Jarrett didn't warm to a bevy of beauties chasing him. "What is the truth? You're not…I mean…" A long, full-length appraisal of a 101 percent male, his clueless look and all, answered her question before she made a fool of herself. "You could just tell them thanks, but you came to spend time with your family."

"I did tell them that I came on this vacation because I couldn't tell my mother and sister no, and that I wasn't into parties and games, and that I had too much on my mind to have a good time, and that I'd be a bore."

"And?" Sunny asked, glad she hadn't asked him outright if he liked girls. She'd been exposed to everything at work and sometimes the worldly exposure jaded her judgment.

"Suddenly I had four sister Gails all determined to bring me out of my shell and show me a good time."

She leaned on the rail, looking out at the ocean, acutely aware of the man next to her. "Why would that be so terrible? We all need to unwind sometime. It's not as if you would have to propose to any of them."

He didn't look at her but stared out at the star-spangled night as if an answer might lie there. "I have reason to want to be left alone. There's something going on right now, and I'm afraid it's going to devastate the family. Until I'm certain of it, I can't say anything."

Alarm invaded her sympathy. How many times had she heard those words, or at least the essence of them? She glanced at him, the nurse in her kicking in. Was Daniel ill? If so, it certainly didn't show. He was a picture of health and vitality.

"Well, there's no sense in dwelling on it, whatever it is, until you're certain. Things aren't always what they seem at first. Professionals make mistakes. Reports get mixed up."

"I hope that's the case. I really do...but everything points to the worst." He grimaced and turned toward her. "I'd have been better off to just stay home and work to keep my mind occupied. Here, there's nothing to do but dwell on it. It's in my face, no matter where I turn." His jaw squared with the clench of his teeth.

Sunny placed a gentle hand on his arm and forced a grin. "Well, if the kids and I can't drive you to distraction, nothing can. But I'm warning you, I do it, too."

"Do what?" Dan gave her a surprised look.

"When something is really bothering me, something I feel helpless to deal with, I tend to bury myself in my work, too. So I know where you're coming from, pardner. But there's something else I do."

"Oh?"

"I give it to God. There are many things I can't make right, but He can. And if He doesn't, then I have to allow that He knows best and that whatever happens…well, it will be best in the long run."

"Sounds good in theory. In practice, it's another story."

"You don't believe in silver linings?"

"I don't know." Dan shook his head. "Maybe mine are tarnished because I've drifted away from church since Mom moved out. Just been too busy."

"I don't think I've ever needed my church family more than during the loss of my folks. It's sort of like the shock is draining you of strength and faith, and hearing God's promises and seeing His earthly messengers helps keep you from running out of it completely."

"Never thought of it that way," Dan acknowledged. "I figured you either have faith or you don't."

"You do. Take blood, for instance: We have it or we're dead. But the quality of it constantly changes with our health and lifestyle."

The face Dan pulled all but shouted one of Allison's favorite expressions: *Ooh, gross!* If he stayed around Sunny long, he'd have to get used to it.

She chuckled softly. "My point is, we get a spirit transfusion at church. We emerge from the heart surgery of loss stronger and wiser. It's hard to see while you're in faith's I.C.U., but beyond the wires and tubes and closed blinds, the sun is shining and waiting for you."

"If you had a head full of red curls and a goofy looking dog, I'd swear you're about to start singing something about the sun coming out tomorrow." Dan's grin softened the edge of his voice.

Sunny took a deep breath, glad that he had lightened the tone of their conversation. Her words of reassurance struck so close to home. She believed in their truth, that God was in charge and that no mistakes had been made, but it didn't make her heart hurt less.

She gave herself a mental smack, determined not to let gloomy thoughts in. She'd come to relax, not to dwell on her loss. She refused to do that. She couldn't…or she'd end up like Melinda, a basketcase. That was the problem with relaxing—it gave her time to grieve. Well, she just wouldn't have it.

"Hey, are you okay?" Concern infused Dan's tone and expression, as if he somehow sensed the emotional war waging within her.

Stubbornly, Sunny opted for a zany exit from the desolation nudging at her. Fluffing imaginary curls, she struck a stagelike pose and started to sing the hope-filled chorus Dan mentioned. "Oh, the sun—"

Her companion grabbed her arm and tugged her from the rail playfully.

"Look, there's plenty of entertainment without having to make fools of ourselves. What do you say we take a load off our feet?"

"Was I just insulted?" Sunny complained, falling into step with Dan's long stride as two couples passed them with indulgent smiles. Humor. It was God's gift to her. Laughter, even at oneself, was a soothing balm.

"How about an after-dinner drink?"

"No, I've worn enough refreshments for one day."

Dan laughed out loud. It was a bone-warming sound. Sunny dropped into one of the lounges placed along the promenade. "I think I'll just sit here and *drink* in this lovely setting. I declare, relaxing is just about as tiring as work."

Dan stood for a moment before taking the chair beside her. "You're right about that. It's a shame to waste all this, cooped up inside. Unless you'd rather be alone," he added hastily.

"Sharing the good things in life is one of its greatest rewards," she replied, hesitating before going on. "Even sharing the bad can be rewarding, I guess."

Maybe with a little nudge, she could get Dan to talk about what was bothering him. After all, she *was* a nurse. He might actually feel comfortable speaking to her about it. It's what she was called to do. It was what she'd trained for. Maybe if she shared first, it would make him feel more comfortable, open the door to the secluded room he seemed trapped in.

Did she dare? If she approached her pain from a professional standpoint, she reasoned, she could. She took the plunge. "I know I couldn't have faced my parents' illnesses without sharing how I felt with God and those He sent to offer support and comfort."

The wooden arms of the chair were cool and moist with the evening dew against the skin bared by her sleeveless dress. An involuntary shiver ran through her. What was it about Dan Jarrett that reached out to her? Regardless, it was clear that he needed someone—a friend. Her needs, on the other hand, became hazier each time he touched her with his hand or his easygoing charm.

A warning bell rang somewhere in the depths of her mind as she waited for a response from her companion. She was fretting over the wrong thing…

Forget digging up unspent grief. What she should be worried about was digging a hole for her heart.

Eight

$\mathcal{L}$IKE THE WALRUS and the Carpenter, sans the beach, Sunny and her solemn companion spoke of many things while watching another liner running a parallel course into the night. It looked like a flamboyant, lighted city coasting on moon-silvered waters. They talked of work, admitting it sometimes took the lonely edge off single life. And yet, no matter how Sunny circled back toward the subject of sharing ups and downs with family, Dan managed to evade her rope.

"I guess it must get lonely out there on the range, now that your mom has moved out," she ventured. "I know I miss not being able to drop in on my folks any time. I haven't even been by the house since it was sold." Sunny shuddered at the thought. "I just can't bear to think of it as any way but what it was."

"I know exactly what you mean, except imagine having to live in it now with all the memories. Ever since I can remember, our house was always full of people. Now I feel like the only marble left in the sack."

"But your mom is still living."

Unlike hers. Pain, sharp and breathtaking, pierced her at the thought. For a moment Sunny thought she might double over, but with a stubborn will she pushed the hurt away. She was here to address Dan's problems, not her own.

"And you wish you had the right person," she rallied valiantly, "like your sister found, and maybe a few kids like Jason and Allison to fill the void, but you just don't have the time or inclination to invest in looking for the right one."

Amazement struck Dan's face at her remark. "Exactly. I don't even like to shop in a store for a pair of pants. Order 'em through a catalog."

"When you've got a perfectly proportioned body, you can do that. I, on the other hand—" Sunny broke off, realizing what she'd said. Okay, so he knew she thought he had a great bod. Big deal. Reason, however, didn't stop the color from searing her face as she continued. "My point is, women have more proportions and different cuts and varieties of clothing to fit than men do. Besides, I love to shop."

"I think that's genetic. Men usually know what they want and just go get it."

"Or order it."

"Or order it. Women are the impulse buyers…even when it comes to men sometimes."

A decided damper had closed on Dan's humor. Sure she was close to a diagnosis at last, Sunny waited for him to go on. Had he been bought on impulse and then tossed aside?

"Who goes out on a cruise, meets a perfect stranger, falls head over heels in love, and marries someone without knowing a *thing* about him?"

The moment it hit her, she was shocked. "Are you speaking of your mom and Charlie?"

His silence answered the question. Dan stared off at the distant liner, his jaw tensely set. So *that* was the burr under the cowboy's saddle. What on earth did Dan find objectionable about Charlie Meyers, besides a whirlwind courtship, which to Sunny was romantic. She'd never met a more affable character than Dan's new stepfather.

Before she could ask, a thunderous burst of footsteps at the stern of the ship distracted them both. No civilized joggers these, but a gaggle of kids pounding the carpeted promenade, like a stampede of elephants in sneakers. To Sunny's horror, Jason was at the lead, running neck and neck with the younger Stuart boy. Allison and the elder Stuart trotted along a good distance behind.

"Jog, don't gallop!" Sunny called out from the shadows in a drill sergeant tone as the boys passed them. Surely the movie wasn't over yet. She punched the glow button on her watch, startled to see the hand moving toward ten.

"You might run down some sweet old ladies out for an evening stroll," Daniel added. "What'd you do, skip out on the pic?"

Jason threw on the brakes and leaned over to catch his breath, hands on knees.

"Naw, it's over. That you in there, Aunt Sunny?" He squinted, uncertain.

"With Dan...in the *dark?*" Allison exclaimed, on catching up with them. She folded her arms across her chest in mock reproval, foot tapping. "And what have you two been up to?"

"Chewing the fat," Dan said.

"Solving the world's problems," Sunny quipped, still astonished at how fast, how comfortably, the time had flown.

"Waiting for some energy-overdosed kids to gallop by at breakneck speed. Call it instinct." Dan rose to his feet, stretching. "But your aunt and I knew that you'd break loose sooner or later."

"Not!" Allison challenged.

He looked at his watch. "What's their curfew?"

"Ten, since we're heading out early tomorrow." Allison had signed them and her mother up for the horseback ride at a Jamaica polo club the next day while Alan played golf.

"Well, they're late." Dan looked as shocked at the time on his watch as Sunny was.

"Okay, gang. Hop to it. That goes for you boys, too. I imagine your folks are looking for you now." Sunny turned to Dan as the Stuart boys trotted off. "I'll meet you in the grand salon after I get these two tucked in."

"You got it, pardner," he agreed, pointing a gun finger at her before he headed for his door.

"Can we watch a movie in our room?"

Sunny ruffled her nephew's hair, the bowl part, which hadn't been shaved close in the latest fashion. "No way, José."

"Did he kiss you?" Allison asked in a stage whisper.

Sunny gave her niece's gathered curls a tug. They were damp from the sweat of running around the deck. "Get real. Dan Jarrett and I are just *friends*."

Dan saw Sunny roll her eyes as she glanced back at him upon reaching her cabin door. Shooing her charges in ahead, she reminded him of a hen with her chicks—motherly, but in the most unorthodox way. Must be habit, he mused, entering his own retreat. A gaggle of kids running amok wasn't much different, he supposed, from an influx of trauma patients. Either way, they had to be dealt with and quickly. Despite her unusual tactics, she handled them quite well—a pied piper, if there ever was one.

Smiling wistfully, Dan sacked the tie, knowing full well his mother would frown if he showed up on formal night without his coat. He could remember sweating through long summer sermons in coat and choking tie, and not the clip-on type Jason bemoaned wearing. Back then he'd suffered because he had to. Now he did it out of respect. He shoved the tie in his coat pocket, just in case.

An explosive *pop* from the other side of the wall, followed by startled shrieks, brought a grin to his face. He'd heard two balloons go that morning. The first woke him. The second made sure he stayed awake. It was hard to tell how many of the original *Bon Voyage* cluster had expired throughout the day. A few were Mylar, which meant a long, slow death.

At least Sunny had a balloon's worth more room in the cabin. He'd seen inside her cabin when the steward was making up the beds. There was single-file standing room only.

Dan surveyed his own accommodation. It boasted no more than phone-booth walk space, and he didn't have to share it. Dropping into the chair to wait for Sunny to leave her cabin, he grimaced. *Lucky him.*

The sound of soft singing beyond the wall drew him from his self-pity. Sunny's laughter should have told him that her voice would be as melodic in song. He thought he recognized the tune, a gunfighter ballad of old. He leaned his head back against the bulkhead and listened, stifling a yawn spawned from a full belly and a day of hard work avoiding Charlie Meyers. Odd, he didn't mind telling a total stranger about his suspicions…

Maybe it was her professional training, but Sunny Elders was a good listener, more interested in others than herself.

Maybe a little *too* interested. Dan couldn't help but notice how she evaded the hard side of losing her parents, concentrating only on how to get over it or accept it. God was capable of all things. Dan believed that. But wasn't grieving a step in healing? Seemed to him the nurse was avoiding that, as if God would let her bypass that step.

When she talked about her parents, she hadn't teared up in the least, but spoken of the loss as if citing an example from a textbook. Dan recalled it had been a year or so before he could talk at any length about his father's death without becoming emotional. Sometimes, it still made him that way.

A crackling announcement over the loudspeaker brought Dan to his feet with a start. What had the announcer said? Something about the start of the late show? A glance at his watch told him it was twenty minutes since he'd come to his room. Sunny was probably waiting for him in the foyer separating the casino and grand salon. Straightening out his jacket and collar, he reached for the door. As he jerked it open, there was a startled gasp on the other side, which stopped him short of running over the young woman emerging from the adjoining cabin.

"Ready?" he asked, relieved that he'd not kept her.

A sheepish look overtook her face. "Almost."

"What…did you forget something?"

"Not exactly." She stopped hedging. "I just closed the door on my skirt as I was trying to slip out without disturbing the kids."

Dan had thought the strawberry-pie episode was a stretch. Now he wasn't so certain. He tried not to laugh. "Just open it."

Sunny sighed. "Can't."

"Why?"

She rolled her eyes to the ceiling. "My key is in my other purse." She held up a small evening bag. "I meant to put it in, but—"

"Want me to get the steward?" A chuckle defied his restraint. He'd caught his jacket here or there while squeezing through tight quarters, but with Sunny, the door looked like it had taken a Pac-Man bite out of her skirt.

"No." At least she accepted his humor in good grace. "Just go in through the adjoining cabin door quietly and open this from the inside…please," she added, dropping her gaze as her cheeks flushed.

The crown of her short hair shined in the passage light as though accented by a golden halo, the kind found hanging crooked on those impish cartoon angels. As Dan took a final, grinning look over her shoulder, he caught a whiff of her shampoo. *Apple,* he thought, unwittingly leaning closer than he had to. A sharp elbow jab saved him from himself.

"Okay, I'm an idiot. Things happen to me that don't happen to others," Sunny avowed beneath her breath, thankfully oblivious to his temptation.

What on earth was he doing? He'd been a breath away from kissing the golden swirl of her pixyish crown. Suddenly Sunny met his gaze. Her eyes widened ever so slightly, as if she'd read what recoiled like a loose cannon in his mind—and like a horse from a barn afire, she bolted, seizing a wisecrack for the ride.

"So go open the bloomin' door, will ya?"

As the cabin door closed behind her amused rescuer, Sunny groaned, refusing to acknowledge the hot flash of awareness creeping through her. Self-deprecation was safer.

First ice cream, now this. Maybe she should just trade her wardrobe in for a clown suit, she thought, struggling with the zipper. *Lord, why can't I be a princess…just once in a while? I'm not looking for a full-time position.*

Behind her, the door opened quietly, setting her free. She stepped to the far side of the narrow passage and managed a short "Thank you."

"My pleasure, believe me." If he grinned any wider, his mouth wouldn't fit on his face. "I didn't get your purse, but I can let you in through my cabin. Unless you're afraid someone might see us and talk." He was playing this for all it was worth.

"I don't think there's any chance of speculation on *that*." Tarnfound it, she added, walking ahead of him. She sensed more than felt Daniel's guiding hand almost touching her back as they entered the main corridor. Then it was gone.

"I guess you *could* work at the hospital," he commented behind her. "They've got those gowns with chunks missing out the back...although the dress is a sight prettier."

"Stow it, Jarrett," Sunny cast back over her shoulder. "I also completed a course in self-defense, but I *could* be persuaded to use it for offense."

At least *that* gave him something to think about, she thought smugly, taking the stairs ahead of her now silent companion. Sunny knew if she looked back, she'd see that knee-melting twinkle in his gaze. Humph, she'd like to catch him in line for a flu shot sometime. She'd put it in the largest syringe they had and wave it in front of him. Grin *and* twinkle would be history.

"What's the rush, pardner?"

Sunny slowed upon reaching the top step of the main deck, unaware that she still was in full retreat from whatever it was that had made her run. Dan had the strangest effects on her, the prevalent one being making a fool of herself. She put her hand on her stomach in demonstrative protest.

"Still trying to run off dinner."

The foyer was nearly empty. The open doors of the casino on the opposite side of the grand salon allowed the shared passage to fill with the ring and hum of slot machines and excited voices of the gamblers inside.

"Ready?"

She slipped through the swinging door to the salon at Daniel's nod.

The show had begun, so aside from the lights on the stage and the dim glow of the tiny table lamps, the room was completely dark. Sunny blinked, trying to adjust her eyes.

"We'll never find them in here," she whispered to her companion. Aside from the guests seated around the stage, the rest of the faces were obscure forms in the shadows.

The ship tacked gently to one side, and Daniel steadied Sunny with his arm, tightening it about her waist. "Just let me guide you," he told her, taking charge. "I know where they said they were going to sit."

Sunny nodded stiffly, despite the warmth invading her senses. It was all a body *could* do, when one had just inhaled one's tongue.

# Nine

*T*HE SHOW WAS entertaining. The juggler-comic-magician was terrific and involved the audience in his act. Charlie Meyers was conned into making a fool of himself all in good humor, of course. He was such a good sport that Sunny wondered again why Dan found him so objectionable. The magician had interviewed Charlie when he was on stage, and his remark that he was here with his wife and family elicited an acrid, "Yeah, right," from the young man at Sunny's side. Fortunately, no one seemed to hear him but her.

In the lull between the act and the band setting up, Sunny listened attentively, hoping to learn more about the Jarrett clan—and perhaps find a clue to the discord. It was such a shame for a nice family to be at odds. Family and time were too precious to waste on hard feelings.

She learned that Dan had taken over the small family ranch, as well as managed his mother's affairs, after his father's death. Was money the real source of conflict? Did Dan resent turning over control of his mom's finances? He was frugal, not greedy—not the way her nephew described Dan's subsidizing him and the Stuart boys at the arcade. Besides, the ranch was his and was doing well, from what she gathered.

No, greed just didn't seem to fit with the Dan she was coming to know...the one who loved kids, animals, and teasing the daylights out of a gal, given half a chance. Granted, she'd known the cowboy only a short time, but she was a pretty good judge of character. Her job required quick and accurate perception. No...this thing with Charlie was like a burr under Dan's saddle.

More likely he was just lonely, she decided. Someone had once said that wet babies were the only ones who liked change. Sunny could relate to that. It was hard to let go of the past. But she was also convinced that where one door was closed, God opened another. Perhaps *that* was her calling—to help Dan see that he needed to get on with his life and let his mother live her own.

"Look at Mom and Dad," Gail laughed, pointing to where the two cavorted to a lively two-step.

"He's your *step*dad, Sis," Dan reminded her, a cynical bite to his tone.

"I know that, little brother, but *someone* has to make Charlie feel welcome in the family, since you seem determined to do just the opposite. Besides, I think it means a lot to him...*and* to Mom. If you—"

"Come on, Gail. Let's join 'em," his brother-in-law spoke up, heading off the lecture brewing on Gail's face.

It was certainly clear that Esther Jarrett Meyers was enjoying her new life with her new love. While the band played on with dance music, the two were a joy to watch. Charlie Meyers spun his wife around on the floor beneath the swirling lights like a western Fred Astaire with Ginger in his arms. Mike Madison was more sedate with his pregnant wife, but they were no less caught up in the romantic spell of the sea.

Occasionally, Sunny stole a glance at Daniel, noting that he, too, seemed intent on the dancers, yet anything but joy showed on his face. A pang of pity tugged at her heart. Instead of pining over losing his mom, he should be taking advantage of his sister's matchmaking efforts. Don't look back, look forward.

"You know, those girls from the volleyball tournament are over there at the bar," she offered. "No sense in your family having all the fun."

"I saw them." Instead of turning in their direction, Daniel leveled his gaze at Sunny until a lump lodged in her throat. "Would you like to dance?"

"Oh, I wasn't hinting or anything. I just meant—"

"I know that. You don't have enough guile for those kind of games."

Sunny opened her mouth to reply, but couldn't decide whether she'd been complimented or insulted. Rather than appear duller than she already felt, she accepted Dan's hand.

"It's about time," Gail Madison chided, passing them on her way back to the table for a brief respite.

"All work and no play makes Dan the dull boy," Mike reminded him, giving Dan one of those male to male grins that always confounded Sunny. *Machismo ultimus,* she dubbed it with a curl of humor tugging at the corner of her mouth.

The start of an older song brought many of the senior passengers onto the dance floor. Sunny tried to avoid succumbing to nostalgia, but it was hard as the strains of "It Had to Be You" began. That was the song her father sang to her mother on the night they met and on every anniversary since. The sentiment—of all the people in the world I could have fallen in love with, it had to be you—was so romantic.

"You have a nice voice," Dan said, twirling her around in a

motion that made the room spin.

Sunny laughed nervously. "I didn't realize I was singing. This was Mom and Dad's song."

"You weren't singing. Not just now. I heard you earlier through the cabin wall," he confessed.

Sunny stepped on his foot and recovered quickly. "Well, you're a good dancer…even after I've just crippled you." How lame could she get? Besides, a good dancer to Sunny was anyone who didn't cripple her first, so Dan fit the bill perfectly. Since she was floating on air in the handsome cowboy's arms, those polished boots never came near her tootsies.

"My mom and dad used to sing this one, too." He pulled Sunny a little closer, and she stepped on his foot.

"Sorry."

"'It *had* to be you,'" He had a wonderful voice, one of those deep ones that could brush velvet. "That's how I'd have to sing it to you."

Sunny pretended to take offense. "Hey, watch it. I warned you I knew kickboxing."

At that moment, it felt as though her heart had been kicked and boxed…with a velvet baritone glove. If a girl wasn't careful, she could easily make a fool of herself over Daniel Jarrett. And this particular woman needed no help where acting the fool was concerned.

"Mom's not coming," Allison told Sunny the following morning.

"What?"

Having gotten in at two in the morning, still stuffed from the midnight buffet, Sunny looked at her niece through half-lidded eyes. She was up and wrestling on a swimsuit in the midst of unmade beds, scattered clothes, wet towels—the usual bedroom disarray now concentrated in the tiny windowless cabin.

"Mom changed her mind. She's afraid of horses and chickened out."

Sunny knew she should have gone down to breakfast. It was just like Melinda to back out on her at the last minute. The only reason *she* agreed to go was that her sister was going too. If Sunny was going make a fool of herself or break her neck, she wanted adult company.

"What about the sixty-five-dollar ticket?"

Allison shrugged. "She said she'd pay that not to go."

Sunny hauled her jeans up over her swimsuit and buttoned them. If she didn't go, then the kids couldn't. *Good ol' Crazy Aunt Sunny to the rescue,* she thought, dourly.

"Oh well, fetch Jason from the arcade and meet me down at the Biscayne deck. Unless you want to try to trade the tickets in on the plantation tour."

"No way." Allison abandoned the room before Sunny could entertain the idea.

"Oh…Lord." It was as much of a prayer as Sunny could muster on five hours' sleep.

She glanced at the Do Not Disturb sign on Daniel's door as she started for the departure deck. Being Cinderella for a night was great, even if the prince was using her to avoid socializing with his stepfather. At least he got to sleep in the next morning.

Upon joining the passengers on the lower deck to disembark, Sunny spotted Jason and Allison standing right next to a familiar figure in a Stetson hat. Dan Jarrett grinned at her from under the brim as she threaded her way to them.

"Mornin,' pardner," he said, the picture of a cavalier tipping his hat.

It had indented his hair, which was damp with perspiration. The hanging strips of clear plastic dividing the gathering area from the door where customs officials had set up for the visit couldn't stand up to the tropical heat and humidity seeping in from outside.

"I didn't think you were signed up for a tour."

Daniel clapped a hand on Jason's shoulder. "I wasn't until this buckaroo shanghaied me into it. Boy, you could sell an undertaker a suit with two pair of pants."

Jason looked up blankly.

"You know," Sunny prompted. "An *undertaker*. What is a corpse going to do with *two* pair of pants?"

"Ooh, that's gross," Allison complained. "It's a pension joke, kid. You'll get it when you're older."

Gradually the crowd started through the makeshift temperature barrier toward the gangway. Sunny and her group moved with them.

"Thought you said you wouldn't pay to ride a horse," Sunny reminded Daniel as they walked onto the paved landing. A cruise employee took a look at their tickets and directed them toward a dingy white minivan.

"I didn't," Dan answered, pocketing the stub. "Jason said he had a ticket and that it would go to waste if I didn't go. Then he buttered me up with how much he could learn from watching me in the saddle and—"

"A little ego boost never hurts, I guess." Sunny inhaled the damp hot air and wondered how anyone with breathing ailments made out in this kind of climate. It was almost suffocating.

"Told you I'm a sucker. I kinda like being needed. Besides, I have to say, I was intrigued at the possibilities of mayhem on a horse."

"Just stand clear," Sunny teased, climbing into the battered minivan after a young couple.

The seats were as worn as the outside, which boasted a white sliding door that had been waxed to a sheen. It looked as if it belonged to another car and probably did. Either that or the customer entrance got the royal treatment. Anywhere else on the vehicle, she could write her name in the grunge.

As they pulled out, she noted the sun, still low and bright on the eastern horizon. "Hey, Allison. The commercial showed a *sunset* ride. Where's the romance here?"

"Aunt Sunny," her niece muttered in embarrassment.

"Honestly," Sunny kept on, her humor finally awakened. "Do you see anything romantic about this, Dan? I mean, so far we've been hauled out of a comfortable bed and packed like sardines on a bus without air-conditioning."

"It *does* stretch the imagination," her companion admitted, tongue in cheek.

Sunny discovered something on the short journey through ramshackle buildings and roadside stands, which sold all manner of tourist goodies as well as some items of dubious nature: Denim conducted heat *and* electricity. At least that between her and the cowboy slumped in the seat next to her it did. If heat came from anywhere, it should have been from the couple on her other side, who obviously found the morning just as romantic as the night. *Honeymooners,* she thought, unable to draw away from either in the tight quarters.

She focused on the lush tropical scenery intermingled with a level of poverty and desperation that was not shown in the vacation ads. One moment they passed a stretch of rich, cultivated fields edged by coconut palms and banana trees or hedges splashed with fiery tropical shades of Eden. Then suddenly there were ramshackle houses, made of everything from concrete and mud to shipping crates, nestled into a hillside.

Just as Sunny wondered if they were headed in the right direction, the scene changed over and again, from paradise to impoverishment. Beauty and beastliness, she thought as the bus stopped to let a donkey cart cross the road. Half-dressed children sat on the top of the produce, while a man led the draft animal to a hodge-podge stripmall of rusted tin roofing and thatch that was notched into the side of a volcanic hill.

"This is unbelievable," she whispered under her breath to her companion. Yet it wasn't. She'd seen adults and children come into the ER in an equally filthy, tattered state, gaunt with malnutrition.

"Maybe they don't miss what they don't know about."

"Oh, they know, I think," Sunny answered thoughtfully.

Dan tilted his hat up and looked over at her. "Nurse Elders out to heal the world, huh?"

"I would if I could."

He grinned. "Guess you would at that, though heaven help them."

Yet the Jamaicans appeared happy, taking time to wave at the tourists. Sunny wondered if it was an act for the visitors, or did they lean on God and the wisdom of her mother's plaque that the secret to happiness was not getting what one wanted, but being content with what one had? Surely it took a manna far superior to that of the cuisine their wealthier visitors would sup for them to keep smiling.

The van turned onto a lovely palm-lined drive. The sign beside the road announced their arrival at the polo club, which boasted riding trails and a beach. The contrast to what they'd just seen was like night and day. The van puttered past perfectly manicured grounds and fields to a parking lot, where cars priced beyond Sunny's income gleamed in the island sun. They passed a large, stucco and tile clubhouse enveloped in tropical foliage—green blended with bursts of golds, reds, oranges, and pinks that could challenge the palette and skill available to man to duplicate. There the paved road curved through verdant pastureland toward crisp white stables ahead.

Other tourists waited in the parking lot while groomsmen in white cotton pants and shirts scurried about saddling horses. Jason and Allison immediately started guessing which of the shiny, well fed steeds might be theirs. When a groom finished tacking up a horse, he led it over to a platform and motioned for one of the tourists to come forward to mount.

"If that don't beat all," Daniel murmured, shaking his head. "A horse-mounting ramp."

Actually, it didn't look too bad to her. Sunny quietly rejoiced, watching a woman about her age climb up the steps to swing her leg easily over the saddle. The groom then led the steed away, tightened the cinch, and adjusted the stirrups. At least the horse wouldn't wait till Sunny had one foot in the stirrup and then take off—or worse, her weight wouldn't pull the saddle to the side so that she'd ride half-cocked over hill and dale.

She watched the leisurely pace with which the other rider reached the end of the forming tour line. The girl hadn't had to *drive* with the reins at all. The horse just followed the others. So did Jason's pinto and Allison's dainty-stepping bay. Piece of cake.

"You're up, ma'am." Sunny looked back to see the groom pointing to her and knew she'd celebrated too soon. He held the reins to a fat palomino, which was switching its tail from side to side, ears laid back. Horse savvy or not, Sunny knew this was not a good sign.

"He doesn't like me," Sunny whispered urgently to Daniel Jarrett. "Look at his ears."

"*She,*" he answered, "just wants to stay at the stable. Besides, she's with foal. Just the one I'd pick for you, you being a beginner."

"You mean it shows?" Sunny felt anything but the humor she

stabbed at as she approached the horse.

"Come on up, miss. Swing Ting, she a gentle mama. You gonna like her for sure."

"Are you sure she should be out in her condition?" Sunny asked as she tried to settle in the saddle. The horse was wide as the barn. Sunny's feet, which the groom fitted into the stirrups, stuck out like oars on a boat.

"Swing Ting be fine, you see." The man's grin reminded her of a piano keyboard.

Swing Ting suddenly shook her head and gave him a loud, wet raspberry through her puckered lips.

"I don't think she agrees with... *nice Swing Ting!*" Sunny launched into a higher octave as the cumbersome horse started toward the end of the line of its own accord. Her knuckles white about the saddle horn, Sunny smiled at Allison and Jason, who looked back at her anxiously.

Lord, don't let me break anything. Or lose my breakfast, she added, despite the fact that she hadn't had any. *And, Jesus, get those ears up for me, please. I claim Your name that You are going to see me safely through this. You said ask and boy, am I asking. Got any angels with horse experience?*

As they rode along the trail, Sunny decided Swing Ting's ears were glued back—and that the animal was a pig in disguise. Every time they passed something green and edible, Swing Ting decided to stop and snack. Sunny had heard of *eating for two,* but Swing Ting had to be carrying a litter. She held up those in the line behind her, making the guides riding up and down the length of it to holler for Sunny to kick the horse.

"But she's pregnant."

"It won't hurt her, Sunny. Just nudge her a little," Daniel coaxed from behind.

Not only was Swing Ting a pig, but she had no feeling in her sides. The mare just dropped her ears farther back and took another bite of grass, her width blocking the rocky trail.

"Have you no pride, Swing Ting?" Sunny challenged to no avail. "Keep this up and there will be no tropical scenery for you to show off, dear."

From the corner of her eye, she saw the head of Daniel's bay gelding coming up beside her.

"What are you doing up here?" She tried to keep her voice calm as the horse stopped chewing the grass and raised its head, as if waiting for the answer too. There was no sense in both horse and rider getting too excited.

"Encouraging Swing Ting." Daniel slapped the palomino on the rear. "Git up there."

He clearly had the voice of authority, for Swing Ting bolted forward in a trot, closing the gap in the line so fast Sunny thought she was going to collide with Allison's horse. Teeth jarring, she held on for dear life, too scared to admit she was terrified.

"D...don't you th...think this p...pace is b...bad for the b...baby?"

By the third time Daniel *encouraged* Swing Ting, they'd reached a beautiful ridge overlooking a bay below that was so blue it looked unreal. It would have taken Sunny's breath away, had she not been holding it as tightly as the saddlehorn.

"My word, that's so beautiful," she managed, momentarily distracted by the scenery. *Lord, You outdid Yourself here*.

"Told you it was romantic, Aunt Sunny," Allison called back to her.

"Okay, it's got possibilities," Sunny conceded wryly, drawn from her abbreviated moment of contemplation.

"You should see the little falls on our north range. I have a hunting cabin up there. The water's not blue like that, but it's crystal clear. Looks like liquid diamonds spilling over the ledge."

"Sounds lovely. Can we reach it in a jeep?"

Daniel laughed at her and gave Swing Ting an encouraging click of the tongue to get the mare going again.

"Go figure," Sunny exclaimed, voice jarring with each step of the steed. "I've clicked till I'm dry and she won't go for me."

"She knows you're intimidated by her."

"Gee, you *think?*" She was afraid to look over her shoulder where Daniel made no effort to hide his amusement. At least *he* was having a good time.

By the time they reached the beach below and turned the horses over to the guides, Sunny's arms ached from wrestling with Swing Ting. The T-shirt she wore over her swimsuit clung to her like a second skin, plastered by the sun climbing overhead. At the base of the incline was an island gazebo, obviously built with the guests in mind. At the bar, cool refreshing tropical punch was doled out generously to offset the effects of sun on the riders.

"Electrolytes. Just what I need," Sunny joked, taking a big swallow. She'd had island fruit mixtures at home, but something about being in the primitive native setting made them taste twice as good. She suppressed the loud "*Day-oh*" it inspired within.

"I thought it was fruit juice." Jason stared warily into his glass as though it had bugs in it.

Dan clapped him reassuringly on the back. "It's nothing. Your aunt just can't leave the nurse behind, even on vacation. It's the same stuff as in that sports aid coaches insist their athletes drink."

"Oh yeah. To replace the sweat."

Sunny smiled at her nephew. "Something like that."

Around them some of the tourists had started stripping down to their swimsuits.

"I don't know about you guys, but I'm ready for my *romantic* swim in the crystal blue Caribbean waters…" Sunny forced a dreamy note to the words. Waving her arms over her head and swaying like a palm in the island breeze, she mimicked the commercial enticement. "I am *come to Jamaica,* mon."

Ten

"SWIM TIME, GOOD people," one of the guides announced loudly, as if he'd overheard Sunny's declaration.

Sunny turned, expecting the staff to be handing out beach towels. Instead, they were passing out horses again—horses wearing nothing but rope halters. She'd seen the guides taking the tack off the animals and thought nothing of it. The horses were all sweaty beneath the saddles. It was natural to allow them to cool off while the guests swam in the water nearby. This just couldn't be, she thought, watching a guide help one of the guests up onto his assigned horse.

"I'll be…" Daniel cut himself off with a dubious shake of his head. "This ought to be interesting."

"Bareback?" Sunny echoed her startled thoughts aloud. "They expect us to ride *bareback?*"

"Cool!"

"Awesome!"

With their simultaneous responses, Allison and Jason broke away and ran to where their steeds waited. After helping them on with ski belts, the guides offered them a boot up with hands and fingers interlocked to form a makeshift stirrup.

Obviously accustomed to the routine, their horses trotted over to where another guide waited, mounted and ready. But for what?

"Ski belts and horses," Dan commented wryly, foreshadowing Sunny's worst anticipation of what was to come. "I've lived too long. Unless they expect us to ride in the water and the belts are to keep people afloat if they fall off."

Riding horses in the water…

The common sense Sunny prided herself on prevailed against Dan's observation. No, it couldn't be. Sunny looked at her companion. Surely Mr. Meat and Taters wasn't going for this, even if some of the others around them were recovering from their shock and starting to go with the flow. She couldn't see Dan Jarrett— much less herself—astride a horse with a bright yellow ski belt on.

"My arms are aching now from playing tug-of-war with Miss Piggy," she complained at his expectant grin. Her eyes widened. He was going to do it! He was going to do it, just to see her make a fool of herself.

"That ain't all that's going to be sore before the day's out, I'll bet."

"Ha, ha, ha," she rallied without humor, but at that moment he followed the suit of the other guests stripping to the swimsuits they wore beneath the riding clothes and peeled his plaid shirt off, stalling her mischief in its tracks. Muscles had no right to ripple like that. She shook her head. This guy could make her forget a body cast.

She gave herself a mental smack. What on earth had come over her? Hers had never been a pitty-patter heart. She'd seen bigger and better specimens, treated them, and sent them on their way without a backward glance, while the other nurses and assistants drooled in the wake. *She* was always the one who brought the others back to earth with some dry wisecrack.

But this man loved family, kids, and animals—he was perfectly tailored to make a heart not only *pitty-pat,* but *thump-de-dump.* He had a good sense of humor that played well with her own. Dan was simply a 3-D catch—honest, kind, a man of character and faith…not to mention those rugged good looks. Granted, his attitude toward his stepfather was sometimes a little ragged on the edges, but if it weren't for that, he'd be close to perfect.

"Hey, pretty lady, dis you turn. Swing Ting is waiting."

Turning from her uncharacteristic stupor, Sunny saw one of the grooms holding the broad palomino's rope halter and grinning widely at her. Pitty-patter collided into one giant thump, followed by prolonged stillness in her chest. Instead of presenting that halo-like aura of expectant motherhood, the mare looked positively menacing, as if all its problems were the fault of one ER nurse from Texas. Sunny swallowed, her mind cleared of Dan Jarrett completely. Penance awaited with a vengeance.

"Go on, pretty lady. I'll cover your…er…well, you know, the south side."

Dan exhaled, puffing his cheeks in a silent whistle. It was the most pitiful show of feigned innocence she'd ever seen, grounding her earlier soar of awareness. He also had a way of ticking her ticker off.

She managed a cutting glance as she stripped off her T-shirt and cutoffs, preparing for the inevitable. If he showed half this enthusiasm with his family, they'd be ecstatic.

Setting her chin in determination, Sunny marched over to where the pudgy palomino scuffed the sand, ears laid back with a resolve of their own.

"Okay, Swing Ting, I won't bother you, if you won't bother me, deal?"

Swing Ting just snorted, a sound riddled with disgust.

Instinct told her to just say no. Enough was enough. In her line of work, Sunny functioned on instinct garnered from years of experience and knowledge. There was no time for second thought. But one glance at Jason and Allison gave her pause enough for it to register. How could she say no to her darlings? They looked up to Crazy Aunt Sunny.

Crazy was right. Sunny put her foot in the guide's locked hands and, with the help of a boost, straddled the disgruntled horse's back. The first thing that registered was that all Swing Ting's *cushioning* was on her sides and belly, not on the hard backbone that jarred Sunny's own as the mare broke into a trot, falling in line like a trooper readying for a charge. A quick glance around confirmed what Sunny thought: The nickering pig had already stripped the beach area of edibles.

At least Sunny wasn't slipping and sliding as she'd thought she would. Swing Ting's back, devoid though it was of comfort, was tacky from where the saddle had been. Closing her eyes, Sunny grimaced.

"Praying for mercy?" Dan drawled as he drew up beside her, seemingly as comfy without a saddle as he'd been with one.

"Scripture says 'rejoice in one's trials,' but heavens to Betsy, I never thought I'd be reduced to rejoicing over smelly horse's sweat. What next?"

"Round here, I'd be afraid to ask that question."

Before Sunny could think of something witty to say, he leaned forward. As if reading his mind, his horse moved on ahead to where Jason and Allison waited. Watching as he exchanged words with the eager listeners, Sunny was once again distracted from her predicament. She never dreamed swim trunks and Stetsons belonged in the same picture any more than horses and ski belts, but they did. And how. Pack that with his way with kids and his protectiveness where his loved ones were concerned and it was down right irresistible.

Suddenly, Dan swung his head around, meeting her gaze from under the shade of the Stetson's brim. Sunny couldn't see his eyes, but she knew they'd shame both sea and sky. Impossibly, they warmed her more than the sun soaking the beach.

Lord, I can't help him if I'm as fickle as this. I want to hug him one minute and smack him the next. I hardly know him and yet I know I'm too involved with this guy. It goes against my grain—not to mention all my training—not to get personal with those we need to help. Besides, I'm just a friend in his eyes. So whatever is bedeviling me about Dan Jarrett, Father, stop it. It scares me. I can't make it stop alone and it hurts so much to say good-bye. Loving on this side of heaven is losing, and I don't think I can stand that again so soon.

From out of nowhere, pain welled up in her chest and burned at her eyes. The weight of her parents' loss—of one funeral followed by another—pressed in on her. Her quandary over Dan faded from her thoughts, replaced by something worse as Swing Ting came to life beneath her. The beast broke its annoying trot and fell into an easy canter, as though suddenly obsessed with passing the horses ahead of them. Fingers fisted around the short rein attached to the mare's halter, Sunny held on for her life as her mount followed the guide, plunging into the crystal blue water of the cay, passing not only Allison and Jason, but Dan as well.

Lord, help! It wasn't much of a prayer, but given the circumstances, God surely understood.

"Ride 'em, cowgirl!"

"Yay, Aunt Sunny!" her charges shouted in unison.

"This was *not* in the brochure!" she hollered to anyone listening, voice breaking in panic. It wasn't the heavenly relief she'd asked for either, but it was effective. God did have a way of reminding a body that it could be worse.

The water hurriedly rose to her knees, then her hips. Swing Ting was now paddling beneath her, neck stretching until the rope strained against Sunny's fingers. Quick assessment told her that to hold it would force the horse's nose under water. She let go the rein. It was worthless anyway, unless she wanted to chafe the mare's jaw. Considering how she'd tugged its mouth back to its ears without effect, there was little point in holding on to the rope.

She'd done right to rejoice in the horse's sweat, because now that it was washed away by sea water, Swing Ting was more slippery than a fish. *I get it, Lord. A little Jonah payback on a four-footed whale. Okay, I'll help Nineveh Dan.* Hands fisted on either side of the horse's massive neck, grabbing desperately with her knees as the ski belt lifted her tush from Swing Ting's back, Sunny glanced about frantically for any pointers. The safety device might serve well if one fell off the horse, but it wasn't worth a hoot if one managed to stay on the beast.

At that moment, a riderless horse passed her, swimming for all it was worth. Well, *almost* riderless—clinging to the float stream of its tail was a man holding on as if to life itself and spitting mouthfuls of water off to the side between breaths. At least the belt held him up. Sunny would have laughed except for the realization that it was only by God's grace that it was someone else instead of her.

"Oh, sugar, hang on."

Sunny recognized the other half of the honeymooning couple from the van laughing hysterically at her half drowned mate.

"There goes trouble in paradise," Dan said from her other side, surprising her.

"Yeah."

Her desperation-strangled answer fell short, for he guided his swimming steed ahead and across her path to help the floundering groom. The cowboy might have been on land, for all the trouble Dan had in accomplishing his goal. Before one of the guides was able to help, Dan hauled the hapless rider back up on his horse by his ski belt.

"Here you go, pardner."

"Thanks, man." The young groom coughed and swung his head toward his giggling bride of a few days with a glare hot enough to make the water around them bubble.

"Way to go, Dan," Jason cheered from somewhere behind Sunny as Dan moved away from the kindling feud.

"Romantic, huh?" he quipped, dropping in beside Sunny.

"Don't tell me, tell Allis—" Sunny leaned too far to the right and would have keeled into the water but for Dan's restraining hand on her belt. "I had no idea a horse could be so slippery."

"Hold on to her mane."

Sunny looked askance at the cropped cut. "I can't. The last rider pulled it all out."

Dan threw back his head and laughed, despite the searing glower in her gaze. Composing himself, he reached over and tugged up her ski belt as high as he could and still remain a gentleman. "It looks silly, but at least your backside won't float off the horse."

She answered with a skitter of a smile. It was an improvement. An even better improvement would be if he pulled her onto his horse, the one that listened to his silent commands. If she were headed for Nineveh, she might as well go first class. Besides, she could shout herself hoarse at Swing Ting and the hoofed whale would paddle wherever it chose.

"This is *so* much fun, Aunt Sunny," Allison said as she passed Sunny. Her long arms and legs were wrapped around her lean steed's long neck and her smile was as wide as Swing Ting.

"Define *fun*," Sunny called after her in challenge.

Jason and Dan were engaged in a race ahead of the lead guide, who called them back. He was turning the water-logged stampede. It was almost over. *Thank You, God!*

Adept at follow-the-leader, Swing Ting circled when the guide led the other riders past them. Sunny did what she'd done from the start and held on for dear life, lest she become a tail ornament for the stubborn horse.

A new horror set in before much comfort in Swing Ting's long overdue obedience could be taken. Floating ahead of her in the water was a small, bobbing island of dubious origin. It didn't take a genius to guess the horse who'd deposited it had had a big breakfast that morning and been snatched into duty before its constitutional was complete. Swing Ting started for it as if sighting something that reminded her of home, where food would be waiting.

"No, Swing Ting, *this* way." Sunny leaned as much as she dared toward the shore.

One of the tourists made a loud exclamation of disgust as his steed beat Swing Ting to it—or rather, *through* it. Sunny could only hope her stubborn mare would take the cleared channel, but that would be accommodating—and if there was anything Swing Ting was *not,* it was accommodating. If she could reach its ears, she'd have pulled them back permanently, but as it was, Sunny had other problems. The "islands" in the stream were spreading.

The thought of swimming through them when she already smelled more of horse than she ever wanted to, was too much. There was nothing to do but abandon ship...er...horse.

Just as she leaned hard toward the shore, intent on swimming, Dan cut her off. Relieved beyond measure, Sunny reached for her tall-out-of-saddle hero, but Dan had other intentions. He caught

Swing Ting's rope bridle and tugged the mare off her course, back toward the beach—just as Sunny went under.

Allison's voice met her along with an entirely too-close view of his horse's behind when she surfaced.

"Hey, Dan, you lost Aunt Sunny."

Startled, Dan glanced back to see Sunny treading water as best she could, considering her ski belt was wedged beneath her armpits. His laugh only added to her sputter. There were a million names she could call him, but at the moment, since he was her best option to get to shore, she held her tongue as he swung around to pick her up.

"You almost made it, Slick," he said, tossing the rein Sunny dropped the moment Swing Ting started swimming to one of the guides. They were everywhere when one didn't need them.

"Aunt Sunny, you were so funny," Jason teased, catching up with them. "She reached out for you, and you just kept right on going," he told Dan.

"You know me. Anything for a laugh," she said, clinging to the strong arm drawing her across the other horse's back.

Dan still shook with amusement, but he was carrying her to land and that was all that mattered. He leaned over and rumbled in her ear, "Are you feeling romantic yet?"

"Just shut up and carry me off into the sunset, Jarrett."

Allison and Jason burst into another round of giggles.

Sunny hoped she sounded sufficiently annoyed, because all semblance of irritation fled the moment Dan embraced her, snugging her close against his chest. No, she was definitely not feeling annoyance. Annoyance, she could handle, but this new sensation was something else again.

Lord, this isn't fair.

"I'm afraid you'll have to settle for the high-noon sun, pardner,"

Dan kidded back, oblivious to the sparks scattering from every nerve center she had.

Sunny made a face at him, all the while wondering how she could reel with the sense of falling when she was firmly ensconced in the steel of his embrace. There was only one certainty amid the chaos of her thoughts…

For the first time in her life, she was grateful that a man was clueless. Maybe a short visit to Nineveh wouldn't be so bad after all.

In a cotton plaid shirt and string tie, Dan picked up his Stetson from one of the three empty chairs at his assigned dining table and slid it under his own as Jason entered the dining room. He waved as the boy spotted him and brightened, increasing the bite of his stride on the distance between them. A man could get used to this family scenario. Dan couldn't recall when he'd had more fun or laughed so much. With Jason buttering him up with adoration and Allison blushing every time he teased her, he'd…well, he'd just bonded with them and that was not like workaholic loner Daniel Jarrett.

But it was Sunny who iced the cake.

Sweet and wacky, he mused, staring over Jason's head toward the door as the boy chattered away about the video game he'd just won. Groups and couples swarmed into the room, splitting to go to their assigned tables like horses to their stalls, but there was no sign of pixie blond hair that looked cute even when it was mussed—or plastered wet around her fresh scrubbed face, freckles multiplied, soft brown against pink, each time it was exposed to the sun.

Like her niece, Dan thought, picking out Allison in the herd of guests that arrived en masse. At the girl's beguiling smile, Sean, the waiter, nearly tripped over a chair and rushed to show her to the table. Dressed in keeping with the dining room's Old West theme, the Irish lad seated Allison and brandished her napkin with a snap of his wrist before draping it across the short denim jumper she wore.

Smooth, Dan mused, a hair of protectiveness bristling. He knew what young men thought no matter how suave they were, and this one was using his continental charm to the max on Allison. It promised no good to Dan's notion.

The teen was so aflutter, she all but giggled, "Thank you, Sean."

Sean's color deepened until it almost matched Allison's. "A privilege, Miss Allison."

"Just call me Alli. All my friends do."

"He's just following rules, Alli." Dan advised her in a paternal fashion meant to remind the waiter as much as inform the girl.

"But you can call me Alli if I say you can, can't you?" she asked Sean, disregarding Dan's observation completely.

Dan recoiled, more in shock that he'd said anything to start with than over being ignored.

He had no right to intervene in Allison's affairs, regardless of what he thought of Sean. He just didn't want the girl to get hurt.

"Aye, that would be fine. Alli it is, then." He winked, despite Dan's flat stare, and turned back to his work.

"Where is your aunt?" Dan asked, drawing Allison's attention back to the table.

"What are you gonna get, Dan?" Jason said, emerging from his menu, oblivious to all but his rumbling belly.

"Aunt Sunny had a body ache, so she decided to skip dinner and take a nap."

"A…body ache?" Dan repeated.

Allison grinned, braces gleaming. "She said she didn't know

what hurt more, her legs, her arms, or her rear. She's normally a trouper —" the girl observed in obvious admiration—"I mean, she quit work and took care of Grandma *and* Grandpa day and night."

Dan recalled how worn out his mother was after his dad's death. She'd said the heavy burden of care at the end was God's way of making her ready to let him go, so they both would have relief— his from suffering and hers from watching him like that.

"Yeah, she had some yucky stuff to do," Jason put in. "Aunt Sunny never throws up." He shuddered. "She doesn't cry, either." He opened up his menu. "Man, I could eat a horse."

Allison chose a roll and placed it on her bread plate before her brother made for the same piece. "I don't know how she did it all. I cried every time I visited. I just couldn't stand seeing Grandma and Grandpa like that, all shrunken and full of tubes and wires."

"Me, either," Jason agreed, sobriety claiming his boyish features. Dan couldn't tell if it came from the conversation or that his sister got the choice of the breadbasket. He riffled through the gourmet assortment until he found one like it.

"*You* wouldn't even go in the room," Allison challenged.

"It made me sick."

"Burned toast makes you sick." With her dismissal, his sister took one of the shell-shaped butter patties displayed on ice. "Anyway, Aunt Sunny took care of everything. She held Mom up and made us laugh when we started to cry."

Laughter was definitely one of Sunny's strong points, Dan thought, but he wondered…was it a defense as well? She was always cracking jokes, making light when things got heavy. Like a diamond, she had many facets, not all of which were apparent to the casual glance. Laughter was the glow, but beneath it was strength and perseverance. And faith, he thought, recalling their conversation. He supposed that was what held Sunny's family together.

He kind of envied that. His mom had that kind of faith too. It simply hadn't *happened* for him. He attended church, up till his mom's wedding. Most of the time, it seemed more social than spiritual to him—or as though the sermons applied to someone else.

"When are we gonna order?" Jason asked again, doggedly.

"Is food *all* you ever think about?" Allison exclaimed with a dramatic roll of the eyes. "We're having an adult conversation. Besides, you're supposed to fold your menu when you've decided. Otherwise Sean won't know when we're ready to order."

"Is *Sean* all you ever think about?"

Pulled back to the situation at hand by the sibling antics, Dan opened his menu. It wasn't like him to analyze a person. He usually took new acquaintances at face value until they were ready to reveal more of themselves. Yet here he was wondering what else he was missing in his appraisal of Sunny, as if he'd found a new breed to introduce to his ranch. He wanted to know all there was about it and fast.

"So what are you gonna order, Dan?"

Jason's question drew him back to the table. "Well, let's see." It was surprisingly hard to concentrate on the print when a diamond still dazzled his mind. "Do they have some kind of beef and potatoes in here? Ah, New York strip steak, probably raised in Texas—" he speculated to no one in particular—"with mushroom peppercorn sauce and baby reds. Sounds good to me."

"Me too," Jason said. "And a big dessert. Wonder what they're having?"

"If it has sugar on it, you'll eat it," Allison said in her most disparaging adult tone.

"Like you wouldn't, Miss Piggy?"

"Miss Piggy is Aunt Sunny's horse."

The banter dissolved in laughter. As they'd headed for the old VW bus to return to the ship, Sunny called "Good-bye, Miss Piggy" to Swing Ting, embarrassing and delighting her charges at the same time. Aware of Sunny's struggle with the horse that ate its way to the beach and back, holding up the line of mounted tourists, their other companions shared in the humor as well.

Dan would bet even money Sunny's ER patients left with a smile on their faces after Sunny was through with them.

"I can see how your aunt got that name...Sunny."

"It's not what you think. Gramma said that when she was having Aunt Sunny, the sun shined through the window so bright she didn't even notice the lights all around her," Jason informed him, as if repeating a story he'd heard many times.

Allison nodded. "It was at daybreak. One minute it was dark and the next, Aunt Sunny was crying and the whole room was full of sun. So they called her Sunny. Kinda like God named her."

"Maybe He did," Dan remarked. "I take it your grandmother was a religious woman."

"She taught Sunday school till she got too sick and died." Without remorse, Jason snatched up a fat roll and broke it apart.

"So did Pop," Allison added a little more tenderly.

Butter now lavished on the roll, Jason took a bite. "Yeah, and we gotta go to church all the time, too. I can't wait till I'm old enough—"

Allison gave him a motherly smack on his arm. "Don't talk with your mouth full."

The boy swallowed, eyes bulging in rebellion at his sister. For a moment, Dan thought he might have to perform CPR, but a big chug of water cleared the way for Jason to finish.

"Women! When I get old enough that I don't have to listen to

Mom and Dad, I'm going to sleep in on Sunday."

Those sentiments sounded familiar. Dan took a sip of water, swallowing it along with his guilt. He couldn't deny it. He had dozens of excuses at hand every Sunday—too tired, too much to do, peeved at God and all those well-meaning folks who rambled on about how wonderful it was that "Esther is moving on with her life…"

Dan grabbed a roll of his own, glancing past the busy waiters' station to where his family laughed and talked excitedly about the tour they'd taken together that day while the men went fishing. His mom was almost glowing. She didn't look like his mom. She looked like…like a woman in love. Next to her, Charlie just stared at her while she chatted, as if she were the biggest catch in his life.

Dan tore into the bread with his teeth. That had better be love instead of greed, or he'd personally knock that smile off the man's face.

"Oh, thank you, Sean," Allison gushed, as the boy filled her glass with iced tea.

"And an extra slice of lemon, isn't it?" Sean replied.

He even squeezed it for her. *That older Stuart kid had better get his act together,* Dan thought, lips thinning. He exchanged a quick look with Jason and had to agree with the lad after all. Women!

Like the saying went, *Can't live with 'em, can't live without 'em.*

Dan's gaze drifted to Sunny's empty chair. Maybe he'd check on her after a while. Even nurses needed some care and concern occasionally, and with this one's penchant for getting into bizarre situations, she especially needed looking after.

Eleven

OOM service!"

Sunny dragged herself out of the comfy hide-a-bed and stumbled to the door in the dark of the cabin, uncertain of the time. It was always dark in an inside cabin. She felt around in her sleep-induced fog for her watch and stopped when she realized that without more than the light shining in under the door, she couldn't see it anyway. With a half smile at her folly, she stumbled over something on the floor—most likely the clothes Jason shed before supper.

Another three sharp knocks proceeded a cheerful, "Room service, lady. Come on. Get up. You can do it."

That drawl didn't sound like any room service steward she'd come across yet. Hand on the latch, Sunny frowned. "Wait, I didn't order anything."

Unless the kids had sent it, in spite of being told she'd just get something later. If anything it sounded like—

She pulled open the door and peeked out. Instead of one of the filipino staff members who'd brought up sodas to the cabin in the past, this "steward" was unmistakably taller and decked out in all

too familiar plaid and denim. It *was* Dan, she realized, not the least
displeased.

"Couldn't pay for your room tab, eh?"

Dan fell in with her jibe. "Have to work it off somehow. I got
wind there was someone here suffering from horse overdose."

Sunny stared at the plate of fruit he'd obviously collected from
a buffet. It brimmed almost to the point of spilling over around a
chilled bottle of water. Well, she had to give him an A for effort.

"Can I come in?"

Reminded of her manners, she stifled a yawn and backed into
the room.

"Watch your step. Jason left traps on the floor."

Feeling along the wall, she found the switch and clicked it. She
blinked at the sudden glare of light. "What time is it?"

"Eight or so." He stood awkwardly just inside the entrance.
"Maybe I should try coming in the other way."

Sunny looked down at the floor where clothes were strewn like
stepping stones from bunks to bathroom, starting with Jason's
jeans, his swim trunks, his T-shirt, and lastly the towels he'd used
to shower. She'd just scuffed her way through the debris, but considering there was only the one narrow passage from one end of the
cabin to the other, it was a gauntlet of sorts.

"Just kick it to the side. I'll kick him later."

She took the food and put it on the small dresser, shoving
Allison's scatter of makeup, jewelry, and hair accessories aside in the
same manner. A bottle of glitter nail polish fell on the floor. As she
bent over to pick it up, so did Dan. Their heads collided.

Laughing, Sunny straightened. "I spend the day riding a pig
disguised as a horse and now, as you can see, I live with piglets."

"Here, let me see that."

The touch of Dan's fingers on her brow, the tickle of her hair as he moved it away, cleared Sunny's sleep-soggy daze in an instant. Suddenly, every nerve was on full alert, registering that she was in close quarters with a man she found entirely too attractive for her own good. And he was touching her oh-so-tenderly...as tender as a kiss might be. As if reading her mind, he planted one where his fingers had been just a moment before.

"There, feel better?"

If there was room, she could do a back flip, which was pretty impressive, considering she'd never been able to do one in a gym with all the space in the world.

"Much. Thanks."

"Somebody has to look after you."

Somebody has to look after you. Now that had an inviting ring to it. It got old looking after everyone else.

"I guess you don't do evenings, either," Dan said, breaking her indulgence in whimsy.

Sunny glanced down at the *I Don't Do Mornings* kitten on the front of her oversized sleepshirt.

"Heavens to mergatroid," she exclaimed, looking about in desperation for something a little more acceptable.

Dan laughed. "I haven't heard that in years. Don't tell me you're a Snagglepuss fan."

Sunny seized a cotton sundress off the hook on the locker door and squeezed past her guest and into the bath cube, as she and the kids had dubbed the bathroom.

"Exit, smartin' all the way!" she called back, mimicking the cartoon character's lisping retreat.

Dan flattened against a locker door so that she could close the bath door for privacy.

"How about if I pick a few things up? A body could get hurt in here."

"If it makes you feel at home, have at it," she answered, tugging off her sleepshirt.

In the mirror, she caught a glimpse of her hair and groaned. That's what she got for lying down with it still wet from her shower—a sci-fi do, spikes and all. The fact that her towel turban had come off and she'd slept on it only enhanced her out-of-this world look with a twisted terry cloth imprint on her sun-reddened face. She looked as if she'd been dragged off into the noon sun rather than carried in the arms of her tall, dark, and handsome rescuer.

"I'll be out in a minute." Or sixty, she thought, turning on the faucet to wash away the remnants of her nap.

Sunny emerged from the sink a few minutes later, feeling human again. A good brushing tamed her hair and a few touches of mascara and liner gave some shape to her sun-bleached eyebrows and lashes. In fact, she was fairly pleased with the outside. It was the muscles screaming beneath her wholesome appearance that dared her to move. Hopefully the aspirin she took would knock the edge off her discomfort. After all, it wasn't every day a man like Daniel Jarrett showed up on her doorstep bearing fruit and mineral water and offering to take care of her.

Dan sat on the edge of her made-up sofabed, dividing the mineral water into two plastic glasses filled with ice. The rest of the room had been equally improved. Sunny narrowed her eyes at him.

"Okay, 'fess up. Who *really* committed this neatness? Was the cabin steward in here or are you really Berto in disguise?"

"Bunk house training…similar to military, I think."

"Do you do windows, too?" She watched as he produced a small penknife and whittled a slice from one of the oranges crowning the fruit plate.

"Like anyone else, I can do what I have to, I guess." With a twist, he squeezed juice into a glass and handed it to her.

This guy was definitely a keeper. Surely the only reason some female hadn't snatched him out of the singles market was his workaholic seclusion. That was it. Someone just hadn't found him yet. Come to think of it, she'd literally stumbled over him. Except he wasn't hers to keep.

She had to remember that.

"Thanks. I was so tired when we got back that I crashed. I feel like Swing Ting has been walking over me instead of me riding her."

"That's why you need to get up and use those muscles. Haven't you heard that if you fall off a horse, you need to get back on?"

"I thought that was to show the horse who was boss."

"That," Dan agreed, "but also to show your muscles who is in charge. I think you need to climb some stairs, maybe do a little line dancing. It's country night up on the Lido."

Sunny swallowed the mouthful of water she'd just taken before surprise sprayed it out her nose. "Come again?"

"Everyone's up on the Lido tonight for a barbecue Texas style. They're serving until ten, so you can make up for missing supper. It'll be just like home."

"I didn't know Satan lived in Texas." At the puzzled lift of Dan's brow, she explained. "If I move too quick, I'll hurt like I'm kicking up my heels at his place, not in our beloved Lone Star state."

Dan was unmoved by compassion for her condition. "Come on, Nurse Elders. You should know better. Gotta work out those kinks."

Sunny allowed her companion to turn her toward the door. "Sadist," she called over her shoulder.

"Wimp."

Sunny jerked open the door, only to be met by a startled gasp on the other side.

"Melinda!"

"Sunny."

Both sisters grabbed at their chests, as if to stop their hearts from leaping out.

"Are you okay?" Melinda asked, backing against bulkhead.

"I was until you scared the bejittles out of me." Sunny caught her sister's glance and cleared her throat. "You…remember Dan, don't you?"

"Well, you told me about him, but we haven't officially met. I'm Melinda Reddish, Sunny's sister."

At close quarters, Dan waited for Sunny to move out of his way so that he could step outside the cabin. He extended his hand. "Dan Jarrett. I was just checking on your sister after her harrowing swim with the horses."

Melinda made no attempt to hide her amusement as she shook his hand. "I heard the whole story from Jason and Allison."

"I know, *another* Crazy Aunt Sunny story for the record books," Sunny complained. "They'll never let me forget it."

"Well, it *was* kind of memorable." Dan had gone from sassy to sheepish at being caught in the room with Sunny, and the change was adorable.

Silence ensued for a moment until the awkwardness threw even Sunny off.

"Well, I can see you're just fine, so I'll go on back to Alan at the piano lounge. They let him sing one song, and now he thinks he's one of the Beach Boys."

"Oldies but goodies. That sounds like Alan."

"Sounds like me, too, actually," Dan admitted. "Give me those rock-and-roll classics over some of this shouting match music on the radio nowadays."

Melinda brightened. "Why don't you two join us?"

Sunny gave Dan a you-dug-the-hole, you-fill-it-up look.

Actually, it didn't matter to her. She enjoyed her sister and brother-in-law.

"Trust me, ma'am, you don't want to hear me sing. Besides, I promised my sister I'd join the family upstairs. She's a line dancing addict. But you folks are welcome to join us. I told the kids to look us up there at ten or be in the cabin by ten-thirty."

Melinda was taken aback. "You have children?"

"No, *you* do," Sunny said. "And they've taken to Dan like fleas to a stray dog."

"So there *is* hope."

Sunny groaned inwardly. She'd heard that calculating tone before. If her sister mentioned how she longed to have a niece or nephew to spoil like Sunny had Jason and Allison, Sunny would force her aching body to stomp her. Fortunately for both women, it wasn't mentioned, which meant that while Melinda looked brighter and healthier, sporting a little sun, she still wasn't quite up to her old mischievous self.

"You haven't cornered the market on matchmaking sisters," she told Dan after Melinda took an elevator to the Promenade Piano Lounge. "If my sister were up to par, she'd be planning a wedding by now."

"Then you're as safe with me as I am with you. Meanwhile—" he nodded toward the double staircase—"we have some steps to climb, some limbs to loosen, some—"

"Sadist," she said, feeling like Cinderella had hit the dirt again.

"Wimp."

Well, she *had* asked God to keep her from getting carried away.

Twelve

$\mathcal{I}$T WAS HARD to believe, but a cowpoke with a devilish grin did what wild horses couldn't: drag Sunny out of a comfortable bed to go to a party she'd had no intention of attending. After Swing Ting, she'd had it with anything that remotely resembled western. In fact, she still might toss the jeans she'd been wearing. For now, all the clothes she and the kids had worn on the shore excursion were tied up, air tight, in a garbage bag to contain the pungent odor of horse, sweat, leather, and something she chose not to think about.

"Come on, Sunny. Lift those feet. Git 'em up," Dan barked at her heels, when she pulled herself around the banister to climb the last of the seven flights to the Lido deck. "You can do it."

Sunny shook her head. "My legs feel like rubber afire," she panted at deck eight. Only one more to go.

"Want to take the elevator the rest of the way?"

Sunny glanced longingly at the elevator doors—polished stainless steel set in modernistic walls of copper and brass. She felt as pitiful as the wide-eyed waif portrayed in swirls of watercolor on the framed artwork hanging on the landing ahead. Snatches of western swing and merriment drifted in each time guests entered and exited the lobby above them, as if daring her to join it.

"No, might as well finish this torture right."

"Here then, let me help you." His arm locked around her waist, lifting half her weight off her feet. "Together on three. One, two, three…go."

"Aww…"

"Move it, lady."

Dan's arm exuded an energy all its own, holding her aches and pains at bay as he coaxed her up the last few steps. People were staring, not that Sunny cared. They'd stare harder if the focus directed at her protesting legs failed.

"Made it," he announced on reaching the top. Sunny straightened, grunting from the bear hug Dan gave her. "I knew you could do it. Your legs'll feel better, I promise."

That close to Daniel Jarrett, Sunny forgot she even had legs.

Neither of them spotted his family after a quick scan of the open deck, so Dan insisted Sunny take a seat at an empty table beneath the red, white, and blue foil flags snapping in the sea breeze. As she did so, he left to fix her a platter of Caribbean barbecue, Texas style. He returned a few minutes later, a napkin draped over his arm and a plate of ribs, chicken, potato salad, slaw, deviled eggs, and fresh pull-apart rolls.

"I'll never eat all that!" Sunny was grateful the loud music covered the eager roll of her tummy, which seemed to indicate she should mind her own business. The Waldorf salad she'd ordered before her nap had been digested and was long gone.

Reaching into his pocket, Dan produced a handful of wet naps and tossed them on the table. "And if these don't work, they have beach towels in a basket by the pool."

"Funny guy."

"Hey—" he threw up his hands in an innocent shrug—"I've seen you eat. You looked pretty good in it, too."

Sunny tore a bit of the rib meat off the bone and growled at him in return. To her dismay, a dollop of the tangy sauce dripped off its end, but Dan was faster than gravity. He caught it with one of the checkered napkins before it landed in her lap.

"This could be a full time job." The devilment in his gaze took the edge off the jibe—as well as Sunny's wit.

Her pulse tripped. She wanted to say "You're hired," but settled for, "It could have happened to any—"

He dabbed the smatter around her mouth.

"Hey, stop stealing my food. I wasn't done with it yet."

"So that's where nephew piglet gets his ways."

"Look, you want me to eat or do you want to wear this?"

His smile disarmed her threat. The man was a nonstop tease, but with his charm, he could pull it off. Oh well, a gal had to take as good as she gave. It looked like she'd met her match.

By the time the band took a break on the half hour, the pile of bones on her plate looked as if a school of piranha had finished with them. Her tummy was right. She'd been hungrier than she thought.

"Not hungry?" Dan said when the waiter cleared the table.

Sunny grinned sheepishly. "Must be the salt sea air."

"Hey, Aunt Sunny! Dan!"

From the rail on the uppermost deck, Jason, Allison, and the Stuart boys leaned over, waving furiously.

"Wanna play some Ping-Pong?" Jason asked.

"I'll pass tonight, pardner."

"Me, too," Sunny chimed in. Digesting her supper was the most exertion she intended to make for the evening.

Without further ado, the herd of sheer energy housed in small bodies took off.

Sunny shook her head in wonder. "Maybe I should start eating Gummi worms instead of taking vitamins."

Dan looked askance at her. "What?"

"They've been going strong since 6 A.M. and show no sign of slowing down. It's gotta be the Gummi worms."

He scratched his head, clearly clueless. "Do I *want* to know what a Gummi worm is?"

Gail Madison appeared behind him, dressed in a Stetson, western boots, and a denim jumper to accommodate her blossoming figure. She gave him a sisterly whack on the head.

"If you got off the ranch now and then, you'd know, dufus."

Sunny laughed at his startled expression, glad the title had shifted to someone else.

Dan smoothed down his ruffled hair with a grimace of brotherly tolerance as Gail and Mike Madison joined them at the table.

"Where's your hat?" Gail asked.

Dan smirked. "I had a premonition that some wiseacre might whack me from behind, so I left it in the room."

"So how was the horseback ride?" she asked, turning to Sunny, her face a picture of innocence. With a bouncy Hamill haircut swirled toward her face, Gail was a feminine version of her brother, with softer, rounded features to his more angular ones. Mike Madison did not have his wife's talent for acting and snickered.

Sunny slashed a glance at Dan but spoke to Gail. "I imagine you've had a frame-by-frame account. Let's just say I'll probably walk like a gimpy John Wayne for the rest of my life…or at least the balance of the cruise."

Gail waved her hand, brushing away the idea. "All you need is a little line dancing to work out the kinks and you'll be just fine."

Sunny groaned silently through her answering smile. It must run in the family. She might have been born and raised in Houston, but she was still a city girl to the bone—every aching one of them.

"I can't believe they took inexperienced riders on something like that," Mike commented after ordering drinks. "Although I've read that even though a shore excursion is booked on an American cruise ship, the regulations are those of the country you're visiting. Most foreign countries don't have the safety regulations we require."

"Now he tells us."

Dan turned to Gail. "Where's Mom?"

"At the bingo lounge. Charlie was on a roll and didn't want to quit just yet."

"He started out with five bucks worth of cards and is still going strong," Mike added. "The man's charmed."

"He's hoping to win a free ride on another ship."

"Why? He's got all the free rides he needs now."

Sunny tensed at Dan's dour comment. Nothing darkened her companion's humor faster than the mention of Charlie Meyers.

"That was mean. He's going to pay Mom back and you know it." Gail backed away to let the returning waiter put tropical punches topped with fans and pineapple slices on the table.

"Seeing's believing," Dan answered.

"Oh, Dan. Lighten up," she chided. "You're in exceptional company, the music is about to start, and the night is young and beautiful. Besides, knowing you, you've made fun of Sunny all day. Now we can make fun of your line dancing."

"Not likely." Dan straightened in his chair, as if backing away from the idea.

"Hey, you pulled me out of a sound sleep to come up here and work the kinks out, so if this cripple is going to get up and abuse her body, she's not doing it alone," Sunny warned him.

A twitch at the corner of his lips was her only reward. Instead of looking at her, his gaze fixed on the automatic glass doors that opened from the elevator lobby of the ship.

Charlie and Esther Meyers came through, arm in arm, sharing a laugh over something. There were as many stars in their eyes as there were in the sky, Sunny thought. At that moment, the band struck up a tune about a hoedown on a Saturday night.

"Well, we might as well get this over with." Dan stood up and held his hand out to Sunny.

"Hey, I'm all for skipping any unnecessary movement," Sunny reminded him.

"Nope, gotta work those kinks out."

He led her to the back of the forming lines. Sunny knew a few of the dances and was able to follow with relative ease. Every self-respecting Texan from knee-high up, city bred or nay, had to know how to line dance and do a two-step.

Dan was no exception. Despite Gail's remark, he wasn't doing too badly at all; he seemed more rusty than inexperienced. He moved with the same ease and grace as he had shown in the saddle, unlike some of the awkward men who ventured onto the dance floor in hopes of meeting someone, or were dragged by invisible ropes by their feminine partners.

That the number passed without anyone being knocked over or her legs giving out made it a winner in Sunny's estimation. By the second tune, she'd found her groove and felt like she could sling hay with the best of them. She grinned at Dan as they bumped into each other and, to her relief, it was returned. Dan was actually having a good time, despite his stepfather's presence.

How many dances they stayed up for was a blur, so when the band slowed the pace, it was a welcome relief. Sunny had a feeling that Dan would dance all night if Charlie was residing over the family table. She knew her brilliant company wasn't that compelling.

Dan swung into a two-step as easily as if it were a broken-in saddle and swept her in circles until the lights overhead swirled. Sunny couldn't tell if it was her balance that dizzied her or the smooth lead of her partner. Here was a man who liked to be in control and when he wasn't, it drove him to his charm's end. He gave her a squeeze and dipped her backward as the song wound down, his face above hers, almost close enough to steal a kiss, if he had that in mind...

Okay, not *quite* at his charm's end.

Dan held Sunny bent back over his arm longer than he intended before remembering her horse-wrangled muscles. He really didn't like to dance, but those lessons his mother insisted on when he was a mortified twelve were coming in handy after all—those and the few times he'd agreed to a blind date with his matchmaking sister and her husband at the Cattle Club.

After pulling his startled partner up, he hesitated to let her go. It just felt right, holding her, drinking in the laughing blue of her eyes. As he'd started to lower her, they'd widened for a split second before he caught her in middip, assuring her he wouldn't let her fall.

She was too much fun to catch, light as a feather on her feet—like a pixie who might vanish in a twinkle of light, and just as mischievous. Yet she was innocent, unlike so many women he'd met—guileless in her femininity. Her predisposition toward disaster seemed to reach out to him and tap a raw vulnerability he couldn't quite identify.

She latched onto his biceps in the split second when she thought she might fall, and he was struck by the strength of her hands—hands that healed for a living. Dan felt it as strongly as if he'd connected with the open end of a power cable. It was a comforting, peace-giving surge that zeroed in on the discord knotting his muscles and straining his usual mild manner. He wanted to tell her, but he didn't quite understand it himself.

"You're something else, Sunny Elders." Now that was one of the dumbest lines he'd ever heard, and a far cry from what he felt. "How're your legs now?"

Sunny pirouetted away, the loose knit of her sundress swirling around her as playful as her humor. "Look, no kinks. Much as I loathe to admit it, you were right."

"After you give a horse a good workout, you just don't pen them up. You walk them down. Not that I think of you as a horse. I just meant—"

"Muscles are muscles, right?"

"Right." He *had* been on the ranch too long.

Thankfully, his companion was forgiving of stubborn klutzes. She just smiled at him.

"I need something to drink after that workout. I thought my aerobics were high impact." She fanned herself with her hand.

Dan glanced at the table where Charlie sat with his bucket of coins. Maybe if Dan hadn't heard the announcement earlier for someone from the Meyers cabin to go down to the purser's office, he could force himself to be congenial. But most likely Charlie had gone over his charge limit—or rather Dan's *mom's* charge limit. Dan felt his blood pressure rising at the thought. And when Gail and Mike announced he was on a roll in the casino, Dan wanted to chew nails and spit tacks. Meyers might not be a big-time gambler, but he was certainly a big-time spender. Dan didn't even want to think about what this holiday cruise cost his mom.

He braked the race of his thoughts with a deep breath before escorting Sunny to the table. He felt like the Lone Ranger with his hands tied. His mother thought Charlie hung the moon. Gail was

just in love with the idea of romance on the sea and an elope-
ment—some mother-to-be hormone maybe. He'd heard women
got extra emotional when they were like that.

Dan plain thought it was all hogwash. He didn't believe in love
at first sight. Sure, he liked Sunny. She was like a breath of fresh air
compared to the few females he'd found the time to date. But love?
Spending the rest of his life holding his breath at what would happen next?

"Ohhh!"

As if on cue, the subject of his thoughts lurched ahead of him.
Dan didn't have time to see what had fouled her step. He grabbed
at her waist before she sprawled over a group of college boys who'd
most likely gathered to watch the single girls and see who could
outdrink the next guy.

"Got—" he pulled her upright—"ya."

"I'm *so* sorry." Sunny grabbed a napkin to wipe off the drink
she'd knocked into a hunk of muscle with a *Love Ahoy* tank T-shirt.

"Hey, *Love Ahoy,* babe. It's cool. It's cool."

And he thought *his* lines were bad. Dan gave the young man a
slashing look, but the kid was beyond subtlety.

"Name's Steer, buy ya a beer?"

Sunny shook her head, chuckling. "No thanks, I'm having
enough trouble staying on my feet as it is."

"S'why I'm sittin'."

"Shush, man. She's with *him,*" one of his friends warned.

The young Romeo rocked back and forth. "Yo, dude, didn't see
ya. No offense, okay?" He grabbed Dan's hand in some kind of
funky handshake. "She *is* with you, right?" The appraisal he gave
Sunny raised the hair on the back of Dan's neck.

To his astonishment, Dan was annoyed to no end. It took a grand
effort not to offer to teach the liquor-induced lothario some manners,

but Sunny didn't seem the least affected by any of it. She was still embarrassed, and in the most becoming way, over tripping. "That's right, *dude,*" Dan replied.

He thought he'd been subtle until the muscle man threw up both hands in surrender. "Yo, man, just askin'. It's cool. It's cool."

"No problem, pardner." What a sap. Dan wiped the sticky drink from the handshake on his jeans. "Glad I won't have his head tomorrow morning," he whispered in Sunny's ear.

"Or *any* time for that matter," she quipped wryly. "I just can't picture you with no hair."

Dan grinned. The boy was bald as an eagle and sunburned to boot. No, he definitely would not like either part of that head tomorrow, inside or out. "You okay, *babe?*"

She giggled. "As my dad used to say, 'Fine as frog hair.' But I can't believe what happened."

It never occurred to Dan that this walking accident would need a reason to sprawl over a table when least expected. Sunny turned her ankle toward him, revealing a dangling sandal. It was a simple gesture, but Dan felt as if he'd just opened the door on a sunbaked truck and been knocked back by the heat.

"I literally blew out my flip-flop," she said, picking at the dangling thong of her leather sandal. "Except I paid more for these than Jimmy Buffett's version."

With a grimace, she dropped into the empty seat next to Charlie.

"Boy, you've literally danced this little gal out of her shoes," his stepfather observed with a hearty laugh.

Turning phrases was cute coming from Sunny; not so from Meyers. They pulled Dan from the heady daze dealt by Sunny's guileless display.

"Esther, I believe they are like the pair we bought for you back home, just before we left."

"You mean *Mom* bought, don't you?" The words churned too bitterly within to keep to himself.

"Yep," Charlie admitted, clearly unoffended. "And as much as she paid for them, they best not bust and throw you down. *Italian* leather, mind you."

"Those man-made materials make my feet itch," Dan's mom said, flashing a look of motherly caution at Dan. "My podiatrist says I have to have leather," she explained to Sunny.

"Yeah, well just remember, Essie, I'm not as quick on my feet as your Dan."

His mom's warning stayed Dan's ready reply, but not the thought. *You're slow like a fox.* The nerve of the man, complaining about the cost of her shoes, when it was her money. And he hated it when Charlie called his mom Essie—as if he were talking to a blooming cow. Dan forced open the hand that had automatically clenched and leaned on his chair. He just couldn't sit at a table with the fraud and watch his family be taken in.

Pulling off her other shoe, Sunny stood up.

"Well, I've about had the course for the day anyway. What little energy Swing Ting didn't take, Dancin' Dan here finished off." She gave him an impish look. "I'll take this as a sign from my fairy god-mother that this Cinderella needs to get some rest."

Help straight from heaven, Dan thought in wonder and relief, just like that freckled face. He couldn't decide which he wanted to do more, kiss the little upturn of her nose or pinch it. But he did neither. He simply stared, dumbfounded by his thoughts.

"Well…" Sunny trailed off, returning his look with uncertainty.

It was all the jar Dan needed. "I'll walk you back," he offered, giving himself a mental shake. He felt like he'd been standing on his tongue and gaping. He hoped he hadn't, but from that satisfied smirk on Gail's face, he feared the worst.

"I'm sure the kids'll be there. I mean, I don't want to take you from your family." Sunny had misread his hesitation entirely.

"Nonsense. It's no fun being a fifth wheel." The moment that was out, he sensed another front rising.

His mother straightened in her chair, puffing like a hen with a threatened chick. "Son, you are not a fifth wheel on this boat any more than you've been at home since Gail brought her Mike home from college and married him."

"Ma, he wants to even out a couple," Gail volunteered across the table, giving her mother one of those womanly nods that meant Cupid had called out all hands on deck.

Dan refused to dignify either comment. Instead, he leaned over and gave his mom a retreating peck on the cheek. He knew when to fold and run. "I'll see you good folks tomorrow sometime."

His mother drew back in hopeful surprise. "You're going on the tour to Marigot with us?"

She'd asked him to go, but Dan had other plans. "No. I thought I'd just kick around the Dutch side. I only meant I'll see you all sometime tomorrow, even if it's at supper."

His mother nodded, some of the sparkle dying in her gaze. Feeling more like a wet towel than a doting son, Dan gave her an extra hug. He really hoped his suspicions about Charlie were wrong, but he couldn't see how they could be.

"Night, Mom…and watch you don't throw a shoe now," Dan teased, hoping to put a smile back on her face. It worked.

With a wave at the others, he turned to follow Sunny. She padded barefoot ahead of him in uncharacteristic silence.

"You sure you want to go this way in your bare feet?" he asked, surprised when she started down the steps in lieu of taking the elevators.

On reaching the first landing, she turned suddenly. "What do you find so objectionable about Charlie, aside from your not believing in love at first sight? You were rude back there."

He drew back. "I'm sorry, I just have reservations about him. That's all."

"Well, I hope you have a good reason for them, because the tension when the two of you are in the same room is so thick you can cut it with that little pocketknife of yours."

She started down again, her skirt filling with the updraft, making her look as if she floated—a butterfly spreading its wings. Stung by her terse comment, Dan watched until she turned for the next set of steps. Shaking himself out of it, he hurriedly followed and caught up.

"I think I do."

"Well, what's the problem?" she said over her shoulder, her momentum carrying her deeper into the ship toward the main deck. "Aside from the fact that he married your mother after a whirlwind courtship and made her happy?"

Dan's already sagging humor was pricked by the judgment in her voice. It was none of her business anyway. "What *is* this? Analyze Dan night?"

At the bottom of the steps, Sunny pivoted so suddenly Dan nearly collided with her.

"Yes, it is! You are too nice a guy to be acting like a cross bear around your family. Your mother's found a new life and she's happy with it. She's a big girl. You have to let her go."

"To *what?*" he exclaimed, louder than he intended to. A foursome passing by in one of the corridors glanced at him curiously.

Eyes widening in warning, Sunny brandished a librarian finger to the lips. "Shush! Some people are already asleep."

It was perfectly harmless, but so was the last straw dropped on the camel's back. First she stuck her nose into something she knew nothing about, then she told him to shush, like some little kid in her ER. Dan burned to tell her that Charlie Meyers was a fraud; that he had rotten credit; and, at the rate he was going, would ruin his mother's credit, too. But he needed more proof than a lousy credit rating.

"I can't believe people fall in love at first sight at their age—or any age for that matter. And Meyers was a retired car salesman on a cut-rate passage so that he'd put a smile on some lonely widow's face, maybe ask her for a dance or two, make her feel special. It was his *job* to charm her, for heaven's sake."

"Oh, that explains it."

Dan hated the word *that* when spoken in that tone. It was condescending and dripping with doubt.

"So all car salesmen are hucksters and all cruise social hosts are predators on old ladies with money, is that it?" Sunny crossed her arms and tapped her bare foot, amplifying the impact of her five-foot-four height with pure attitude. Teachers perfected such intimidation. He supposed it had its place in the emergency room setting too, except that the women who were usually cast in such roles were big and brawny enough to move a refrigerator single-handedly, not petite and too feisty for her size. "And I suppose you chew tobacco and sing to your cows every night?"

"What?" Dan rebelled against that guilty schoolboy feeling she was evoking, top teeth grating against bottom.

"If you're going to stereotype Charlie, you might as well have a taste of what it feels like, pardner."

"No," he grated out, "I don't—"

"That's stereotyping. Occupational prejudice. And frankly, I never took you for a man who would harbor such ridiculous notions."

Occupational prejudice? Dan scowled. He'd never heard of anything so ridiculous. Leave it to a woman to stir black and white until everything was a baffling gray.

"It's not exactly any of your business." He finished on a note that said *end of conversation*.

It went unnoticed. One fair eyebrow leapt a good half-inch higher than its mate in challenge. "It is when you are using me as an excuse to avoid your family. It is when I see a nice person acting like a jerk."

A *jerk*? "At least when I see a problem I deal with it. You *run* from yours." Nothing like a good offense for defense.

That halted her in her tracks. "What does that mean?"

"It means you busy yourself *healing* the world, all the while avoiding facing your parents' death."

Sunny's mouth dropped open. "I...how can you say such a thing? I cared for them. I watched them die. How in your face can you get with it? And I'm a nurse—"

"Yeah, I know, healing's your job. But part of healing is grieving, and you're running from grief like a scalded pup. You haven't even cried." Dan shuffled uncomfortably under Sunny's astonished scrutiny. He hadn't intended to reveal he'd been privy to all this, but she started it.

"You don't know what I have or haven't done. You...you don't know me."

Now he'd done it. His anger deflated like a slashed tire at the sight of tears gathering in her eyes, which were now a rainy gray instead of sky blue—at least what he could see of them.

"Okay, I'm sorry." If he'd had a white flag, he'd have waved it...or at least offered to dry her tears.

His reprieve, if he even was going to get one, was preempted by rapid-fire, heavy, descending footfalls. He turned to see Jason, Allison, and possibly every child on the ship capable of walking.

Regardless of the numbers headed their way, no relief came to ease his sudden misery.

So do you feel better? an inner voice demanded, and his silent answer was an emphatic "No!"

Jason was taunting his sister. "I saw you flirting with Sean in the pizzeria. Wait till I tell Marshall. Marshall's going to be jealous. Marshall's going to be jealous."

"Like a nine-year-old twerp would know," his sister retorted. "Get a life."

Not the least fazed by Allison's derision, Jason vaulted over the banister of the last set of steps, skipping the landing altogether. "Hey, Dan! Hey, Aunt Sunny!"

Dan nodded, lips thinning into a semblance of acknowledgment, which was more than his companion did. It was as if she'd somehow sensed his misery and drawn fresh wind from it. No rain now, just storm.

"You are a control freak who doesn't like change, but life stands still for no one and it has its own mind," Sunny said under her breath before grabbing Jason's arm, slowing him to a walk with a stern look.

"Okay, okay," the boy complained to her in a hushed tone, misinterpreting her sharpness as being aimed at him. "I forgot."

"That's because he doesn't have a brain." Allison displayed a full rack of braces as she passed by them, suddenly demure as a princess. "No brain, no memory."

No brain. Though her remark was not intended for him, even Allison made him feel like a guilty schoolboy. Women. They must come out of the womb with that gift.

Dan ran a hand through his hair, as if that somehow could help him sort out why he was arguing with Sunny. She knew even less of Meyers than Dan, who knew less of her situation than she. If this wasn't the pot and kettle in the same stew, what was?

"Just think about it," Sunny said, turning after her niece rounded the corner and walking back to him. "Is your problem really with Charlie or is he just one needle on that burr under your saddle? If you really want to know, God'll show you the answer and help you deal with it." Before Dan realized what she was up to, Sunny rose on tiptoe and gave him a kiss on the cheek. "Good night, pardner. Despite your stubborn streak where your stepfather is concerned, I had a good time."

Struck dumb by the sweetness of the kiss, Dan struggled to regroup, following his barefoot Cinderella to their respective cabin doors in the offshoot of the hallway.

Sunny retreated inside the cabin, her kiss obviously his dismissal.

Stalled in his tracks by her surprise tactics, Dan watched the door close behind her, still waiting to see which of his scrambled emotions would emerge from the blow of her kiss-and-run attack, when the door opened again. Just a crack.

Just enough to release the rest of her swingy skirt.

He couldn't help himself. He laughed. Only Sunny could end an argument on such a parting note.

But once inside his cabin, alone and alienated, not only from his family, but from the welcome refuge he'd found in Sunny, his smile faded. God. Only God could figure out what just happened, and Dan didn't feel like they'd been close enough of late for the Big Guy to share—not since Dan's mom had married and moved out.

Dan had always taken her to church. God was something they'd shared together, leaned on together through thick and thin. God lived in his mom, but Dan couldn't honestly say that was so in him. At least, he didn't feel like it. Who knew? Maybe he needed to be around folks like her to feel that way...maybe her leaving and his not joining the others each Sunday had something to do with the distance he felt from God lately—like a friend who'd moved away.

But even when he had regularly gone through the motions of Sunday worship, even when he was as quick to help his neighbor as the next man, and even though he believed in God and praising Him, he still felt he didn't have the communication his mom and some of the church members seemed to have. Sure, he prayed dutifully, covering all the bases—his family, the ranch, the prayer list at church. Sometimes, though, it seemed like a canned program, regular as chores, even though he meant what he said. He simply wasn't much of a talker and figured God was too busy for small talk anyway.

Dan scowled, still smarting and bewildered by Sunny's turn-coat treatment. Besides, he'd prayed for his mom, that she'd come to her senses, and still Charlie Meyers had her snow-blinded like a calf in a blizzard. Prayer hadn't done one whit of good as far as Dan could see.

"If you really want to know, God'll show you the answer and help you deal with it."

He mulled over Sunny's words as he got ready for bed. Praying for his mom's eyes to open hadn't worked, but Dan hadn't prayed that his would. He felt uneasy praying for himself, when there were so many others with more important needs than he had. But if God would help him get the evidence on Charlie, then Dan could show his mom.

Lord, I know I've been pretty busy lately and haven't had a lot to say, but I'd appreciate it if You'd help me show Charlie Meyers for what he really is. A lot of people's happiness depends on it, Lord. Amen.

Thirteen

*M*ELINDA LOOKED MORE like Allison's older sister than her mother as she and Sunny walked off the floating plank from the tender. The small boat transported them from the *Love Ahoy* to the dock at Phillipsburg, the Dutch capital of St. Maarten. With small, pewter-framed sunglasses and her dark hair swept back by a little bandanna, the capri-clad mother of two had deckhands rushing to help her off, while Sunny made her way on her own.

"Thank you, hon." Melinda addressed the deckhand like the late teen he was, her soft drawl setting the sun-bleached Dutch on his bare heels.

"You're most welcome, miss. Enjoy our island," he answered, grinning all over himself.

Sunny sighed, wistful and amused at the same time. Just one more fallen swain to step over in her sister's wake.

"So where's Dan? I was beginning to think you two were joined at the hip," Melinda asked, after she'd abandoned her court to walk toward the doll-like town of island pastels spread on either side of them.

Sunny concentrated on the map the steward left in the room the night before while ushering her thoughts from her sister to the disgruntled cowboy she'd bid good night. "I'm not sure. He skipped the family tour of the island. That's all I know."

Dan hadn't come down for breakfast, and she couldn't blame him if he was avoiding her. She should have minded her own business. Except that she couldn't, not when she saw him making himself and his family miserable. Time was too short not to make the most of it with those you love. She knew that firsthand *because* she grieved. She spoke up *because* she grieved, not because she was running away from her parents' loss. What on earth had possessed him to say that?

Of course, she had acted as if he'd pulled her out of bed on the wrong side, jumping all over him because of his cynicism toward Charlie. But maybe today would be the end of it.

Lord, whatever he thinks he's going to find out today, I pray it will put us all out of our misery.

"It's just that you two have been so cozy." Melinda was a pit bull when it came to sniffing out reticence to discuss a relationship. "I certainly never expected to see him in your cabin last night. Why, you could have knocked me over with a feather."

"Or a pillow full of them." Sunny ventured, switching to mischief as was her sisterly right—besides, that was far easier than fretting over the things she and Dan had said to each other.

Melinda stopped in front of a stall selling trinkets and T-shirts. "Oh, for heaven's sake, Sunny, tell me about him."

"He is a bachelor, a rancher, and stubborn as the day is long when it comes to his new stepfather. End of story." She hadn't said enough and she knew it, but she honestly didn't know what else to say. If there had been anything building between them, they'd cut it down with their words last night.

"I mean about you and him," her sister said, snatching away the T-shirt Sunny was eyeing to get her full attention.

"Nothing to say. Like me, he's weary of matchmaking sisters." She gave Melinda a pointed look. "And unlike me, he's avoiding his family because he doesn't like his new stepfather. You'd think the man was featured on *America's Most Wanted*, the way Dan acts." Sunny pointed to the shirt. Her sister wasn't the only one who could stay a course—Sunny's just happened to be one of evasion, rather than pursuit. "You think Ruth Ann would like that? I have to get shirts for my biweekly Saturday night gang—something that reflects them."

Melinda heaved a sigh of defeat and shook her head. "I'd go with the golds and maroons for the redhead. The Caribbean blues look more like Carol."

She suddenly looked panicked and began to dig in her purse— a large, straw bag capable of handling an overnight change of clothes, maybe two. "Thank goodness," she exclaimed, when she came up empty-handed. "I thought the kids had forgotten their tanning lotion with the sunblock. The boys burn so easily."

Now that was more like Melinda, quick on her feet, switching from matchmaker to mother in an instant. Alan and kids had gone windsurfing at Simson Baai Beach, leaving the women to shop.

"The *boys*?" Sunny teased. "You call Alan a boy?"

Melinda made a face. "Well, he is when it comes to taking care of himself." A devilish twitch toyed with her lips. "And when it comes to taking care of me…"

"You *are* better." Sunny sniggered. *Thank You, Lord.*

Things were definitely looking up regarding Alan and Melinda. Her sister was returning to her old self. As for Sunny herself, seeing others get better was the best medicine. The vacation with people she loved certainly wasn't contraindicative. Now Phillipsburg, a shopper's paradise according to the brochures, was at their disposal. What more could a gal want?

The port was laid out simply, in a ladder configuration parallel to the crest of sand edging the harbor upon which it was founded. By noon, Sunny had trailed Melinda into every shop along the rails—or its two main streets, aptly named Front Street and Back Street. They walked up one and then worked their way back on the other, taking little forays into the connecting alleys called *steeges*. Imports from all over the world underscored the historical reputation of the Dutch as international traders. The town itself was founded in 1733 as a free port, which meant all the packages Sunny carried in a newly purchased imitation straw bag of her own were tax-free.

With the packages, mostly souvenirs and enough T-shirts to set up a shop, Sunny felt as though she'd single-handedly helped the Dutch uphold their dominance, at least on St. Maarten. Despite its compact metropolitan atmosphere of traffic and modern stores, there was enough island atmosphere to charm tourists to empty their purses. Sunny felt like a modern pirate with duty-free wares.

"It's a good thing we're finished. I don't think I could carry any more," her sister said, shifting a large shopping bag from one hand to the other.

Melinda looked like a pile of packages with two legs. There were all the kids in her Sunday school class to buy for, not to mention special purchases for her coworkers. From the looks of their fellow passengers meandering toward the incoming tender to head back to the ship, they were not alone.

"But look at all the money we've *saved*," Sunny chortled.

Ahead of them, she spied the straw hat with the red-and-green tropical print band that Melinda had insisted her husband wear when he was out on the golf course or in the sun. Both he and the kids wore new T-shirts touting the name of the beach and a screen print of windsurfers. Jason was the first of the crew to spot Sunny and Melinda.

"Hey, what'd you two do, buy out the place?"

Sunny exchanged a startled look with her sister. "As long as Jason lives, Dad'll never die."

"You got that right," her sister agreed. "You know, I just can't help but think Mom and Dad are enjoying us enjoying ourselves as much as we are…like they're here too," she added wistfully. "I miss them, but I know they are still with me, as long as I have memories."

"Sure they are, Sis. And you know Mom was drooling over the jewelry with us." She'd made a joke simply to cheer her sister, Sunny told herself, not to run from her parents' loss as Dan suggested. Confound him, his accusation just wouldn't leave her be.

Regardless of her motive, the ploy worked. Melinda grinned, her touch of melancholy fading. "I know. I'll tell Alan I bought the gold bracelet with the cats etched on it in Mom's memory. She did love her kitties."

Praise God, life went on. They all were learning to smile at the memories rather than cry. It was a choice, not an escape. "Like he'd complain," she teased, keeping the tone light. "Especially if you wear it with that Parisian flimsy thing you bought at the lingerie shop."

A look of sheer devilment lit in her sister's gaze. "That's right. I bought something for me and something for him."

"You are bad." Sunny grinned. And Dan's notion was plain silly. "Emptying the man's pockets and making him smile while you do it."

"Hey, this is my payment for solo parenting during all those long hours he'll put in between now and April 15."

"He owes it to you, right?" Sunny chimed in.

An emphatic "Right" came from behind the shifting packages.

"Did ya get me anything?" Jason dove into the largest bag greedily, oblivious to the drift of their conversation.

"Yes," Melinda told him, snatching it away from him. "Dad and I got you a cruise. Are you having fun?"

Jason was so taken aback, he just stared at his mom for a second. "Ah, man," he exclaimed in that I-have-been-had tone and helped relieve Melinda of some of her packages.

"Hey, what about me?"

"A body can only carry so much, Aunt Sunny."

Sunny objected facetiously. "That's why I need help."

"Here, Aunt Sunny. I'll take them," Allison obliged, yawning widely. "I'm ready for a nap."

"Allison cover your mouth when you yawn," Melinda chided.

The young girl's eyes bulged with incredulity. "How can I do that when I'm loaded with packages?"

"Can't be a femme fatale and a packhorse at the same time, Sis."

Melinda threw up her hands, now free except for her straw handbag. "I don't know which of you is worse."

Guided by Alan's arm, she stepped aside to let the passengers coming off the tender get by them. Sunny fell in behind, warmed at the gesture, yet not without a green twinge of envy. Her sister was the kind of woman that just cried out, *Someone take care of me*, and men jumped to attention. With Sunny, they stood back, waiting to see what she'd do for herself first.

"Hey, pardner," a familiar voice hailed from among the debarking travelers.

Ahead of her, Jason held out his elbow, his hands encumbered by his mom's packages for Dan to slap—the teen equivalent to the handshake.

"Thought you were going windsurfing," Dan said, looking beyond Jason until he found Sunny in line. She wanted to ignore him but couldn't. His look was as tentative as she felt, as though each of them was waiting to see how the other reacted.

"We did. Man, it was awesome. Dad took a dive, I mean big time."

"I wasn't exactly alone," Alan reminded his offspring. "I seem to recall three members of this family floundering in the tropical blue water."

"Always wanted to try that. Waterskiing is about as far as I've ventured from a horse's back." He glanced at Sunny again, as if waiting for her to say something.

She obliged. "And when you can combine horse and water in one activity, you've got it made, right?" She gave a wry twist of her lips. Face it, if the man wasn't a jerk sometimes, he'd be perfect. So who was she, the family klutz, to hold imperfection against anyone?

Dan shoved his hands into his jeans pockets. "I have to say, it was a memorable experience."

"So where are you off to, Dan?" Melinda asked.

"Marigot." He turned to Sunny. "Want to ride along?" He pulled a shy, sheepish look that had a greater melting effect than the tropical sun overhead. "I mean, if you're not too tired from cleaning out all the stores."

Melinda intervened. "Go ahead, Sunny. Alan and I'll look after the kids. You deserve a day to yourself." She gathered Sunny's loot in her arms. "I'll have the kids put your loot in your cabin."

"I'll take 'em. I'm taking a nap," Allison reminded her with a decidedly I'm-big-enough-to-take-care-of-myself attitude.

"An' I'm going to tour the bridge and engine room with Marshall and his dad," Jason spoke up.

Relieved of her local booty, Sunny shrugged and added another point to Dan's character scorecard. Forgiveness wasn't foreign to him. "Well, looks like I'm footloose and fancy-free." She stopped suddenly, pulling her arm back from the one Dan offered her. "Wait. There aren't any horses involved in this, are there?"

"Scout's honor."

"You two have a good time, but remember, be back before sailing time at four," Melinda called after them as Alan managed not only his wife's packages but an adoring arm to usher her up the gangway.

Sunny barely heard mother Melinda's warning. She was too relieved that the hatchet she and Dan had buried between them hadn't severed their friendship. And she was too distracted by Dan's gentle but firm touch at her back. It was so easy to relish the feel of his guidance, as if she had a strong, protective arm of her very own. At least for a while, the color green was not part of the rainbow-colored glasses through which she viewed her sister's life.

One of the cruise crew, clad in crisp white, hailed a cab for them. Dan tipped the man and held the door for Sunny before climbing in behind her.

"We'd like to go to the express office in Marigot," Dan told the man in the front seat.

The driver, a perfect example of the island's melting pot of cultures, turned and asked in a French accent, "Do you wish the scenic route along the coast or—"

"We'll take the shortest route. We're in a bit of a hurry with the ship sailing in a few hours, and I'd like to take this little lady to lunch while we're there."

Like one of Pavlov's dogs, Sunny's stomach growled. Confined in the cab, the sound was hard to miss.

"Make that a big hurry," Dan laughed, settling back on the seat beside her.

"I am Roy. Sit back and make yourselves comfortable and enjoy our island," he announced with all the aplomb of an airline pilot.

His small, European compact car launched into the line of traffic as if it could fly, gears shifting, tires squealing. Sunny grabbed on to the door with one hand and checked her seat belt with the other, while Dan squared his hat with a firm tug. The air rushing in whipped around them, playing havoc with her hair.

"Guess they don't use air-conditioning much in these things," he said to her, one hand still steadying his Stetson lest it take flight.

Small talk was a good place to start, given their heated discussion the night before. "When flying this low, I guess you don't need it."

The car swerved sharply into another lane, its turn signal ticking loudly.

"This looks like a case of too many cars and not enough island," she added, loosening her death grip as the vehicle straightened out from the turn. She'd been on bumper car rides that weren't this hectic.

"This riding on the opposite side of the road takes some getting used to," Dan agreed. "We're definitely not in Kansas, Toto."

In a few minutes they were heading inland, away from the bustle of Phillipsburg traffic. The road ahead was less traveled, but no less challenging. Barely wide enough for two small cars, it snaked up and around the scrub-covered lava stone landscape rising before them. Here and there, tucked in the shade of a variety of sun-baked palms tipped in dried yellow or tattered umbrellas, were colorful produce stands where island squashes, yams, and plantains were displayed in cardboard boxes or on straw mats—picture perfect. Too bad the car whizzed by them so quickly that only high-speed film could capture their quaint, tropical beauty.

"Imagine having a banana tree or coconut tree in your own yard," she mused dreamily.

"They'd not do that well in our neck of the woods," Dan observed, pragmatic to a fault. Somehow the spell of paradise fell short of his grasp. Maybe it was a man thing—although Alan was excited about identifying the tropical birds.

"There was some mix-up with the information I was waiting for and the express office sent it to Marigot instead of Phillipsburg, where the cruise ship is," he volunteered after a few more hairpin turns. Sunny wondered if his sudden desire to chat was born of nerves.

"Oh?" Still speaking, offering to buy her lunch, and not afraid to broach the subject that had set off their tiff—here was a man who could take a licking and keep on ticking.

And so could she. "I'm sorry I was so short—" she started.

"I'm sorry about last—" he said at the same time.

They laughed. Sunny pointed to him. "You first. I like my men to grovel."

"I shouldn't have accused you of not grieving for your parents. What do I know?"

Sunny shrugged. "I don't know. Maybe you're right. Keeping busy is my way of handling stress. I always thought of it as a tool, not an escape."

"You're probably right," Dan observed pensively. "If I'm upset, I work. Problem is, there's no work to do on a cruise."

"Look down to the right," the driver instructed, seemingly oblivious to their conversation. "That is the Great Salt Pond."

In a few short exchanges, they'd climbed far enough into the interior of the volcanic island that the water could be viewed. The car slowed just long enough for Sunny to turn her head before accelerating again at whiplash speed. She grabbed the small grip on the door.

"It was that which provided my ancestors with income hundreds of years ago." The driver looked over his shoulder and gave them a toothy smile. "My ancient family must have spent its fortune and so—" he shrugged—"I drive the cab."

Dan, she noticed, had a good hold on his side as well. The car approached a sharp turn ahead, which it took with protesting squeals of the tires, giving Sunny a thrilling view of a straight drop-off with no rail to block it. She caught her breath and glanced at her companion. A mutual anxiety bonded their gazes until Dan broke way, leaning forward as far as his fastened seatbelt would allow.

"Hey, pardner, you think it's safe to drive this fast on these hilly roads?"

The driver tossed up both hands. "I drive these all the time. You will get used to it. Ten minutes tops."

Sunny let out her trapped breath as he returned his hands to the wheel. She managed a weak smile at her champion for at least trying. Fifty cabs had been lined up at the dock, and they had to get one with an aspiring top-gun pilot.

Going downhill added a whole new dimension to the travelog term *breath-taking views,* particularly when a small herd of goats meandered across the road just around the corner. The squeal of the brakes drowned out Sunny's cry of alarm. Strapped in by a seat belt and not a shoulder harness, she caught herself against the front seat. Although she heard Dan's exclamation of surprise, she was probably just as well off not to understand it. Certainly the braking car left a trail of rubber right up to the goats, who scrambled in all directions, save one little frozen animal. It was the only obstacle in the middle of the extremely narrow road, so that there was no bypassing it on either side.

Cursing in French, or some version thereof, the driver leaned on his horn as hard as he had the brakes until a barefoot child appeared from the scrub and shooed the animal off to the side of the road. Waving his fist threateningly, the driver slammed the accelerator to the floor, and they were off once again.

Dan's expression would have made Sunny laugh if her heart wasn't demanding all her attention to find a normal beat again. He looked torn between saying something and possibly setting this maniac off even more and swallowing his Adam's apple, which appeared to be inordinately high in relationship to his throat. If it was possible, he was actually white beneath his tan—not that Sunny felt a drop of blood was left in her face, either.

"What's another two miles?" she quipped, wading through her alarm toward sympathy and commiseration.

Marigot was as close to France as Sunny had ever been and a world away from the other side of the island, she thought later as she waited for Dan to sign for the all-important packet regarding his stepfather. It had Paris's old world charm but its own island style, with sidewalk terraces and unfurled umbrellas lining the streets. The quaintness set it apart from the Dutch side, which was more commercial with its businesses fitted cheek-by-jowl wherever development would allow.

Red tiles topped Marigot's stuccoed buildings, which were mostly white interspersed with island pastels and landscaped as only the tropics could be. Bougainvillea of every color adorned foundations and vibrant flowers bloomed in gay profusion everywhere, shaded by the lazy umbrellas of moss vine-wrapped trees. Open restaurants and shops, their working shutters folded back or raised to allow the island breezes in, offered more of the same Euro-tropical ambiance, reminiscent of an era when time was plentiful and sultry elegance was a way of life.

It was enough to make a gal feel rich, even if she'd only cruised there on someone else's account.

Sunny's stomach growled in appreciation of the scent of the

many flavored coffees blended with those of fresh-baked croissants and pastries. The pickiest tummy would do somersaults for a sample and hers was not the least bit choosy.

Wiping the perspiration from her brow, Sunny glanced up at the bright awning overhead, grateful for what shelter it provided from the heat. The glass door—a strange modern contrast to the cozy, weathered, shuttered windows on either side—opened, and Dan emerged, tugging his hat down on his forehead, the open packet under his arm.

From the thundercloud expression on his face, Sunny was almost afraid to ask. Almost.

"So what's the verdict? Is Charlie an ax murderer or an international con artist?"

If looks could kill, her niece and nephew would be an insurance policy richer any moment now. Dan's face was a livid red.

Sunny grimaced. "Sorry I asked."

Instead of replying, Dan took a bracing breath, letting it out slowly, not unlike a pressure cooker cooling down. He was upset, but he was trying to put a lid on it.

"No, *I'm* sorry," he said at last. With a few sharp tugs, he ripped the express mail to shreds and deposited it in a garbage can close by. "But I didn't bring you along to take out my frustration on. I thought we'd do lunch at a place the purser recommended."

Sunny ditched the "So, you're ready to eat crow?" that popped in her mind for something more tactful. Obviously he didn't get what he wanted…or he did get what he wanted and it was worse than he thought. Either way, he needed a pal. She linked her arm in his as they started walking along the umbrella-lined street.

"Look, for some reason, we've been practically joined at the hip from the get-go," she said, borrowing her sister's observation. "First it wasn't by choice, of course, but now you're just asking for it."

He grinned. It gave new life to his frown-frozen dimples. "I still think you are a walking disaster waiting to happen." It was an effort, but he was doing his best to be cordial.

She elbowed him. "Hey, it's what I handle best. It's my job."

They stepped around a street vendor selling snow cones with tropical flavor names from a cart. The treats looked luscious, but Sunny hardly gave them a second glance. Like it did quite often during patient traumas, her nagging stomach took a backseat to Dan's dilemma.

"Anyway—"

"Wait a minute. There's that café the clerk told me about. She said it was only a block from the express office. *Le Fleur de Lis.*"

He stumbled over the French syllables like skates over cobblestones, but the name was so appropriate for the place, who cared? French wasn't exactly a requirement for wrangling cows and horses. Sunny looked around while he gave the host his name. She'd hoped for one of the tables along the street, thinking gay Paree—the hustle, the bustle, the smells, the romance. Instead, Martin, according to his name tag, showed them through a wrought-iron gate and into a courtyard, to a bistro table for two. Next to it was a stone fountain of nymphs pouring water from their wands.

It was like a fairyland—a tropical one—with light shafting through palms and arbors. Spikes of bougainvillea bloomed wild, while vines climbed along painted brick walls cracked by time and the elements. Balconies surrounded the area and were dressed in lacelike ironwork surely fashioned by the hands of another world, another century. The restaurant, Martin told them, had once been the home of a French nobleman who'd been exiled after refusing to look the other way while his wife's favors were demanded by the king. He and his wife escaped and lived out their lives in isolation, but forever in love. Martin told the story with such emotion, Sunny thought he was angling for an Oscar instead of a tip. After he left, Dan leaned forward. "I didn't know whether to offer my handkerchief or not."

"It was a lovely story though. Just think how old this place is."

"Just so the burger is fresh."

True to form, the cowpoke ordered meat and potatoes—burger and fries this time, with a French tag to make it sound fancy. Sunny opted for a chicken salad and fruit bowl, the bowl itself being a pastry, although there was enough fruit in the house punch to run up a diabetic's blood sugar.

"*This* is the life," she said, sipping from a long straw. It was a shish kebab of fruit slices in itself.

"Okay, so we're joined at the hip for the cruise. What are you getting at?"

The magic popped like the last balloon in her cabin, bringing her back to earth. Right…joined at the hip. Now where was she?

"Oh yeah. I was going to say that we seemed to be destined to share whatever it is that is bothering you, because when it eats at you, it nips at me, too. In other words, you don't feel like you can share this with your family because it will distress them. I'm not directly involved. Maybe God thought you needed someone to talk it over with."

"God put you in my path?"

She shrugged. "It could happen. Don't you believe God looks out for us?"

"Well, yeah, but…"

Sunny put her drink down. "Look, I'm not here to discuss religion, although I'm game if you want to. But there are some things we shouldn't handle alone. Sometimes it helps to have a friendly ear to reason out whatever is bothering you. I just happened to be on hand."

Dan pulled out the fruit kebab from his drink and started picking at it thoughtfully.

"I'm just offering," Sunny said nervously. "You'd be surprised at
some of the family situations I find myself pulled into with my job.
I'd like to think that I've helped in some way. At least I pray that I
say the right thing at the right time, when and where it's needed
most."

"An ER angel, huh?"

She paid him back, grin for grin. "I don't know if I'd go *that*
far."

"Okay, Nurse Elders. Here's the long and short of it. I was worried that Mom had married too hastily. There's all manner of men
out there willing to steal a senior widow's money through her heart.
So I had Charlie investigated, and the way he's been throwing
money around, I think I was right to do so."

"Investigated?" She didn't think Dan's suspicion had gone that
far. On one hand, it was sweet that he cared that much for his
mom, but still… "And those were the results? What you tore up
back there?"

The waiter approached the table with their food. "So what did
the report say?" Sunny prompted.

Dan waited until they'd been served before he answered. "The
same as the preliminary report, except that this is from another
credit agency on another Charlie Meyers—this time a *married* one
from Jacksonville. But whether Mom's Charlie is married—and if
he is, so help me, I'll wring his neck—or not, both Meyerses are
coming up with bad credit ratings all over. They are up to their ears
in debt and have more people waiting in line to sue them than the
tobacco companies do. Jacksonville or Miami Charlie, he's lying
about something."

"I can't believe it," Sunny whispered to no one in particular.

Was Charlie a fraud *and* a bigamist? She simply couldn't see it.

Dan threw up his hands in exasperation. "It's hard to tell what lies he's told us, particularly Mom. He did say his credit cards were tied up in a credit mix-up. More like a freeze, if you ask me."

"Oh man," Sunny groaned, shades of her nephew. No wonder Dan was upset.

"So he's been spending Mom's money like there's no end to it...and if he's *married*—"

"I know, you'll wring his neck. But credit reports *can* get mixed up. You hear about it all the time."

"That is why I've kept this to myself...at least I've tried to," Dan admitted upon seeing Sunny's sharp look. "I really don't want to even hint at this to anyone until I'm sure, especially the bigamy part." He spoke as if the word hurt him as much as it would hurt his mom. He really did care.

"Well, that's wise," Sunny acknowledged in approval. "But I just can't believe it. He acts like he's totally head over heels for your mom."

"Key word there is *acts*."

To Sunny's surprise, Dan reached across the table, placing his hand over her arm. His gaze was almost pleading. "I'm not a jerk, Sunny. I just love my family and I want to protect them."

With him looking at her like that, touching her and setting her senses on full alert, she could believe pretty much anything he said. But she'd known all along Dan wasn't a jerk. Not really. He was simply the kind of person who could never be labeled as two-faced. He wore his heart on his sleeve...and at the rate she was going, he'd be wearing hers as well.

She swallowed hard. "I know that, silly. I just couldn't figure out why you were acting like one just because Charlie had sold used cars and married your mom too quickly for your taste." She felt like saying more, although what, she had no idea. Never one at a lack for words, she retreated to her strong suit. "Now eat your lunch. You need protein to handle all that stress you've been under."

"Yes, ma'am."

As he drew his hand away, she felt a part of her longing to hang on, as though as long as they had each other, they wouldn't have to deal with the pain that possibly lay ahead for Esther Meyers. Such a perfect couple as Esther and Charlie destroyed by greed as surely as *her* folks had been destroyed by cancer. There wasn't a lot of difference.

Oblivious to Sunny's uncommon distress, Dan bowed his head and asked a short blessing. "Heavenly Father, bless this food to our use and us to your service…"

The simple prayer hit Sunny with the force of a tidal wave. It was the same one her mother had taught her as a child. The depleting force of the memory took her by surprise. Through a glaze of emotion, Sunny watched her companion bite into his burger. She stuck her fork in her salad, as if to drive the darkness away.

No protein there, she thought in frustration, popping it into her mouth. It was tasteless. She chewed and blinked, but to her dismay, all that did was force tears to her cheeks.

"Hey, what's up?"

Great, now Dan *noticed*. Sunny grimaced and tapped her chest, like she was choking. She was actually. The salad would not go down her constricted throat.

His eyes widened. "Are you okay?"

She nodded fervently. The last thing she needed was the Heimlich maneuver. Daintily, she rid herself of the salad in her napkin. "Something didn't sit right," she explained, trying a drink of water.

This was ridiculous. After all she'd been through, a child's grace was her undoing? Try as she might, Sunny could think of nothing witty or funny to drive away the terrible anguish that knotted in her throat and chest.

"That...that grace. It was—" a sob distorted her words—"my mother's." She waved her hand in front of her face, but the memory held out with pit-bull stubbornness.

Dan got up and hailed Martin. "Box this up," he instructed the waiter, handing him a charge card. "And hurry."

People were staring. Sunny hadn't noticed anyone else in the courtyard until now. For the first time, she knew tragedy as one of those stricken—knew what it was to be self-conscious, yet unable to contain herself.

"I'm all right...really," she announced, as much for her sake as for Dan's.

But why now, Lord? Why with Dan?

Dan signed the receipt when Martin returned with the bill and boxes for their meal. Sunny concentrated on packing the food, hardly cognizant of what she did or why. She just wanted to get away from the curious onlookers and get a handle on this emotional onslaught.

"Ready?" Dan asked, slipping the credit card back into his wallet.

Sunny put the last of the boxes in a bag Martin provided and nodded. What was she going to say to Dan? How was she going to explain this when she didn't understand it herself? She followed Dan outside, where he hailed a cab.

A pale blue clone of the taxi that brought them to Marigot pulled up. The driver leaned down so that he could see them through the passenger's window. "Where to, folks?"

"Phillipsburg...the *Love Ahoy*," Dan told him, opening the back door for Sunny.

"You in a hurry?" the man asked over his shoulder.

"No!" Dan and Sunny answered simultaneously. They burst into laughter, and she felt her tension slip a notch as a grinning Dan climbed into the cab beside her.

The driver gave them a tolerant, crazy tourist grin. "You *sure* you're in no hurry?"

"Take your time, pardner. We have a good hour left to board and wouldn't mind a leisurely ride back at all."

Dan took the bag of food from the seat between them and put it on the floor by his feet. As the cab putted away from the curb, sounding like it took all its effort just to merge into the slower traffic of the Marigot street, he crooked his finger at Sunny.

"Come here, Nurse Elders. You need a consultation."

How a heart could leap in a sinking chest, Sunny had no idea. It wasn't in any of the textbooks she'd ever studied. But her weary, hurting heart was suddenly pitty-patting in time to the tap of the taxi's engine. She was having a heart attack. She was certain of it…just not the kind she'd been taught to handle.

All she knew was she needed a doctor's care—so long as the doctor wore jeans, boots, and Stetson big enough to shade the two of them.

Fourteen

*A*MAZING. WHO'D HAVE thought a broad shoulder was better than any thrombolytic medication Sunny had ever administered for coronary trauma? Or that a western, plaid shirt hardly showed the tears it soaked up, although the pearl-covered fasteners biting into her cheek would surely leave a curious mark. Not that she cared. Surely heaven wasn't this comfortable, she thought, listening to the beat of Dan's heart.

It was accelerated, like her own.

"I'm sorry, Dan. I really don't know what came over me. One minute I was salivating for food and the next—"

"Sunny, penning up emotion isn't much different from penning up a horse. Hold it too long and once that critter's out, it's uncontrollable."

Now that was one for the psychology books. Unorthodox but appropriate, given the source. She wanted to answer, but a trembling sigh was all this critter could manage just yet. She soon found even that was a mistake, for a sob was right on its heels.

Dan tightened his arms around her. "Mom tried holding back

after Dad died. It wasn't until after everything was over and done with that she finally broke down. Till then, she was too busy seeing that everything went smoothly for me and Gail."

He rested his chin atop her head. The fit was perfect.

"Anyhow, we packed all Dad's clothes up. Things got back to normal. Then it hit her."

Sunny wasn't Esther Meyers, but Dan's words worked like a balm on her shattered emotions. Who'd have thought *she'd* wind up being the one who needed comforting when they left the ship that afternoon?

"One day, out of the blue, I came in the house from feeding the stock and found her sobbing her heart out. She'd found one of Dad's socks tucked down in the recliner and went all to pieces." Dan stroked the length of Sunny's arm and closed his hand over hers. "Go figure. She'd packed up a whole wardrobe like a trouper and given it to the church, but a few months later one little ragged sock set her off. She cried more over that sock than I've seen her cry in a lifetime."

Lifting Sunny's chin, he leaned around and looked at her face. His mouth was poised for a smile, but clearly he was uncertain if it was premature. Sunny felt the corner of her own mouth tug a little of its own accord. Maybe it was God's signal that it was okay, not just to smile, but to cry, to give in to her grief.

"Yep, she finally gave it up," Dan said. "And it's high time you did the same."

The words struck Sunny like a thunderbolt. She'd praised God and focused on His mercy for her parents…but she hadn't taken it for herself. She hadn't given into her grief, and that was right. But she hadn't given it up, either.

"You're right—" She drew away from Dan, but not too far, in wonder—"this has been like the cancer that took Mom and Dad.

It's just lain dormant, ready to rear its ugly head and gnash me to bits when I least expected it."

"Or it's like the horse ready to kick up its heels," said the cowboy with a lopsided grin.

"Or like the horse," she agreed, melting inside.

Oh, Lord. I am SO over my head. I don't know whether I should thank You that there's only two more days left of the cruise or ask for an extension. It would be so easy to fall head over heels in love with Dan Jarrett. He was the kind of guy that a girl hoped for for a lifetime, never quite able to describe exactly what she wanted, but sure she'd know when she saw it.

She was yanked from the drift of her thoughts when the taxi driver turned abruptly off the paved road and onto a dirt one that led toward a ramshackle house.

"Hey, pardner, this isn't Phillipsburg," Dan exclaimed, clearly caught as unawares as Sunny.

She scooted over as Dan reached to unbutton his seatbelt.

The driver looked back at them through the mirror. "You said you are in no hurry, no?"

"No," Dan admitted, "but—"

"So I stop by my house." He pointed to the sky. "See, the clouds are thickening. My wife, she hangs the clothes out this morning over there."

Sunny exchanged a grim look with her companion. Neither of them had any idea where they were. For all she knew, this could be a robbery about to happen. To the driver's credit, though, there was a line full of clothes in the yard next to the dwelling.

"She works in Phillipsburg at a jewelry store, so I stop to take in the laundry, okay?"

Dan blew thoughtfully through his lips, apparently weighing the situation in his mind.

The yard was empty, save some chickens, a rusty tricycle, and a few scattered toys. On the clothesline were male and female garments, as well as those of children. It looked legitimate.

"Okay, but leave the car running," Dan said at last. Keeping his hand behind the driver's seat, he showed Sunny a small pocket-knife, as if to assure her that all was in control. A gash from that would hardly need stitches. Her nerves were so frayed, she almost laughed—but at that moment, the driver stopped the car in the yard.

"Fine," the driver agreed, putting it into park. "Now I go get the basket off the porch and take in the clothes."

He did as Dan asked and got out, leaving the engine running. They watched in disbelief as the driver took down the first garment, a pair of worn trousers, and neatly folded them before laying them meticulously in the basket.

"His wife's got him trained well," Dan observed dryly.

Sunny nodded in agreement. "We did insist we weren't in a hurry."

She looked over at her companion, only to find him looking back. As their eyes met, they burst into laughter.

"This could only happen to you," Dan accused good-naturedly. "I just happened to be along for the ride."

Sunny made a face at him as he glanced back to where the driver now labored to fold a dress just so.

"At the rate this guy is going, you might as well break out that food," Dan suggested as the man shook out the dress and started over.

"A picnic. What a novel idea." Sunny giggled, giving him a sly look. "You had this planned all along, didn't you?"

"Busted," he admitted facetiously. Then he sobered with second thought. "You're a good egg, Sunny. Maybe God did send you, because I certainly feel better knowing that at least someone doesn't think I'm a selfish jerk."

"I know, a little cracked, maybe, but a good egg." Oh yeah, being thought of as a good egg was every woman's dream. "Actually, I prefer the title of ER Angel." What she really wanted to say was that maybe God had sent them to each other. Oh well, a gal could dream, couldn't she?

Nearly two hours later, after what should have been a twenty-minute ride, the driver pulled up to the dock in front of the *Love Ahoy,* his basket of folded clothes on the front seat beside him. What could Sunny say? The people on the island evidently spoke *literal* English. If one said hurry, it was at breakneck speed, and if one said *no rush at all,* there was time for a picnic in the high country and laundry.

"Hi, Aunt Sunny!"

She turned from where Dan paid the driver to see Allison standing a few yards away, near an empty freight crate. A few off-duty members of the ship's crew clad in civvies lounged about in the shade provided by a large cargo bin. Sean was among them. He lifted his hand, brandishing a smile on his lips and in his eyes. Sunny couldn't help but recall the saying about when Irish eyes are smiling, they are up to something. Not that she had to think too hard to figure out just what.

Allison was as picture pretty as her mom and looked entirely too old for her age, even if she was wearing shorts and a cutoff tee. Maybe it was those mammoth sandals. Sunny watched the sixteen-year-old clomp across the paved dock as though she had a plank of wood attached to each foot.

Sunny held back an instinctive, "Does your mother know where you are?" She glanced over at the crew members. "What's up? I thought Sean worked all manner of hours during wake time."

"Oh, Aunt Sunny, it's the coolest thing. Something in the ship is broken, and we have to stay in port until the part comes. Like, there's no A/C or lights in some parts of the ship. The elevators are down—"

"And this happened when your aunt was not on the ship?" Dan exclaimed, catching up with them.

"Hey, *I'm* not the one who said I wasn't in a hurry or take all the time in the world, pardner," Sunny mimicked. This was one freak incident the cowpoke was not going to lay on her.

"Why, what happened to you guys?" Allison looked from one to the other of them.

"Sunny! Dan! Up here!" Sunny looked up to see Melinda waving from a balcony room on one of the upper decks.

Relieved that her niece wasn't hanging out with the crew of the ship unsupervised, Sunny waved back and tucked her tongue into her cheek at the sight of the binoculars around daddy Alan's neck.

"Come on up to our room when you've checked in," Melinda told them. "There's a glorious breeze and cool drinks. You can tell us all about your trip."

"You, too, Allison," Alan called down in a fatherly tone.

Allison pulled a face. "Do I have to?"

At her father's sharp thumb-jab toward the boat, she fell in ahead of Sunny and Dan, her disappointment lasting no more than the dozen or so clomps it took to get past the customs officials waiting at the gangway.

"So…what happened to you guys?" she repeated as Sunny picked up her purse from the scanner belt.

"Let's just say we saw more of St. Maarten than we ever thought we would." Sunny grinned over her shoulder at her companion.

"Yeah," Dan agreed. "In fast-forward *and* slow speed."

"We didn't know if we'd be mugged or what."

"I had everything under control," Dan reminded her.

Sunny laughed shortly. "Oh yeah. The little penknife. What were you going to do if it was a mugging? Catch the sun on the blade just right and blind him?"

Dan made a pained grimace.

"So what happened?" Allison exclaimed, curiosity brimming over.

"We'll tell you all about it later," Sunny promised. "Right now, I'm in desperate need of a quick pause to refresh at the cabin and then those cool drinks your mom promised."

There was no light in their inside cabin, save the one shining in from the door Allison held cracked open. Sunny dug through a bag of souvenir goodies and fished out a candle she'd bought for her bathroom at home, and soon there was light enough to move around without falling over each other or the souvenir packages.

Fortunately, the air-conditioning had been contained being shielded from the direct sun, so the temperature wasn't as insufferable as it must have been in Dan's window view room. When she had Allison offer him one of the other candles she'd purchased for a friend, he reminded her that he had a window.

"What I need though—" he called through the closed connecting door—"is a can opener to get it open."

"Try your penknife," Sunny called back. She grinned at his sarcastic, "Ha, ha."

Thankfully, the plumbing worked. Sunny was able to shower away a day's worth of tropical sweat and grime and pull on a fresh cotton capri set, while listening to repeated apologies and updates over the sound system on the technical snafu. Free refreshments and finger foods were being served in all the lounges and up on the open Lido deck to the sound of music for all tastes and ages. The ship's staff was going all out to make the best of an unfortunate situation.

Judging by the comments drifting in from the corridor outside their cabin, so were the passengers.

Jason made the mistake of checking in as she towel dried her hair to make his daily announcement of the main dining room menu: a choice of cold soups, cold salads, cold sandwiches, and desserts.

"Me, I just ate a hot dog and hamburger on the pool deck, just in case it's more of that funny looking stuff I don't recognize."

"You are *such* a pig." Allison curled her lip. "It wouldn't hurt you to try something new…or miss a meal, the way that gut is poking out."

"Better a cute little pig than a fat hog," Jason shot back, snorting for full effect.

"Well, piglet," Sunny teased, "you've still got time to get out of that rank T-shirt and grab a shower before the food's served."

She pictured her nephew waiting at the closed dining room doors for the staff to put out the newest menu at least twice a day. He had developed a reputation among the staff and passengers for not missing any meal served on the ship. And Sunny grinned at the sight of a little paunch that hadn't been there when they boarded.

"But the ship's broke down," he protested.

"Ah, the key word is *broken* down, not *going* down, in which case no one would have to smell you for long," Sunny reasoned. "But since civilization is destined to share the same air space with you, Jason, you're just going to have to get wet."

It was more than his sister could stand not to put in her smug two-cents worth. "And use soap."

After another sibling exchange of names, Jason grudgingly disappeared into the bath cube. He sounded like a miffed bull in a small trailer, bumping, thumping, and mumbling.

"Ah, brotherly love. It just echoes from the walls around us."

Sunny gave a wistful sigh as she bent over and picked up the offensive clothes her nephew tossed out. Wistfulness giving way to mischief, she looked at Allison.

"His pillowcase?" her niece suggested hopefully.

Sunny grinned. "His pillowcase."

"Man, I pity our room steward."

"Yeah, instead of cute little pup and bunny towel figures, he's going to start leaving gargoyles on Jason's bed."

Allison dissolved in giggles. "Oh, Aunt Sunny, you are so much fun. I hope you and Dan get married so I can visit the ranch and go riding and have a place to stay when Mom gets in one of her bad moods."

Sunny didn't know which of her niece's words rocked her more, the remark about marrying Dan or the reference to Melinda's mood swings. Definitely the first was more startling, but she addressed the latter. It was at least realistic.

"Hon, you know your mom has been sick, what with Grandma's and Grandpa's deaths."

"It didn't make *you* sick," Allison pointed out.

"Allison, we don't all grieve the same way." Sunny sat on the edge of the bed. "I deal with life and death every day. It's part of my job, so I've learned to hold back some of myself. It's like I care, but I can't care too much or I'd have nothing left to give anyone." Even as Sunny spoke, she knew her parents' deaths had left a terrible void in her, whether she'd kept emotional distance or not. "But your mom only knows one way to love, and that's with everything she has. So when our parents died, I think they took a bigger chunk of her with them than they took from me."

Allison waited expectantly as Sunny groped for words, not really understanding it all herself.

"And for what it's worth, I cried like a baby this afternoon. I've been postponing it." Sunny reached for a tissue and blew her nose. One would think she'd dried out by now.

"Aw, Aunt Sunny…" Her niece took a seat beside Sunny and draped an arm over her. "Did Dan hug you?"

Sunny's mushy gaze hardened. "You stinker." She gave Allison a playful push. "Are men *all* you think about?"

A metal-dashed grin spread on Allison's face. "Mostly. And clothes." She hesitated, caught in thought. "And Mom and Dad lately."

It was Sunny's turn to sympathize. "Honey, remember how I said that Grandma and Grandpa's loss took a chunk out of your mom? Well, she needs time to heal, to fill it up again so that she can go back to being all she was before. That's where *our* love comes in. We'll never replace Grandma and Grandpa, but we can fill your mom with our love and support, even when she loses her temper and comes unglued. We have to help her when we can until she gets her strength back, emotional and physical. When one goes, very often the other goes with it."

"She doesn't want me to do anything or go anywhere. Everything I do is wrong. She's been pretty nasty…even with Dad."

The catch in her niece's voice touched Sunny. She pulled Allison to her. "That's not your mom being nasty, it's all her hurt and pain striking out. Kind of like when you slam your finger in a drawer. The words that sometimes come out aren't always yours, because you hurt so much you can't speak. It's the pain that does the talking, especially when you've been drained or battered emotionally and spiritually like your mom has been. Does that make any sense?"

Allison nodded and pulled away. "I think so. Now I know why Dad has put up with some of the things she's said to him."

"Your dad is a special man."

"And Mom does seem better. I mean, I don't think she's gone off on anybody since we got aboard. The airport was a little freaky though."

Sunny chuckled. "An airport is always a little freaky, especially if you're as afraid of planes as Melinda."

Allison walked over to the closet and tugged out a pencil-thin shift. "I thought I'd wear this to dinner tonight. What do you think?"

"I think you shift gears faster than one of those fancy Italian sports cars."

"Huh?"

A sharp knock on the cabin door preempted Sunny's explanation.

Dan's voice came through the door. "You ladies ready?"

"Almost," Sunny told him. "Allison's decided to change again at the last minute. She's been that way since she stopped pulling off her diapers."

"Aunt Sunny!" Allison was clearly torn between mortification and laughter, but laughter won. "You go on ahead. I'll bring the pig along, if he hasn't drowned himself in the shower."

Sunny banged on the bathroom door. "Yo, Jason. Save some water for the rest of the passengers."

At her nephew's unintelligible acknowledgment, Sunny shook her head and walked to the door, doing her best to convince herself that the sudden jump of her pulse was because of the delicious food—*not* the man—waiting for her.

# Fifteen

*S*UNNY STEPPED OUT into the hall to find Dan looking freshly scrubbed and totally delicious in casual twills and an island print shirt splashed with palms, fruit, and flowers.

"Well, well, I see the island spirit has finally come upon you."

And it was as becoming as his basic plaid, she thought, as they started down the corridor. Despite the open doors and island breeze, the heat and humidity were starting to build. Behind them a door opened.

"Aunt Sunny," Allison called after them. "Mom just called and said to meet them up on the Lido deck. There's hot food up there. Me and Jason are going to eat in the dining room with the Stuarts."

"Thanks, Allison." Sunny gave Dan a hapless shrug. "Sisters. That okay with you?"

"Why not?" He pulled with equal frustration at the front of his shirt. "My sister bought this for me. I look like I had a head-on collision with Chiquita Banana—or the Fruit of the Loom gang."

But he wore it for Gail anyway, the sweet guy. Restraint prevailed over an uncommon sweep of warmth that urged Sunny to hug him, fruit, fronds, and all.

"Where are the kids?" Melinda asked as they located her and Alan amid the throng of passengers making the most of roughing it on the high seas. They were seated on lounge chairs on the Sun deck overlooking the Lido.

"They're eating supper with the Stuarts in the main dining room."

Clad in an equally loud island print, Alan rose to give Sunny a peck on the cheek and shake Dan's hand. "Hope you don't mind the change of plans. The breeze changed directions right after you all boarded, and it started getting a little stuffy, even with the balcony doors open. So we opted to join the rest of the stranded souls topside."

"The only places left to sit were up here," Melinda apologized. "Seems everyone is set on taking advantage of the free drinks."

"Are you kidding?" Sunny exclaimed, looking down at the Lido, packed with passengers and the island musicians. "It's gorgeous up here. And we can actually hear each other talk over the music."

"We're not keeping you from your family, are we, Dan?"

"Not at all, ma'am."

"Melinda. Call us Melinda and Alan. No need to make us feel older than we are."

Dan smiled. "Melinda, then. Anyway, I had a message from my sister that Mom and Charlie decided to do room service and call it an early night."

"They must have one of the rooms with air then," Alan put in.

"Only the best for Charlie." To his credit, Dan shifted to a brighter note. "Anyway, Gail and Mike are *drifting,* whatever that means."

"There's a lot of that going on, even if the ship is without some of its auxiliary power," her brother-in-law pointed out.

"Did you hear about the shipboard credit?" Melinda interrupted. "The captain is giving a $100 shipboard credit to each person who booked full passage."

Sunny laughed at her sister. "I can see the dollar signs flashing in your eyes as you speak."

"The way the kids have been running up the tab with those frozen drinks at five bucks a crack, we'll need every penny of it," Alan observed with a laconic twist of his mouth.

"We checked their tab on the television accounting menu and Alan nearly hit the ceiling, so he laid down a limit of no more than two of the fancy drinks a day. Kids!"

"Least you have two good kids," Dan said. "I get a kick out of them, but I've seen some I'd like to kick."

Sunny took one of the aforementioned frozen concoctions off the tray a waiter put in front of her. Dan special ordered the drinks without the rum du jour before they came upstairs. Until this trip, Sunny had no idea that rum came in so many flavors, but then she was hardly a connoisseur. She lifted her *Love Ahoy* glass in toast.

"Here's to hoping the wee ones don't take too much advantage of the freebies and stay up all night on a sugar high."

"Here's to hoping I don't stay awake all night on a sugar high," Dan kidded.

"I'd hate to think I brought those all natural juices for nothing," Sunny thought aloud.

Dan sniggered. "Oh yes, a cooler full as I recall."

Sunny gave him a warning glare and then preceded him out the door he held for her. "And the little stinkers have hardly touched them."

"Welcome to the world of parenting," her sister teased, "though we wouldn't trade it for the world, right, dear?"

Sunny was still picturing Alan's pained expression as she and Melinda made their way through the food line later at the outside grill and salad bar. The men were saving their places on the top deck since, with the main food deck already being packed to capacity, more and more of the passengers were headed for upper level. Given the circumstances of the breakdown and the lack of the formal meals that made cruise travel famous, good humor prevailed.

By the time she and her sister made it up the steps, Gail and Mike Madison had joined Dan and Alan. Sunny ate her dinner off the footrest of her lounge chair, with a full service of utensils wrapped in multicolored cloth napkins at her disposal. When Dan joined her, she'd finished, but scooted forward to give him room for his plate. Doubling up was the only way all six of them could sit together, and no one seemed to mind. Especially Sunny.

Tiki torches, electric for safety, provided just enough light to create an island ambiance. It looked like Polynesian night, Fourth-of-July picnic style. From their vantage point, they could view the audience participation games below, run by the cruise staff to provide entertainment during band breaks.

When Gail asked how the trip to the other side of the island was, Sunny took the floor before Dan had the chance. "Just let me tell you that when Dan-the-man tells a taxi driver he's in a hurry, no grass grows under the wheels."

Sympathy and incredulity echoed among their audience at the end of the account of the ride to Marigot, but Sunny checked it, holding up her hand. "It gets worse. We found another driver on the way back and told him we were in no hurry—"

"And wound up at some country road farmhouse waiting while he took in his laundry," Dan finished. "What a hoot."

"Well, I never!" Gail laughed. "You two sure have your share of adventures. First that horseback ride and now this."

"Sunny *always* has her share of adventure…plus someone else's," Melinda told her. "The stories I could tell."

"No, you can't." Sunny gave her sister a warning look.

Melinda wasn't the least bit intimidated, but before she could expose some of the secrets her children hadn't already shared about Sunny's misadventures, Melinda and Gail discovered they'd belonged to the same sorority and the conversation took a blessed turn in that direction. Behind her, Sunny heard Dan snort beneath his breath.

"Saved by the sisterhood." Whether he meant to or not, he brushed the bob of hair on the back of her neck.

Sunny caught her breath, feeling as if every strand jumped straight up at attention. Part of her wanted to rub away the spreading sensation of awareness with her hand. The rest of her clamored for more of the same. All she had to do was lean back against him, like Melinda did with Alan….

As if he'd read her mind, Dan invited her with a gentle pressure on her arm. His closeness made it impossible to concentrate on the conversation as it swung to tomorrow's plans, where a nature walk to the falls on Dominica was in store. Both families were booked for that particular tour, including the Meyers's and the man at her back.

"Why would I want to go traipsing up a mountain to see a waterfall when I have one in my own backyard?" Dan challenged his sister.

"There'll be all kinds of birds and wildlife we just don't see in Texas," Gail informed him. "There *is* life outside the ranch, dear brother."

"We'll have a good time," Sunny assured him over her shoulder in an effort to keep peace. "Where's your sense of adventure?"

"Scared out of me on that ride to Marigot." Seemingly resigned, he propped his head against the back of the chaise, hands folded behind his neck. "But if you're going, it just might be worth tagging along to see what will happen next."

The wink he gave her made Sunny's heart do a somersault. He wouldn't go with his family, but he'd go for her. Sure, it was because he never knew what to expect when she was around, because she was a good egg, but still…

"Then it's settled." Melinda eyed Dan and Sunny with a twinkling calculation. "It'll be fun. Just one, big, happy family."

"Here, here," Gail chimed in, lifting her empty glass of what had been a vegetable juice and lime twist.

Sunny didn't comment, nor did Dan, but their exchanged glances blended their thoughts as one. *Sisters!*

The evening passed pleasantly, despite the obvious romantic conspiracy hatching between Melinda and Gail. Of course, Esther and Charlie Meyers weren't present, which explained Dan's ease and, consequently, Sunny's. With his arms resting on either side of her on the lounge, she felt snug as the proverbial bug in the rug—safe in the knowledge that not only was she in his protection, but that, if necessary, he'd been willing to defend her with his courage and a poor excuse for a knife.

The protective nature he demonstrated for his family was reserved for her as well—at least for the duration of the cruise. She wouldn't dwell on the possibilities beyond that. If she didn't count chicks before they were hatched, then she wouldn't be disappointed. Her motto was clear: Give the eggs your best care, but not your heart, and let them go when you've done all you can.

For now, she was content to savor the dreamy combination of Caribbean, calypso, coconut, and cowboy.

Especially cowboy.

Sixteen

AT ELEVEN O'CLOCK, Sunny's and Dan's siblings and spouses made excuses to retire. The update on the auxiliary generator failure promised that all was well and that power was being restored to the ship section by section to avoid an overload. Actual departure would be at midnight. The lost time would be made up at sea so that shore tours at Dominica the following day would proceed as scheduled. The captain made the last announcement himself, again extending apologies and offering the shipboard credit as a token of staff appreciation for the inconvenience endured with such grace by the passengers.

"So how're you going to spend your extra money?" Sunny asked, yawning in spite of herself after another day in paradise.

When the others left, Dan had made no effort to take another seat—and neither had she. She was so comfortable it honestly hadn't occurred to her. It was probably the same with Dan—good old Sunny, comfortable as an old shoe...

"I think I'll just stock up on all that duty-free gold and perfume."

She snorted in amusement. *Oh, that was real ladylike.* "Perfume, eh?"

"Sure. So what if I won't get much use out of it. The price is right."

"Well, mine should just about cover the shipboard souvenirs I've bought."

Somewhere beyond them, they heard the approach of someone running at a gallop as opposed to the usual jog reserved for the sports deck.

"Wonder who that is," Sunny said with a wry grin.

"King Kong in combat boots."

Dan chuckled, and she shook with him. Same sense of humor—that could be scary if it weren't so much fun.

"Hey!" It was Jason. He slowed to a trot before nearly knocking one of the unoccupied deck chairs over. "It's eleven o'clock!" He checked his watch, just to be certain he'd not missed the adjusted curfew set by his parents earlier. Cheeks flushed, T-shirt damp, and blond curls disheveled, he was all boy.

"Where's Allison?"

Jason shrugged. "Back at the cabin, I guess. She left us after the Stuarts put the little girls to bed. Said she was too old for video games." His expression told exactly how absurd a notion that was.

Sunny slid forward and rose to her feet reluctantly. "Well, I guess I'd better go check on my charges."

"Mom said we could go to the midnight buffet since we didn't get much for supper," Jason informed her, plopping down on the edge of the lounge she'd just abandoned. "It's just a half hour or so."

She thought better of strangling him for not speaking sooner—and for usurping her seat. "In that case, let's go tell Alli before she gets ready for bed."

"I think I'll stay up here with the men and watch them set up.

It's gonna be down there tonight." Jason looked at Dan for approval.

Sunny hadn't even noticed the staff clearing everything away earlier. Their impromptu six-some had been involved in their own party and discussions and the wait staff made certain they weren't lacking for anything.

"Actually, I couldn't eat another bite, pardner. I think I'm going to turn in."

Dan stood up and stretched. The breeze molded the soft rayon of his shirt to his chest from his wide shoulders to his narrow waist. It was a sight that made a woman want to slap herself to stay grounded.

Reaching under his chair, he retrieved his hat and pulled it on. "Nice evening, all considered."

Sunny nodded, slipping her arm into the crook of the one he offered her. "One of the best," she agreed, willing her feet to confine their spontaneous little dance to less conspicuous toes only.

"The pizzeria isn't open yet, though," Jason said, wedging between them as if he belonged. "I'd rather have pizza than all that fancy stuff, wouldn't you, Dan?"

"The pizza is good, I have to admit."

The smile he gave her over Jason's head curled her toes tight enough to squeeze the fancy out of them.

Personally, she was ready to suggest they toss their clueless intruder over the side. Instead, she steered him around the chaises of those passengers who'd decided, since their rooms were evidently among the last to receive power, to sleep pajama-party style under the stars. Little groups of four to eight were camped out with pillows and blankets from their cabins, their makeshift beds cushioned with pads the deck staff put out earlier in the evening in anticipation of the worst.

As Sunny and her companions coasted down the steps to their

cabin, a message came over the speaker system: All the elevators were in working order now, in lieu of the two they maintained in operation for handicapped use during the power failure. Air-conditioning would continue to be turned on in relays. The announcement ended with more apologies, thanks, and a reminder of the shipboard credit, which could be paid out to individuals via a check to those who did not spend the entire amount aboard before the end of the cruise.

"Guess that saves me carrying home a boatload of stuff I won't use." Dan grinned at her as they reached their respective cabin doors. The air-conditioning had returned to their rooms. It was obvious at a glance, however, that Allison had not.

A note was left for Sunny on the makeup- and hair accessory-covered vanity, written with a funky purple glitter eyeliner pencil.

Dear Aunt Sunny… She didn't like the way it started. Formality was not typical Allison—unless, of course, her niece was up to something. *I'm meeting Sean on the sports deck for a little while. He doesn't work until later because of the power mess or something. I promise to be back before twelve-thirty. Love, Allison.*

Sunny glanced at Jason, who'd read the letter over her shoulder. "Does your mom know about this?"

"I dunno. I didn't even know about it. Mom just said we could stay up for the buffet."

"Everything okay?" Dan asked from the door Jason left open behind them.

Sunny handed him the note. "Probably, but I'm not sure."

This chaperone bit was getting a bit worrisome now that Allison was older. When Sunny had seen her niece on the pier with Sean and his companions, some inherent instinct had bristled, but she'd ignored it. Now she realized it probably wasn't the eldest Stuart boy Allison had worn that dress for at supper, the little braces-toothed vixen. *Give me back the Barbie days, Lord,* Sunny prayed, trying to ignore all the frightening stories she'd heard about young women getting into trouble while traveling alone.

"I don't think Alan would like this," Sunny admitted, guilt setting in.

"Neither do I. That boy's a good five years older than she is." Dan firmly set his hat on his head and adjusted the brim in a let's-saddle-up-boys attitude.

"I'm sure he's a nice boy," Sunny said as he herded her out into the corridor.

"He's over twenty and male. I wouldn't want my sixteen-year-old daughter alone with him, no matter *how* polite he is."

Jason skipped after them, bringing up the rear of the self-appointed posse. "Man, is she in trouble now."

"Allison is *not* in trouble. We're just going to look and see if she's okay. And she's not totally naive, Dan," she added, as much for herself as for her ruffled companion. *Boy, when he takes someone under his wing, he means it.*

"She's never been twenty and male, and neither have you." His lips thinned. "'Nuff said."

Dan punched the elevator button in the lobby as if it were Sean's eye. A mingle of alarm and admiration stirred in Sunny as they entered and started the ride up to the top deck of the ship. There wasn't a lot up there apart from the gymnasium, beauty salon, and spa. Outside there was room to jog around the deck's perimeter, as well as space for shuffleboard and Ping-Pong, where the deck widened to overlook the sun and pool levels below.

"We'll just walk around the deck like we're on a moonlight stroll…" Sunny began.

"With *him?*" Dan pointed to her nephew.

Sunny stopped so suddenly, Jason bumped into them.

"Jason, wait by the elevator," she ordered.

Her nephew screwed his face up. "Man!"

"We'll just be a few minutes," Sunny assured him. "If we see Allison is okay, like with a group of boys *and* girls, then we'll wait nearby for her."

"You guys get all the fun."

Dan pointed an authoritative finger at him. "Stay."

"Want me to roll over and play dead too?" Grinning, Jason lifted his paws and slid down the wall. "Arf, arf!"

"Wiseacre!"

"Smart alec!" Sunny chimed in at the same time as her companion.

Flattening his hand at Sunny's back, Dan guided her through the foyer leading to various fitness and beauty enterprises. The doors to all of them, the gymnasium included, were closed and locked. That could only mean Allison was out on the open deck. A revolving glass door separated that from the interior of the ship.

As Sunny stepped inside the door and started to push, she saw a group of young people, both boys and girls, playing Ping-Pong. It only took a second to spot Allison. She sat, as demurely as her sixteen years would allow, watching Sean and another of the waiters from the dining room in a fierce competition.

Sunny froze. One more quarter of a turn and Alli would see them spying on her.

"There she is. Hurry, she'll see us."

Before Dan could question or react, Sunny shifted into high gear, pushing the revolving door for all she was worth to keep from being caught. With a soft *whoosh*, it returned full circle and spit her out into the lobby. She stumbled to a halt and turned, colliding head-on with Dan as he, too, shot out of the whirling carousel of glass.

Who caught whom was hard to say. Suddenly they were together, tangled in each other's arms, face to face, then lips to lips. Her pulse, which had already been racing at double-speed, kicked into triple-time.

Dan was kissing her! Her reeling senses laughed hysterically at her brain's slothlike registration of a contact that was everything she'd thought it would be. And then some.

Thoughts assaulted her mind, seeming to lift her like whirling helicopter blades into a weightless ecstasy, where toes were too flustered even to curl. Good night, she didn't even know if she still *had* toes.

Dan's hands spread, warm and strong, against her back, as if it was their sole duty to preserve this one moment in time. The vital warmth of him enveloped her…and then, like fireworks that explode and blossom in a full array of colors and light, the afterglow flickered, fading and cooling until they both held their breath, wondering, waiting, not wanting it to end.

Dan was the first to catch his breath, and with it, some semblance of reason apparently followed. He backed away, leaving Sunny grateful for the glass-block wall at her back. Her knees weren't trustworthy enough to hold her without help from somewhere. She watched him lick his lips, as though to confirm what had just happened…as though he was no more convinced of it than she.

But it *had* happened. Breath-robbing, sense-rattling happened.

"I guess I forgot I was male and over twenty, too."

The low, husky comment—and the sheepish, almost boyish look that peered out from under his thick to-die-for lashes—nearly knocked the wall from behind Sunny. But Dan held her hands, drawing her away from the support. "Just tell me one thing, Sunny Elders," he whispered as he pressed his forehead to hers.

At least *he* had a voice. Sunny could barely squeak some semblance of a question in response.

"What in the devil did you see on the other side of that door?"

Seventeen

HE WHITE TOUR bus jostled through the sun-faded streets of Roseau, capital of Dominica, the following day, carrying thirty-some passengers toward the Emerald Pool. Seated next to Allison, who was keeping a low profile after her adventure without her family's permission, Sunny listened to the guide, Alfonse, tell the history of the island and point out the various points of interest along the way.

Unlike many of the predominantly Afro-Dominican guides who'd waited outside the buses while the tourists debarked, Alfonse was a direct descendent of the Caribs, complete with coppery skin, Asian features, and shoulder-length straight hair that was as black and shiny as Chinese lacquer. He wore it gathered at his neck with leather and beads. His parents, he told them, lived on the island reservation for the last of the pure-blooded Carib Indians. Clad in capri-length cotton pants of the same natural texture and color as his loose shirt, he lent a primitive promise to the pristine rainforest adventure lying ahead. The bus stopped, immediately surrounded by islanders hawking wares from handmade soaps to

Dominican coins glued on a used plastic phone card. In the duration of a stoplight cycle, Jason handed over three dollars of his allowance for the coins on a card, while Allison purchased two soaps, one for her and one for Sunny.

"Here, Aunt Sunny. It's not much, but I hope it makes up for the worry I caused you," the young girl said, handing over the fragrant bar packaged in plastic wrap.

"Where's mine?" Dan asked from the seat ahead of them.

"Sorry, but I didn't think you'd want to smell like us women." Allison jumped up, planted a hasty kiss on his cheek, and sat back down, her own color rivaling some of the tropical flowers growing along the way.

"I appreciate your not telling Mom and Dad," she said in a voice that was meant for their immediate circle only, certainly not the early-bird members of the family clustered together near the front of the bus. "I really didn't think it was a big deal, since everyone's always saying there's safety in numbers."

"Yeah, well, that's all that saved your hide," Sunny told her. "Dan and I thought you were meeting Sean alone and that made us feel uneasy, not that we didn't trust you—"

"We just didn't trust Sean," Dan finished in a and-that's-that! voice.

Allison slumped against the bus seat, all protest deflated.

A body would have thought Dan was the outraged father. The role was endearing—almost as endearing as his kiss. No, the kiss was something else again. It was downright soul-consuming. Sunny grew even warmer than the humid, ninetyish air blowing in through the open windows. She hadn't known she had such response in her as she'd given to Dan last night. Where on earth had it come from? Flushed, she glanced at a small shelf cut into the side of the volcanic rise that the road now climbed, a fertile grove of coconut and banana trees, splashed with tropical colors and rich red soil. *Lord, he's found a me even I didn't know existed…and I don't think I've ever been so frightened.*

She wasn't certain of what. She only knew that the feelings Dan had stirred in her were so wonderful they alarmed her. *If something seems too good to be true, it usually is.* Sunny could hear her father say those words clearly. Dan was addictive, and she couldn't allow herself to indulge in such a temptation—not when he'd be back at the ranch in a few days, and she'd be in triage, too busy assessing others' traumas to be plagued with her own. It just wouldn't do.

He seemed to sense her uneasiness and backslid from Romeo to pardner. Granted, it was in a shy, embarrassed manner, as if the kiss had taken him by surprise too. Then this morning he acted as if it had never happened. She'd been relegated back to good egg status.

The moment the bus rolled to a stop in a stony sand parking lot lined with rented cars, motorbikes, and other tour buses, the breeze disappeared. The morning sun beat down on a small open market of tables with more soap, coins, and island wares. Ladies and a few tagalong husbands checked out the goods. As they finally embarked on the climb up through the dense rainforest, the group packed a few more bags than they started out with. Sunny was no exception; she wore the lovely handiwork of a beaded cross she'd purchased at one of the stalls.

"This is beautiful, just beautiful." Esther Meyers exclaimed from the rear of the family assembly as the guide paused at one of the terraced landings to point out some of the wildlife and a little waterfall. "It smells like God's own private garden. And look at the heliconia. Charlie, get a picture of that."

Sunny glanced back to see Esther pointing to one of the sun-flamed flowering plants that grew amid gently arching stems everywhere along the way. Dan's mom posed by the plant.

"For heaven's sake, Esther, we have a hundred pictures of flowers at home."

The atypical bite in Charlie Meyers's voice startled his new bride. Sunny saw Dan practically bristle nearby.

"Toss me your camera, Charlie," Sunny offered, in an attempt to head off a confrontation. "I'll get a picture of you two with the flower."

Esther pulled Charlie over by the tropical blossom and leaned her head on the shoulder of her less-than-enthused mate. Sunny took the picture and handed the camera back down the line of family.

Sunny had noticed that her own Prince Charming regressed to frog that morning after something about the shipboard credit came up in the general conversation. Charlie remarked that the windfall gave him a few more dollars to while away in afternoon bingo. Since then, a little thundercloud hovered in Dan's once blue-sky humor, ready to strike. While Sunny understood it to some degree now, she still felt he had too little proof to justify his impertinence.

Thankfully, Alfonse unwittingly distracted them. The guide pointed to a flat rock by a running rivulet of clear water. "See the bullfrog over there? We call it *crapaud*. He is almost twice as large as the North American one, weighing about two pounds when mature. But when it's fried, we call it *mountain chicken*. I recommend that you try some for lunch after the tour."

"Ewww," Allison and Jason said, agreeing for the first time that day.

"But it tastes like chicken," the guide teased the youngsters.

"Yeah, that's what they all say," Jason shot back, with all the authority of his nine years.

Alfonse laughed, pointing to the boy. "And *that* is the reason our restaurants do not show patrons the creature before it has been cooked."

After a few minutes more of picture taking, they resumed the steep climb. Sunny was glad for the sneakers she'd worn as opposed to the sandals some of the hikers opted for anyway in spite of the advice in the brochure.

She was also ready for the stops they made along the way, reminding her that she really needed to get back to the exercise regimen she'd had before her parents became so ill.

"You be glad there is no rain today." Alfonse looked as unaffected by the hike as the wildlife flitting from tree to tree above them or skittering over the moss-covered rocks along their feet. "Or the trail is very slippery for climbing."

Sunny was grateful, and the nurse in her kept a trained eye on a number of senior citizens in the group. They'd lingered toward the back of the line so as not to hold up the younger, more athletic tourists. Some huffed and puffed with the exertion but remained in good spirits, clinging all the while to the rail lining the path. Full of youthful vigor, Allison and Jason, as well as a few other children in their age range, had moved all the way to the front, preceding the guide.

"If they could can and sell that energy, neither one would have to work a day the rest of their lives," Dan commented to their parents. He'd placed as great a distance between his own family as he could.

Alan laughed. "Tell us about it. We stay in good shape just keeping up with them."

It was true. Unlike Sunny, her sister and brother-in-law had hardly worked up a sweat. In their khakis, backpacks, and heavy-duty climbing shoes, they looked like cover models for a hiking magazine. With her swimsuit under a pair of cutoff jeans and an oversized T-shirt, not even the forest-cooled air breathing down the trail could offset the effects of the climb for Sunny.

At the base of the falls was a mineral pool, according to previous visitors Esther and Charlie, which was guaranteed to refresh and restore body and spirit. Water spilled from a crevice in the rock cliff overhead into a forest glade literally lined with cascading lianas and ferns. It was greener than green, Sunny thought, as she took in the silver pool where the water was dammed temporarily by rocks before it spilled down to the next little pool. Eventually the brook made its way to the Belle Fille River on the windward slope of the island.

"Look up through the trees," Alfonse told them as the older members of the group caught up at the falls. "Today, you get to see our liquid sunshine." He pointed to fine mist hovering in the air, backlit by the sun. "Too bright for rain, too wet for sun, eh?"

"No wonder I feel like I've been walking through a sauna." Sunny grinned at her sister, who immediately captured the phenomenon of the mist on video.

Cameras rolled, clicked, and flashed all around, while some of the guests stripped down to swimsuits to test the invigorating waters. Carefully stepping down into the pool so as not to slip on the moss-skimmed rocks, Sunny followed Allison and Jason, while Melinda taped it all on video.

"C'mon, Mom," Jason hollered up to her. "Don't be a sissy. The water's warm."

"Not in this lifetime." Melinda's response reflected the very words that ran through Sunny's mind. Leave it to Melinda to spend a fortune on a swimsuit that would never see water—but she always looked good in their home movies sitting on a pool deck or a beach. Sunny always looked like a drowned rat.

Sunny put one foot in the water and shouted at Jason. "Liar, liar, pants on fire." She shuddered. "It's freezing."

Dan stepped down to join her on the same flat rock. "Tenderfoot."

She moved as close to the edge as room would allow, welcoming the close warmth of his presence—until she felt the pressure of his hands at her back. "What are you doing?"

"Just moving things along."

Reacting instinctively to his unsolicited help, Sunny curled into a fetal ball just before she hit the water. The moment her feet touched bottom, she bolted straight up through the icy water to the surface.

"Nice guy," she shouted sarcastically, pushing hair out of eyes bulging with shock.

Dan sprang up beside her, grinning like a donkey chewing brambles.

"C'mon, gotta keep moving." He slipped an arm around her and pulled her toward the spot where the water splashed down from above.

"I know," she gasped, still breathless from the change in body temperature. "Those c-cursed k-kinks."

The longest minute in her life—adjusting to the cold—started the shortest half hour of the same as the playful side of Dan emerged. Sunny had seen him frolic in the pool with the kids, but this time she was part of the fun. She gave as good as she got in the water fight, and when Dan tugged each of the kids across the deeper well in the pond to where the waterfall hammered the otherwise smooth surface, Sunny waited her turn.

"Feels like a heavy-duty nature massage." She blinked furiously, trying to clear her eyes in the downpour to see Dan's face, even though she was in his arms. He was as warm as the water was cold, a refuge she could get used to if she wasn't careful.

"Adam and Eve's shower," he concurred, his voice closer than she'd realized. His lips were not far behind, finding hers as he drew her into the full force—and cover—of the falls. Or was it that Dan stepped farther in and her hands, snaking around his back and up the ridges of his shoulders, simply carried her along for the ride?

Her senses were assailed by his warm kiss and the icy pounding water, and her mind reeled with one giddy thought: She was going to drown in paradise...

And, frankly, she didn't care.

"I've wanted to do that all morning."

The words, although shouted above the roar of the water, stroked her ear like a whisper of yearning, shattering all semblance of reason. As Dan moved back into view, leaving paradise behind, Sunny floated speechless, her arms still around him and his around her.

A whistle split the air, evaporating the primal remnant of the lovespell.

"Time to get out," Alfonse announced from his lifeguard perch above the water.

Jason protested the entire climb back up the rocks to the terrace of the hiking trail, goaded by his sister the entire way. Getting out was far more treacherous than going in, but Sunny followed her niece and nephew, herded like a mindless steer by the swimsuited cowboy who'd made her that way. She slipped once, banging her knee, but she hardly felt it—not with Dan's supporting hands on her waist. For all she knew, she'd just drifted up the steep incline like the last puff of smoke sparked by Dan's fervent affection. Not even a brisk toweling could eliminate her light-headed aftereffect.

The trip down was much quicker and easier on all, especially when one's heart was on the wing, rather than the hoof.

"I'd like to show you the little falls north of our ranch," Dan told her. "Not that you'll see all this tropical stuff, but it's just as pretty in its own way. I've spent many a quiet hour up there."

If she'd been a dog, her ears would have stood straight up and her tail would be thumping as wildly as her pulse.

"You mean later, like…I mean, after the cruise?"

Thankfully, he managed not to smile at her babbling. "Well, I don't think Hopper Falls is on the ship's itinerary, do you?"

"I know that. I just meant…well, you know."

Oh, brother! Time to put her chin on the ground and cover her head with her paws.

Dan grinned then and ruffled her hair, as if he'd spied the pup in her. "Yes, after the cruise—"

A startled shriek from behind them cut him off abruptly. "Charlie!"

Sunny turned in time to see Charlie Meyers crumple to the ground, despite Esther's effort to hold him. His weight nearly took the older woman down with him. Sunny jumped into action, pushing her way through the line of gapers between them before she reached his side.

"What happened?" She felt his forehead. It was dry. Blood had fled his face beneath his tan, taking with it his characteristic healthy glow.

"He said he felt like he was going to be sick and then he just collapsed."

Dan pulled his distraught mother to her feet. "Come on, Mom, give Sunny some room to work. She's a nurse."

"Could be the heat," Sunny suggested. "Someone open up his shirt."

She seized Charlie's wrist, unerringly finding his pulse, and counted its staccato beat while watching the second hand of her watch. She didn't have to wait long to know it was faster than it should be. His forehead was clammy.

Mike Madison knelt down to help, tearing open Charlie's floral shirt so fast that one of the buttons flew off and pinged against the rocky wall beside them.

Heat stroke would explain Charlie's irritability earlier as well…
"Probably the heat," she told Alfonse, when the guide backtracked
through the gathering to see what the problem was. "Go ahead and
call for emergency assistance."

"What can we do?" Dan asked in what she hoped was concern.
It was hard to tell.

"Get some towels and soak them in that cold spring water.
We'll wrap him in them. Then get him down to the parking lot as
soon as possible."

"Oh, my heavens," Esther wailed helplessly. Her daughter took
over comforting her, while Dan and a man Sunny didn't recognize
took the innumerable amount of towels produced by the concerned onlookers and climbed under the rail down the slippery
rock surface to the stream a few feet below.

The mother in Esther prevailed as she watched the men.
"Gracious, son, be careful."

Not even the seriousness of the situation could extinguish the
sibling mischief in Gail Madison. "Dan was born part monkey,
Mom. Don't worry."

Esther almost smiled as she turned from Dan back to her husband.

"He's coming to!" she exclaimed, upon seeing Charlie move his
head on the backpack someone had provided for a pillow.

"I have a bath-sized towel in my knapsack," Sunny told
Melinda. "Get it. We can use it for a stretcher. Esther, do you know
what medications Charlie is on?"

Esther dug in her purse and produced two small prescription
bottles as Charlie rallied.

"Hey, guy," Sunny said cheerily. "You've just scared the wits out
of us."

Charlie glanced around. "Wh…what happened?" He started to
get up, but Sunny held him back.

"Whoa, there. Just relax a few minutes."

"Charlie Meyers, what am I going to *do* with you?" Esther bent over him and kissed him on the forehead.

"I don't reckon I'd best say in front of all these folks."

Sunny grinned. His humor was returning—that was a good sign. "Do you have any heart problems, Charlie?" A glance at the prescription bottles Esther showed her told her he did, but it was best to hear it from the horse's mouth.

"It's not my heart. It's this blamed cold I woke up with this morning and the humidity. Don't know how these folks breathe down here."

"They're used to it, dear," his wife reminded him.

She took an embroidered handkerchief out of her purse and as she mopped her husband's brow, Sunny caught a whiff of spearmint. It took her back to Sundays in church when her own mother dabbed at her little girl's runny nose with one like it. The fabric had absorbed the scent of the spearmint gum always present in her mom's purse.

Dan and the other man returned with four dripping towels. "You still need these?"

Sunny nodded. "Charlie, if it's just the heat, this will help us get you stabilized." She took a wet towel and made a compress, placing it on his chest. His pulse was erratic and his color wasn't good. "Your meds suggest a heart condition. Do you have any history of heart problems?"

The man nodded. "I had a heart episode a few years ago. It's why I retired. I loved the car business, matching people up with the right car…" He shook his head slightly, as though clearing it. "Haven't had any trouble since."

"You never told me that," Esther exclaimed. "I thought these were just blood pressure pills."

"You haven't been married long enough to know everything about him, Mom."

Sunny groaned at Dan's cryptic reminder. Talk about a pit bull in a Stetson.

"Didn't see any need in worrying you, Essie." Charlie sat up, brushing Sunny's resistance aside. "And I'm fine now. Honest." He glanced around. "I've held these good folks up long enough."

Sunny and Mike helped the man up, and it was clear he was still a bit wobbly on his feet.

"Why don't you let the men carry you down in a towel sling?"

"I think that'd be a fine idea, dear," Esther agreed.

"Now Esther, you know I'm always this knock-kneed when I first get up. Stop your frettin'."

"At least hang this towel around your neck." Sunny draped another of the damp, cool towels over his shoulders, not nearly as certain as Charlie that he was over his spell. Heat stroke was nothing to take lightly, especially if the patient also had a heart condition.

But he proved himself right and walked the remaining way down the hiking trail to the parking lot just as an emergency medical vehicle screeched to a halt, scattering dirt.

"Aw, now you've done it," he accused Sunny. "I wish you hadn't sent for doctors."

"She did what she thought was best," Dan piped up in her defense. "And she's a nurse, so I'd take her word over yours any day."

"At least let them check you out," Sunny cajoled, wincing inwardly at Dan's offensive tone. "It'd make us all feel better."

The tour bus left on schedule, carrying the other passengers back to the ship, after Alfonse arranged for a private cab to take the family back or to the hospital, depending on the outcome of

Charlie's checkup. Grumbling all the time, the patient submitted to Esther's and Sunny's insistence that they were not going anywhere until he'd had a few on-the-spot tests.

Dan waited a short distance away, watching the scene with a skepticism Sunny wanted to smack off his face. He was so intent on proving Charlie a fraud that he'd lost his common sense of decency.

The medics reported an irregularity in Charlie's heartbeat, but he insisted it was nothing new. "Had it since I was in knee britches."

"Maybe—" Esther started.

"I feel great," Charlie overruled her. "And I want to get back to the ship before it sails. Now let's get goin'," he said after signing papers relieving the medical personnel of responsibility.

Fifteen minutes later, they were in a minibus taxi headed back to the *Love Ahoy*. As soon as they arrived at the ship, the ship's doctor checked his vitals once more. Sunny gave them her cabin number and insisted that, if she wasn't there, they have her paged if they needed her. Then Esther spirited Charlie off to their cabin to rest for the remainder of the day.

"Well, I'm glad that's over," Dan said as he walked with her toward their respective cabins.

"Yeah, you were all heart."

He gave her a hard stare. "What's *that* supposed to mean?"

"It means, Daniel Jarrett, that your stepfather, the man your mother *loves* whether *you* approve or not, could have been seriously ill back there—and you showed as much compassion as that crapaud."

"Cra—*what?*"

"A frog, Dan," Sunny told him heatedly as she slipped her key card into the lock of her cabin door. Her head ached, and she couldn't make the contraption work. "A *bull*frog," she reiterated, jamming the card in again. "I'm going to shower and take a nap. See you later."

Dan caught the door before she could open it enough to get inside. "You know why."

"A man is innocent until proven guilty, at least in the part of Texas I'm from. You've got Charlie Meyers sentenced and practically hanged, Mr. Almighty-Judge-and-Jury."

"Well, if we're going to call names, Nurse Fix-It-All, take a good look at yourself. Instead of trying to fix my problems, why don't you concentrate on your own?"

A shower of ice water couldn't have shocked Sunny any more than the cold comment. "Wh…what do you mean by that? I give *everyone* I meet the benefit of doubt that they are good people. The Bible says to do that."

"And Scripture also says take the plank out of your own eye before you go accusing others of their flaws."

He was clearly groping for some way to divert attention from himself, and she wouldn't let him. "One should be suspicious of a suspicious nature. And just what do you mean *plank* in my eye?"

"I mean you are so busy trying to fix others that you don't look at what needs fixing in you."

Sunny felt anything but sunny now. She folded her arms across her chest in head-nurse fashion. "Oh, so now you're judging me too…and don't lay that running from grief accusation on me."

"You're a coward, Sunny." Dan's clipped words fell on her ears like a gavel on the judge's bench. "You've been running from your grief over your parents. You just keep shoving it aside and ignoring it by staying busy, by spreading artificial sunshine and poking your nose into other people's business."

How could he say such a thing? It felt as if he'd plunged a blade of betrayal straight into her heart. "I'm butting my nose in your business *because* I am grieving the loss of my parents."

He jabbed his fingers through his hair and looked at the ceiling before continuing. "You're saying that you miss your parents, so you think everyone should cherish theirs? Well, some parents may not be worth cherishing."

"What about honor thy mother and father?" She stood her full height as she ground out her charge, but inside she bled from his accusation—all the more because it was true, at least part of it. She had been running, just like he said, but he'd helped her see the error of her ways. Just like she'd tried to help him see his problems more clearly. The last thing she intended was poking her nose into someone's business.

"I did and I do. But that man is *not* my father and—"

"You've been around cows too long, Dan." She could bear no more. "You're bullheaded and you know *nothing* about people. Now step aside, because I won't hear another word of this."

He was half again her size and could easily have stopped her, but apparently the gentleman in him prevailed. At least in his actions. "That's *fine,* because I've said all I intend to say." With that, he stepped back, jaw clenched, and allowed her to open the door.

Once inside, Sunny leaned against the door, surveying the room her niece and nephew had abandoned. Their purchases were scattered on the bed and damp swimsuits were draped over the open bathroom door, but she hardly noticed.

So this was how Cinderella felt at midnight. The ball was over, and all she wanted to do was kick an ungrateful frog instead of kiss the prince.

Eighteen

DAN SCOWLED AT the closed cabin door for a moment before retreating to his cabin. Sunny Elders saw the world as just a little too sunny sometimes. It was a jungle where predators didn't have to walk on four legs to be dangerous. She was like his mother, too trusting, too open and willing to share her love of life with others. Sure, God protected people, but not from sheer stupidity. Scripture said to love one another, but Dan believed there was a limit to that love. When you moved beyond that limit, you provided the means for another's continuing folly, be it the lure of drugs, gambling, or some other destructive pursuit. Considering Sunny's line of work, she ought to know that.

He snatched off his clothing and headed for the shower. That woman was carrying this angel of mercy stuff too far. More like angel of blindness. It wasn't like God or some little angelic figure was perched on her shoulder, telling her specifically what to do or not to do, for cryin' out loud.

He turned the water on with a jerk. That woman was going to drive him nuts. He felt like a compass too close to the North Pole when he stood close to her, so charged that common sense went haywire. Maybe they were in or close to that Bermuda Triangle—not that he believed in the woo-woo stories about it. Its phenomenon was scientific, Dan was certain, unlike what he felt around the lady he could hear on the other side of the wall, singing about being a roaring woman.

Well, no matter how much she bragged that she could be bent but not broken, she was flighty as a kitten and just as maddening.

Dan stepped under the water and worked shampoo into his hair, as though to wash away his frustration. Even when he stepped out of the shower, squeaky clean all over, Sunny continued to plague his thoughts. Why did he even care, he thought, toweling hard enough to remove body hair. She was a walking accident waiting to happen. She was a klutz…although it was in an endearing sort of way. Kind of like a kitten.

Endearing. The word echoed again in his thoughts. He closed his eyes. It was true. Who could resist wanting to tease or protect Sunny…or love her?

His eyes shot open. *Love* her? He didn't believe in love at first sight, remember? True, they'd seen each other for five days running, but even that was too fast for him. Sunny was just so different, he was more likely intrigued by her—by that reckless and crazy approach to life that ruled one minute, and her no-nonsense, head-nurse side the next.

Images from the waterfall danced in his mind. She'd had people hopping, orchestrating his stepfather's care like a conductor with a wand. No one questioned her; her tone of voice wouldn't allow it. They just followed her orders, including him, to help the man lying unconscious on the ground.

He frowned at that. How *dare* she imply that he didn't care that a man had passed out? Even if Charlie turned out to be number one on the most wanted criminal list, Dan would have helped him out. But he wouldn't hand over trust—much less his heart and wallet to the man—like his mom had done.

The last thing Dan felt like doing was taking a nap as he put on fresh jeans and shirt. He was too worked up. Even if it cost an arm and a leg, he was going to call the investigative firm from the ship. Surely they'd found something else out about his stepfather by now.

He wasn't sure what the news would be, but he knew this much: He'd had all the uncertainty he could take. He had to know which of the bad credit report Charlies his stepfather was, the car dealer with lousy credit or the two-timing bigamist. It was time to put this whole thing to rest. One way or another, he thought, picking up the cabin phone and opening the information booklet provided with directions on long distance calling. It might cost a bundle, but it would be worth it just to *know*.

It took several minutes for the call to be processed. At least it felt that way. Meanwhile, Dan heard Jason and his herd of friends barge into the room to get more quarters. The boy had announced it in a voice that might have carried up to his parents' room. At that rate, Sunny wasn't going to get much sleep, which meant her humor might not improve before supper. Dan muttered under his breath, annoyed that she'd crept back into his thoughts again.

The receptionist at the agency answered the call, telling Dan that the man he needed to speak to was not in. He squelched a few more unsavory words and thanked her politely, before slamming the phone back in its wall cradle. When it failed to catch and fell to the floor, he just let his frustration go. After placing it more carefully back into its cradle, he stormed out of the room. Maybe he'd feel better after looking up Jason's crew in the video arcade and blowing up some tanks and artillery. As boisterous as that heavy-footed bunch was, a body'd have to be deaf to miss them. The elevators were so jammed with the inflow and outgo of tours, not to mention the late-seating lunch, that Dan took the stairs up to the promenade to cross to the front of the ship through the mall.

Unfortunately, any passengers not engaged in the tour or lunch activity appeared to be lined up on the mall level to spend their shipboard credit. The lines spanned the full circle of the promenade balcony, which overlooked a large, glass-domed gallery. Dan eased his way past the hoards to get to the other side of the circle, while glass elevators that moved from the top- to bottom-most public levels of the ship spilled out even more shoppers.

"Hey, where are you going in such an all-fangled rush? You look like you're about to shoot somebody."

Dan switched his focus from his goal—the double doors leading out of the mall to the deck on the outside of the ship—to his sister. "The video arcade," he explained with a twitch of his lips.

"Boys will be boys."

"I know you like to shop, but this is ridiculous." He cast a disdainful look at the line that seemed to grow exponentially.

"It's for Charlie. Tonight's his and Mom's monthly anniversary. He ordered a sapphire dinner ring for her, but isn't up to waiting in the line. The heat took the starch out of him today."

Before the furrows deepened in Dan's forehead foretelling his displeasure, Gail held up a warning finger. "Don't you say a word. I think it's sweet."

"I was just going to say she's got a ring on every finger now. What is this one, a thumb ring?" It wasn't really what came to his mind, but far be it from him to tell Gail that he hardly considered it *sweet* for a man to buy a woman a gift with her own money.

"No, it's to replace all that worthless costume jewelry she wears. He said she deserves the best."

Dan's temper exploded like an old-time photographer's flash.

"Like the ring we gave her for Mother's Day when I was in high school?" It was a gold-plated pinkie ring with two specks of imitation birthstones—Gail's and his—but to his knowledge, his mom had never taken it off.

"That old thing? Get real, Dan. I'd ditch it in a heartbeat."

"Because it didn't come from your kids' hard-earned money." He looked away, trying to give reason a chance. "If that baby gave you a ring, handpicked and purchased by it alone, would you want to get rid of it for something flashier? I can tell you right now, that little ring we gave her is more genuine than what you're about to pick up."

"If you'd just give Charlie a chance, get to know him better, instead of being a supreme pain in the—"

Pivoting abruptly, Dan pushed his way through the spread-eagled line before his socially unacceptable reply to his sister choked him. The more he learned about Charlie Meyers, the less he liked the man. Was he the only one on the planet with eyes and common sense?

Thanksgiving Day on the Caribbean Sea dawned perfectly cloudless. The *Love Ahoy* glided across the water, leaving a wake that was soon absorbed into a flawless, glasslike surface. A small holiday service was held after the formal breakfast in the Palace Theatre for those interested in attending. Pastor Stuart reflected on that first Thanksgiving Day. Dan sat in stony silence with his family around a low lounge table.

Dan had to admit to himself that Charlie didn't look well. The deep coloring from the sun looked more like a mask, rather than natural health. Dan's mom clearly realized it too and was constantly asking her husband if he wanted to go back to the cabin and lie down. For better or worse—he hoped it wasn't for the worse—she loved the man…. Dan hated to admit it, but Gail was right about one thing. Their mom hadn't been this happy in years. If Charlie was a fraud… *God, I don't want to hurt anyone,* he cried out in silence, when it came the time for quiet prayer. *So far, that looks like all I've done. I'm no good at saying one thing and thinking another. You know I don't wish my stepfather any harm. I just want…* Dan floundered in a sea of emotional confusion. *I'm not sure what I want. But Lord, I can't believe what I said to Sunny last night. She's one of the kindest, most thoughtful people I've ever met.* The blade in Dan's throat cut both ways, making it hard to swallow. *I believe You sent her to me, to all of us…and this is how I thank you both. Just give me a chance to make things right.*

As the congregation repeated the Lord's Prayer, Dan looked over to where Sunny sat with her family, then turned his focus back to the minister, who was beginning his sermon. Sometimes the pastor at Dan's church sounded more like a provoked mosquito, droning on and on.

Maybe that's because you tuned him out…

He couldn't deny it. He'd treated the man like white noise while thoughts about work or what he had to do later occupied the forefront of his mind. He shifted uncomfortably in his seat, closing his mind to the potshots of guilt assailing him from within and trying to no avail to concentrate on what the pastor was saying. His attention kept wandering to where Sunny listened with angelic attentiveness, wholly unaware he was about to burst with penitence.

Last night he'd chewed on cold shoulder at dinner. It wasn't that Sunny wasn't polite. She simply focused most of her attention and conversation on Jason and Allison, rather than him. Dan felt the wall of distance between them growing higher and wider by the minute.

He'd asked if she was going to the show later, hoping to get a chance to apologize, but she'd coolly informed him she'd already arranged to go with her family. It was the same with breakfast and the service this morning.

Reason told him that not only had he hurt her, but he'd monopolized her time. She *should* spend the holiday with her family.

He clenched his teeth. He didn't care what she *should* do. He wanted her with him. He missed having someone to talk to, to pal around with. Someone? Let's face it, he missed *her.* He missed that on-the-edge feeling of not knowing what to expect next when he was with her. He'd reveled in holding her during their cab ride, in offering her support for a change. She'd brought him more joy and laughter than he'd known in a long time. And she'd made him think. Thanks to Sunny, this whole cruise thing hadn't been such a bad trip after all.

Until now. Now it was taking a decided downturn. And he couldn't stand not being able to mend the fences between them.

"These people took the Word of God to heart," Pastor Stuart said, his voice strong and fervent, yet soothing to Dan's ear.

Lord, tell me what to do, he pleaded as the minister went on about the Pilgrims and Indians burying differences and working together for God's glory. Dan's attention piqued, and he found himself listening more closely.

"Did the Pilgrims judge the strangers at their tables based on previous stories told to them or by the Indians' skin or strange customs? Or did the Indians judge their visitors from the way trappers and explorers before them had treated the red man? No. They took the time to get to know each other. They took time to learn to trust."

Trust. Dan blinked, his heart giving a sudden leap. *Is this for me, God?*

Sunny turned, giving Dan a pointed look before looking at the pastor again. He nearly smiled. No cartoon angel messenger for him—just an earthly one telling him to pay attention. Dan glanced at his family, hardly believing what he was thinking. Was this how it worked? Was this how God *spoke* to those who'd listen? He shifted in his seat, only to be elbowed by his sister.

"Be still!" Gail whispered. "You're fidgeting like a worm on a hot brick."

"I've sat on rocks more comfortable than this seat," Dan grumbled, feeling even more like a delinquent.

"They would not allow the planks of prejudice to blind them," the pastor preached on, "but rather leaned on God's Word, knowing He would take care of them."

Yeah? Well, what about those who trusted and were scalped? Dan's lips thinned. He didn't doubt God was with them, but there were some people who plunged recklessly into danger without taking precautions.

Pastor Stuart paused. "I know what you're thinking."

Dan smirked. He doubted it.

"What about those who were massacred? Were they killed for trusting?"

Chills ran down Dan's neck, traveling across his shoulders. Man, this was unreal.

"There were those who would use these unfortunates as planks to blind others, to fuel hatred and mistrust, but you and I both know those who died in Christ were not lost but saved because of their faith. While those who walk blinded by vengefulness live on the edge of damnation. Which would you choose?" Pastor Stuart shook his head. "It's not an easy choice, is it?"

No, it wasn't, Dan thought. How could he just discount what he'd learned from the investigators? Was that really trusting God to take care of his mother? Shouldn't he do all he could to make sure she was safe and protected?

He didn't know. All he knew for sure was that he'd made a royal mess of things trying to handle it on his own.

Pastor Stuart leaned forward on the podium, leveling a gaze that encompassed the whole of the room. "But when we earnestly take up the cross, we must be prepared to face hard choices, sometimes choices that go against our human grain, because, friends, that grain is just that: human. And as such, it is imperfect. Only One made the perfect choice, the choice to die in order to fulfill His Father's will."

Straightening, the minister closed the worn Bible from which he'd read earlier. "And so I leave you with this thought today: When we give thanks, remember not just those strangers who chose to trust and obey by sharing God's bounty that first Thanksgiving, but remember also Him who set the example for all of us to follow. And ask yourself, do I trust Him? With that, let us stand and sing this hymn of grateful praise."

Mrs. Stuart struck up the portable keyboard set up next to her husband. Dan chimed in. He usually sang the familiar Thanksgiving melody mechanically, but the more he sang, the more meaning the words held for him—lyrics of gathering to thank and praise the Creator for the beauty of the earth and sky, which Dan often paused to admire during his days on the range. Today, however, Dan sang in thanks for more than the material things. He sang in gratitude that God let him know his prayer had been heard. God had spoken, not directly, but in his heart. Dan knew it without a doubt.

He needed to talk to Sunny. He wanted to tell her, if she'd even speak to him. If not, at least he'd apologize. He stood on tiptoe, trying to see which exit she and her family were taking, but Gail tugged sharply on his arm, holding him back. Turning in annoyance, he saw his mom standing over Charlie.

"What is it, dear? Are you in pain?"

Charlie held his arm across his chest, his breath short. "I'll be fine. Just give me one of my pills." He reached inside his shirt and fumbled with a metal chain. On its end was a tiny vial.

Dan had seen some of the seniors in his church wear them. They contained nitroglycerin. The heat couldn't be blamed this time for Charlie's spell, for the lounge was air-conditioned. That meant this was something decidedly more serious.

"Want me to find Sunny?" he volunteered.

His mother's concerned gaze met his. "No, go have the doctor paged."

"Now, Esther—"

"Go," she told Dan. He went. When his mother spoke in that tone, man, woman, and child listened.

Dan pushed through the crowd with as polite an urgency as he could muster and still make headway, searching for the first uniformed crew member he could find. Spying one of the social directors standing near an elevator, he hailed the young man. On telling him of the situation, the Scandinavian featured fellow walked straight to a phone concealed behind a door made of the same crinkled metal as the wall covering. In a few moments, his accented page for the doctor came over the speaker system.

"Dr. Emerson, Code Red to Palace Theatre. I repeat, Dr. Emerson, Code Red to the Palace Theatre."

Torn between returning to his family or finding Sunny, Dan asked to use the phone to dial Sunny's cabin. He let it ring a dozen times and then hung up, making his way back to the lounge. *Lord, I know I had reason for my suspicions of Charlie, but I was wrong to condemn him. If something happens to Charlie and I've been wrong all along...* Panic infused Dan's thoughts as he pondered the consequences. *Lord, I'd deserve not getting a second chance to make things right, but Charlie doesn't deserve to suffer for my ignorance. Please let me get this mess straightened out. And take care of that man. Not just for my sake, but for my mom's. And Lord...let me be wrong about Charlie.*

Charlie had taken his second pill by the time Dan made it back through the crowded deck to the lounge. He hadn't brought on his stepfather's condition, but for some reason Dan couldn't shake the guilt he felt. *Father, I'll admit I was wrong in front of everyone. Just let Charlie be okay.*

"Let me through. I'm a nurse."

Dan almost shouted in relief as Sunny shoved her way toward him. He didn't know if this was a sign that things were going to be okay, but he'd take it that way. When she reached him, he grabbed her arms and gave her a quick hug. "Boy, am I glad to see you."

"Just stay out of the way, and for heaven's sake, don't say *anything* to upset anyone."

He backed away as if slapped, then stepped aside to allow her to get to Charlie and Esther, painfully aware he deserved Sunny's disdain. She began a methodical series of questions, all the while taking Charlie's pulse and watching her watch. It seemed to Dan she did a dozen things at one time, as though pulling together a health chart in her mind. By the time the doctor arrived, she gave him a full report.

Then suddenly, everything slipped into fast-forward. Charlie slumped down in the lounge seat. Dan's mom screamed his name. Sunny and the physician stretched the unconscious man out on the sofalike bench. Between the physician's sharp series of compressions on the patient's chest, Sunny tilted back Charlie's head and breathed into his mouth.

Dan pulled his mother out of the way as a uniformed nurse moved in with a small, portable crash unit. Almost simultaneously,

Charlie's shirt was ripped open—Sunny had already removed his tie and opened it at the throat—and the electric paddles were applied. Medical jargon snapped back and forth between Sunny, the doctor, and his assistant with the same electric urgency as the paddles that shook the gray-complected man on the floor. Not even Charlie's tan could hide his pallor now.

Esther cried into Dan's shoulder. "Pray, son. Please pray!"

"I am, Mom. I am." And he was. Over and over… *God help us, especially Mom and Charlie.*

"He's going to be okay, Mom," Gail said from beside them.

Pastor Stuart broke through the wall of observers, along with Melinda and her family. Before he could offer prayer or words of comfort, Sunny announced excitedly, "Got a pulse!"

"A Med-a-Vac unit is on its way," the assistant added, shoving a portable radio into a sheath hanging on his belt. "I'll see to the cart." Without waiting for the doctor's nod, he started back through the crowd. "Ladies and gentlemen, please clear the way. The doctor needs room to work and we need to move the patient."

Dan's mother looked up at him. "What do they mean *Med-a-Vac?*"

"A chopper from a nearby island to transport Charlie to a hospital," Dan guessed. "They'll explain when they're done working on him." His mother chewed on her knuckles, and Dan's heart constricted. She'd done the same thing the night Dan's dad died.

He drew her to him. "Mom, it's going to be fine. I know it." The authority in his voice shocked him. *God, Your message was for trust, so I'm counting on You.* "If they do take him by chopper, I'll go with him. I've worked with air rescue in my emergency volunteer training."

He'd even taken flying lessons, but all that had ended when the full responsibility of the ranch fell on his shoulders. It was a day just like this one that precipitated it all, but this time, Dan intended to look on this as a beginning, hopefully for all of them. He couldn't undo what he'd already said and done, but God willing, he could change how he approached the future with Charlie.

"Indeed you will not. I will," his mother declared, bristling at the idea of abandoning her husband.

Dan shuddered to think of his mother being airlifted by rope into a helicopter or climbing a rope ladder in the terrible draft, but instead of arguing, he gave her a hug. "Why don't we just wait and see what Dr. Emerson has to say before you and I have to duke it out."

By the time the doctor was able to speak with them, Charlie was wired and tubed, with all manner of machinations hooked up to him. An air-rescue helicopter was indeed on its way from the nearest island with a hospital. One person, and only one person, would be allowed to accompany the patient. The doctor agreed that it should be Dan.

"Miss Elders and I concur that there is an irregularity in Mr. Meyers's heart rhythm that could be a problem in need of immediate attention," Dr. Emerson informed them.

"But he said he'd had a heart murmur since he was a child," Dan's mom said in a small voice.

The doctor smiled. "And that may be all it is. We do not have the equipment to determine that, however, which is why we've arranged for his transport to the island medical facility."

"Mrs. Meyers—" one of the ship's officers who'd been with the family since Charlie was moved into the ship's hospital spoke up— "a boat has already been dispatched from the island and our captain has adjusted the course for a rendezvous. It will take you to the island. You'll arrive a few hours behind the helicopter. You and your family can join Mr. Meyers and your husband then."

"Actually, Charlie is my son's—"

"Father," Dan stated firmly. At his mother's surprised look, he smiled. "Mom, if he's dear to you, he's dear to me. I've been a jerk, I admit it. But I promise, I'll take care of him."

"I *knew* you'd come around…slowly but surely," Gail remarked, ever the sibling thorn in his side. Dan afforded her a sharp glance but otherwise ignored her. Just dessert was in order.

The cart arrived by elevator, ushered by the physician's assistant and Sunny, who'd picked up more supplies from the infirmary. Charlie was conscious, but still a deathly color and too weak to talk. While Sunny and the Madisons waited for the next elevator, Dan's mother stood glued to her husband's side, holding his hand on the ride to the upper deck where the rescue helicopter would pick him up.

She argued the entire way with Dan and the ship's physician about going with her husband on the chopper until Charlie squeezed her hand and shook his head repeatedly. Finally she acquiesced.

The copter arrived and lowered its platform, which was caught by crew members and steadied. Dan waited while Charlie whispered his love to his wife—words he saw rather than heard above the roar of the whirling blades. A memory stirred in Dan's mind, and the image of his father saying good-bye flashed though him. Steeling himself, Dan made a silent vow that his mother would not suffer that terrible anguish again, so long as he could do anything to prevent it.

He gave his mother a hug and helped wheel the cart to the chopper basket. After Charlie was transferred and hoisted safely, Dan turned once again to his mom.

"I promise," he shouted, crossing his heart. "I won't let anything happen to Charlie."

His mother stared up at him through swimming eyes. "I know,

son. I'll see you shortly," she shouted through cupped hands.

The sight of his mother's anguish burned like an acid in the back of his throat, filling him with even more resolve. Dan blew her a kiss and started up the swinging ladder. Suspended in midair, he stopped and looked back to where Sunny stood at the crowd's edge with her family. He nodded solemnly.

Allison blew him a kiss. Jason waved. Sunny nodded back, her face a mask of concern, but with no trace of that extra warmth he knew her to possess. The vitality and passion he'd but sampled the night they'd hunted Allison down was gone.

He only prayed it wasn't for good.

He climbed the rest of the way up the ladder and into the craft. Once seat-belted in place, the EMT waved to the pilot. With a tilt, the helicopter lifted and veered away from the tall columns of the bridge and engines. The people on the deck below shrank to the size of dolls on a toy model and then could not be distinguished at all.

Next to Dan, the rhythmic sound of the monitor attached to the patient became more erratic. The paramedic flipped off his seat belt and started working on Charlie again, increasing his efforts when the instrument flatlined. His own heart stopping, Dan reached down and grabbed Charlie's hand, awash with an over-whelming sense of helplessness.

"Come on, Charlie!" he shouted over the roar of the blades and engine. "Blast your hide, I promised Mom you'll make it! So you'd better, or I'm going to thump on you myself."

Lord, please! Dan fervently linked Charlie's ice-cold fingers in his own, praying *for* his stepfather in both senses of the word. *Give us another chance…both of us.*

Nineteen

$\mathcal{T}$HE SHOW MUST go on, wasn't that how the saying went?

As Sunny watched the boat that took Dan Jarrett's mother to join her husband and son fade in the sunset, she shivered. The close contact the ship's communications officer maintained with the medical authorities informed them that Charlie was in the medical center cardiac unit and had stabilized. Tests were being run to determine what course of action to take, but it was likely that, since he was stable, he'd be flown to Miami where his own physician and medical records were located. At least, that was Dr. Emerson's recommendation.

"The medical staff and facilities on the island are excellent for the area, but they are no match for Miami's cardiology team and capabilities," the ship's physician explained to the family as he passed along the information from the communications room. "If a patient is in serious condition and can be transported, I recommend it."

Before leaving, Esther insisted her daughter and son-in-law remain aboard for the rest of the cruise. "There's nothing you can do for Charlie, and Dan is already at the hospital."

The woman's stern, calm voice silenced Gail Madison's objection to the idea. Whatever Dan had said to his mother acted like the sedative she was offered and refused. Esther was stronger than Dan gave her credit for, and in Sunny's estimation, a better judge of character than her son. The woman's feistiness and obvious love of adventure and life struck a common chord in Sunny. They might have been born years apart, but their hearts were the same.

And they'd both been swept off their feet by the Caribbean spell.

Sunny fought back tears. She hadn't meant it to happen to her, but somewhere between knocking Dan's hat off and telling him off last night, she'd lost her heart at sea. It had to be floating on the briny waters somewhere…either that, or in Dan's pocket, because it sure didn't feel like it was in her chest. Her romantic rendezvous had become a collision course, and she was sinking fast.

"Besides, " Esther pointed out, "if we do fly to the States, it will be in a small plane, and I doubt there'll be room for the whole kaboodle of our family. Someone has to stay and see to our luggage. And I know it would upset Charlie if we all gave up the cruise." Esther's tone flatly implied she'd allow nothing to upset her husband. "He so wanted this to be a treat for everyone."

Gail backed down reluctantly. Sunny accompanied them to the lower level where Esther prepared to make her way toward the bobbing plank connecting the ship to the tender that would take her to the island dock. A taxi waited landside, courtesy of the cruise line, to carry her to the local hospital—and her husband and son.

"And Sunny—" Esther gave her a hug as the crew secured the short, bobbing gangway between the two vessels—"How can I thank you for taking care of Charlie? You've been a godsend, dear."

Embarrassed, Sunny brushed off the thanks. "It's my job. It's what I do. You just take care of that husband of yours. He's going to need lots of TLC."

She also knew what *not* to say. Charlie was in serious condition and, based on the evaluation she and Dr. Emerson had given him, would need to be flown to Miami as soon as possible. Yesterday, Charlie's cold, the heat, and the exertion of climbing the hiking trail masked as heat stroke what could not be masked today—not given the edema and bluish tint to his extremities.

"You can betcha he's gonna get plenty of that," Esther promised, hugging her once more.

"Okay, Mrs. Meyers. We're ready if you are," one of the officers informed them.

Esther started away and then looked back. "And if my Dan has one lick of sense, I'll be seeing you again, dear."

"We'll keep Sunny informed. You just make sure Dan calls us," Gail ordered, blowing her mother a kiss from the opening in the side of the ship.

Sunny had accrued enough experience to know that the best intentioned promises to see her again got lost in the flurry of resumed lives once emergencies were over. Dan was right in one respect. She'd run from her own problems and they'd likely caused her to be more sensitive to his treatment of his family. But sticking her nose into others' business was hard not to do in her line of work. It was part of her job, to help families adjust or accept what had happened to their loved ones. Heaven knew she'd meant well with her advice to him, but then, so had he in his treatment of Charlie.

Trying not to cry over words that could not be taken back, Sunny focused on her patient. Once the medication purged the excess fluid build-up in Charlie's chest, there'd be less strain on the heart and lungs. Then surgeons could deal with the cause. She only wished she'd insisted Charlie be taken in yesterday when the medic reported an irregular heartbeat. That twenty-twenty hindsight.

How would hindsight treat Dan, she wondered, given the suspicions he would not give up regarding his stepfather. She prayed for everyone's sake that Dan too would look back with regret—that Charlie would be the man Esther believed she married. Who knew? Maybe she'd find out if the Meyers family story had a happy ending before the cruise ended.

Or maybe this whole episode would be just another passing trauma, the outcome of which she'd never know.

That Dan might fade into life's oblivion followed Sunny to the dining room and reduced the moist slices of Thanksgiving turkey and the heaps of mashed potatoes, dressing, and all the traditional trimmings on Sunny's plate to something tasting like the cover of a cooking magazine. Keeping with tourist tradition, Sunny had taken pictures of the large ice turkey a member of the kitchen staff carved earlier on the pool deck, as well as the other lavish displays of culinary art—squash birds with carrot beaks, melon Indian faces with full headdresses, pumpkin soup and sauce tureens, bouquets of rose buds made from curled beet and squash slices. The imagination and skill of the presentation would awe her fellow nurses back at the ER, and the dessert table would make their mouths water. As for Sunny…she wasn't even tempted.

"You must be coming down with something," Melinda observed, looking up over her own plate of pie slices, tarts, and Indian pudding. "You might have left most of your main meal on your plate, but I have never seen my sister turn down dessert."

"How come you don't make her eat everything on her plate?" Jason protested over a last fork of brussels sprouts. He eyed the skewered, round member of the cabbage family as if it were laced with arsenic.

"Because she's *your* mother, not Aunt Sunny's," Alan reminded the boy.

"When you turn eighteen, you can choose your own diet," Melinda added.

Jason pulled a face and shuddered. "Aw, man, brussels sprouts for another nine years."

Sunny had to laugh. For a few seconds it relieved the emotional constriction of her heart—or the hole where it had been. She'd let Daniel Jarrett and the Meyers family get too close, and now she was suffering for it.

It was a rare slip, and she determined it wouldn't happen again. She'd recovered before, she'd do it again. Granted, romance had never entered the picture before, but she'd let herself care for patients, for their families. Fortunately, the heart was a resilient thing. She had a pulse. She knew it was there. It just didn't feel like it. But it would heal. Once she was back to work, away from the setting where she and Dan had somehow clicked, she'd be fine and dandy.

"I can't eat another thing," Alan said, finishing the last of the dessert his wife left on her plate.

"That's because every plate on the table is empty," Melinda teased. Even Jason had wolfed down a giant piece of walnut cake smothered in soft vanilla ice cream in all of what seemed like five seconds.

According to a table of seniors, who'd spied his heaping dessert plate and taken good-natured bets on how long it would take him to inhale it, it was actually three minutes. As the family rose from the table, one of the white-haired gentlemen among the group shook Jason's hand.

"Son, you just won me another dollar."

To Sunny's amazement, he handed Jason fifty cents of it.

"Keep it up."

"Jason Allen Reddish!" Melinda was the picture of an appalled mother.

"It's all right, Mrs. Reddish. We've had as much fun watching that boy eat and cavort around with his pals as we have on the tours. Don't get to see our own grandkids that much, now that they're grown."

"This is *totally* humiliating," Allison grumbled at Sunny's side. "Let's go check out the pictures in the photo gallery. I had mine taken with Sean last night at supper."

Melinda and Alan authorized Allison to purchase pictures of the family for their ship's album, then headed for the lounge to save seats for the last Vegas-style show of the cruise. It was Sunny's first time in the photo gallery, which, like the shopping mall a level above, was on a balcony overlooking the glass tower that rose through all the decks. There were literally hundreds, if not thousands, of pictures lining the walls and dividers. Aside from themes, like Formal Night, Late Seating, or St. Maarten, there was no rhyme or reason to the myriad of happy faces smiling back at Sunny and Allison. At least every other guest on the ship had posed with a waiter or busboy, making that particular section so big that everyone looked alike.

The imp in her could not resist finding amusement in some of the expressions, particularly of those whom the photographer's flash caught off-guard. "Another deer in the headlights," she snickered, pointing one out to Allison.

"Oh, look. There's you and Dan."

Sunny picked up the photo. It was from the night she'd gotten her dress caught in the door. Behind it was another—she was on Swing Ting and Dan was on his horse. Did it have a name?

Another was of them basking in the sun on the pool deck, Dan soaked from his frolic with the Stuart girls. Then there was Dan, looking like an Adonis among a bevy of volleyball beauties. His eyes were on the ball; theirs were on him.

They were all different scenes, but someone had gathered them together and left them that way—a chronicle of five days in paradise. Heavens, she thought, staring at the picture of Dan helping her out of the Emerald Pool. It looked as if they were among the honeymooners, the way they looked at each other. The electricity she'd felt was right there, captured on film—and not in just one picture, but several. And she'd attributed all the flashes to a camera, not her heart.

Lord, make my boo-boo stop hurting, she cried like a child in silent prayer.

"He is one handsome dude," Allison said, looking over her shoulder at the pictures of their table on formal night, "even if he *is* permanently attached to that hat." She pointed to another photo of Dan alone as he debarked at St. Maarten, just before he'd met up with her for that wild taxi ride. He wasn't smiling that day. "That's his sullen, bad-boy pose."

"Amen," Sunny agreed with her niece's verbal drool.

No doubt about it, the man was gorgeous in denim or a suit. He was boyishly charming, yet rakishly male. He was loving and fun one minute and a royal pain the next. He believed in God and unconditional love, even if he didn't always practice it. But then, no one was perfect. And perfect or not, Daniel Jarrett was everything Sunny had dreamed of. And he was gone.

She bought the pictures and headed for her cabin as the first song they'd danced to played over and over in her mind. Now she understood the darker side of the love's protest that *It Had to Be You.* Her last words to Dan ended the haunting music on an even more depressing note.

Just keep out of the way, and for heaven's sake, don't say anything to upset anybody.

And he hadn't. Not even good-bye.

Twenty

*S*TANDING IN THE hall of the island clinic, Dan watched a nurse check Charlie's vital signs. The ashen patient's slightest disturbance would register on one of the sophisticated monitors surrounding his bed. After an hour's effort, the physician in charge had finally reached the Miami doctor who had Charlie's medical history. Since Charlie had just moved to Texas after the wedding, his records hadn't caught up with him.

Both doctors agreed that the best option was to stabilize the patient and fly him to Miami. There he'd undergo surgery to repair the nearly blocked arteries in his heart that the initial tests revealed. The boat dispatched to bring Esther Meyers from the cruise ship was expected at any time.

"You may go back in now, sir," a young nurse said, interrupting his reverie.

Her accent was a pleasant Euro-Caribbean one—as telling of her ancestry as her dark hair and sea green eyes—and soothing to the ear. Even so, Dan was anything but soothed as he walked inside. The cubicle was darkened by closed blinds. Dim light infused the room from the head of the single bed. The chipped beige-enameled rails that kept Charlie from rolling out of the bed served as a reminder that this was not the best equipped facility, although Dan had seen nothing but top-notch care. At least in his lay estimation, his stepfather had received the best treatment available.

As if he sensed Dan's approach, Charlie opened his eyes. "Some way to wind up a cruise, huh?" Whatever medicines they pumped into him, Charlie was at least coherent.

"Can't say it hasn't been exciting," Dan acknowledged.

Earlier, Charlie had been disoriented, babbling about cars and children—*grand*children to be specific. Dan couldn't help but think of the last report he'd received about a second Charlie Meyers, the one with a wife and family in Jacksonville. Maybe the Miami Charlie had grandchildren from a previous marriage that the agency hadn't uncovered yet, Dan reasoned, struggling against his nature to think the best of the man. Or he could be exactly what he claimed to be: a man who was genuinely excited to be part of a family after years of loneliness.

Lord, I'm trying to trust. Dan dropped down into a chair beside the bed. "Mom should be along soon."

Charlie smiled at the mention of Dan's mom. He stared off for a moment, as if picturing her in his mind and liking—no…*loving*— what he saw. A warmth broke over Dan's heart.

His stepfather turned to him suddenly. "Glad you came with me. I'd have worried about her in that 'copter, scared as she is of flyin'."

"That makes two of us. She's game enough to try it."

They shared a grin. "Nonetheless, I appreciate it, son."

Charlie's presumption always set Dan off, but he let it slide. "No problem."

"Just a figure of speech," Charlie explained hastily. "Listen, Dan boy, I don't expect to take the place of your father. Wouldn't want to."

He couldn't, Dan thought rebelliously. *Lord, I don't know if I'm ready to get this chummy. I'd like to get used to him first.* Heaven knew, he hadn't tried before.

Charlie closed his eyes. "I don't know what I did to put you off, but—"

"Why don't you just take it easy and rest till Mom gets here?" The last thing Dan wanted was to upset the man.

"I can understand how you might be uncomfortable with my coming into the picture and changing the setup you were used to," Charlie insisted. "I'd like to think that maybe in time, we could even be friends."

"Maybe so," Dan said, reluctant to commit beyond a polite reply.

"Least there's one thing we both agree on." Charlie's lips curled tiredly.

Dan waited.

"We both love your momma and want the best for her."

The way he said it, Dan wanted to believe him. He knew nothing more about the man than he had after picking up the information in Marigot, yet he'd held Charlie's hand in the helicopter when his vital signs took a downward spiral. He'd encouraged the semiconscious and disoriented man…and he'd meant what he'd said. He wanted Charlie to make it.

"Esther told me how you came home from that fancy school and took over the ranch. How you took care of her and looked after her affairs after your dad died."

For once, Dan didn't stiffen when Charlie mentioned his dad. What had changed between him and Charlie confounded Dan's logic, but only momentarily. The answer surfaced from his heart, not his head. He'd followed Sunny's advice and asked God what to do. And God spoke to him. He recalled his mom remarking time and again that when God speaks to a person, it changes them. Not that Dan was ready to embrace Charlie completely, but he was light-years ahead of where he'd been this time yesterday.

From the bed, Charlie drew in a deep breath and let it out all at once. "And now it looks like I have to lean on you, too."

"What?" Suspicion gained ground. *Lord, please don't let him ask me for money.*

"Look in my bag of things and fetch my wallet."

Feeling as though he were walking on an invisible tightrope, afraid to lean too far one way or the other lest he plummet to the cold ground below, Dan did as he was told. He rummaged through his stepfather's discarded clothing until he found the wallet and hesitated, as if touching it might undo what little spiritual progress Dan had made. "You sure you don't want to wait for Mom—"

"I don't want to alarm her."

Dan met Charlie's frank gaze. What was in the wallet that would alarm his mother? Meyers's true identity? With a sinking feeling, Dan handed it over. As eager as he'd been to find the truth, he wasn't so certain this was the time or place, much less the manner. Somehow it seemed something like this would come better from a disinterested party.

His mind raced with the possibilities. What if Charlie made a confession? What would that do to his newborn attempt at trust? *Lord, I suppose I have to trust You and let Charlie take care of himself.* It seemed the logical answer.

Hampered by IVs and wires, Charlie opened the billfold and thumbed through it. Finally, he pulled out a worn business card and squinted at it in the dim light over the bed.

"This gettin' old ain't what it's cracked up to be." Once certain that the card was the right one, he handed it over to Dan. "Call my attorney. Tell him what's happened and that I need him to make certain all the bases are covered for my new will to take effect."

"Will?"

At Dan's startled echo, Charlie managed a halfhearted chuckle. "Don't worry. I'm not planning on having it go into effect for a long time. It's just in case."

Dan didn't know what to say. He nodded, staring at the card. *Breckenridge, Taylor, and McGrath, Attorneys at Law.* Dan had heard of them. McGrath specialized in estate planning. It was his card.

Estate planning? Dan looked at Charlie, who'd closed his eyes momentarily, as if even that little bit of effort had taken a toll. There wasn't anything to do except what the man asked.

"I'll call him for you, but you'd best take it from there yourself. After your surgery," Dan said as Charlie glanced at him askance. "You do anything to upset my mom, and I'll haunt you clear to the other side of Jordan. Got that?"

The man on the bed snorted. "I do believe you would, son."

A lawyer's card in itself didn't mean a thing, but Dan could not avoid the guilt shaking its finger at him over his suspicions. Sunny said God would show him the truth if he asked for it… Was this message from God or Charlie Meyers? Dan wished he knew if his mother had put her money in her husband's name.

His mind as well as his conscience seesawed with the possibilities. If she had put her money in Charlie's name, what was the man's rush to have his attorney act? It wasn't as if Charlie could spend it if something went wrong. And if everything went smoothly with the operation, there'd be time later to get his hands on everything. Unless Meyers knew Dan was investigating him.

"Esther is a lucky woman to have good kids like you and your sister."

Shame washed over Dan's musings, warming his face at Charlie's vote of confidence. As rough as he'd been on Charlie, here the man was trusting him with heaven knew what. *So put up or shut up, Jarrett,* Dan told himself sternly.

"Yeah, well, she'll have my hide if you do anything stupid, so you just rest until she gets here to tell us both what to do."

"Now *that* she can do." Charlie laughed, but the mirth turned into a cough that drained him of color and strength.

"Easy, pardner." Without thinking, Dan placed a reassuring hand on Charlie's arm. The old man was right. Even if they had nothing else in common, they had one bond: Dan's mother. Even if Charlie wasn't worth a hoot, he knew how to make her happy. Dan wanted his mom's happiness…

He frowned suddenly. He did want her happiness, didn't he? A gnawing awareness grew in his gut. Or had his previous wariness been, at least in part, motivated by selfishness? By…jealousy?

He groaned inwardly. He hadn't realized how lonely he'd been until he met Sunny. *And you've ruined your chances with her,* an accusing voice told him, but it wasn't too late with Charlie. Or with God. Dan wanted to take off his head and shake it. Now that he'd opened his heart, he was having a problem separating human thought from spiritual instruction. All he knew was that Charlie might be a fraud, but he wasn't faking his illness. That pasty gray coloring couldn't be conjured.

"Can I get you anything, Charlie?"

"Just go make that call before your momma gets here," his stepfather said. "I don't want her hearin' anything about wills and such." He closed his eyes again. "And tell McGrath that you're my appointed representative, and if he doesn't like it, bull…fedders…"

Alarm invaded Dan's confusion. Charlie was starting to slur again. "I'll get the nurse."

"Repeat what I just said."

Nothing slurred about that. Dan obliged him. "You said to tell McGrath that I'm your appointed representative and if he doesn't like it, bullfedders."

"Bull*feathers*," Charlie said, lifting his head off the pillow, as if to drive the word home. "Feathers!"

"If he doesn't like it, bullfeathers. Got it." Dan searched the monitors for any sign of a diminishing state of health, but they appeared consistent. As for mental health, what the devil was bullfeathers? "What is that, some kind of code?"

A sigh escaped Charlie's mouth. "You're a smart boy," he said, peering at Dan from beneath half-lidded eyes. "Stubborn as a mule, but smart all the same." Suddenly his thick, pale lashes flew up like a sprung window blind, brushing the hedge of his eyebrows. "Now git and make that call."

It wasn't until he was in the hall that Dan's thoughts caught up with him. He'd scampered like a dog dodging a boot tip, as if Charlie actually packed some wallop to the punch of his voice. The coughing that resumed from inside the room quickly killed that notion.

No matter what else he might be, Charlie Meyers was a sick man who'd asked Dan to do him a favor. And that was exactly what Dan intended to do—right after he asked the nurse to check on Charlie. Then he'd give McGrath's name to the investigating agency.

Just in case, Lord. Just in case. Dan wanted to be prepared for his mother's sake.

And yet, even as he fished change for the call from his pocket, he hoped with all his heart that he would turn out to be the fool.

Twenty-one

$\mathcal{T}$HE LAST DAY on the *Love Ahoy*'s itinerary was spent on the cruise line's private island in the Caymans. People who'd been total strangers at the onset of the cruise now gathered in friendly groups around picnic tables under swaying palms, enjoying the tropical fare from the cabana. The bamboo shack was a combination of bar and barbeque. Hot dogs and burgers grilled there, filling the air with the fragrance of temptation.

Sunny and the crew at her table helped themselves, while claims rose here and there regarding an impending diet on the agenda as soon as the ship landed in Miami. Jason and the Stuart children were in their glory with a meal where ketchup ruled. The smallest tourists wore theirs on face and clothing, while the smeared T-shirts of their older counterparts betrayed their indulgence in the favorite sauce du jour.

Sunny wiped a renegade droplet from a french fry off her print sleeveless top with a napkin.

"Here…" Melinda produced a purse-sized container of wet wipes from her straw bag.

"It's okay. I got it, I think. At least it blends with the print."

Melinda, whose clothing was predictably spotless, tucked the wipes away. The woman could walk through a food fight and come out clean. Sunny, on the other hand, could get dirty under surgical conditions. Fortunately, medical uniforms in color and prints were now the norm.

"Look at Alan!" Her sister laughed. "You'd think he was twelve, the way he's going after that ball."

Sunny looked over at the impromptu volleyball game that had formed in the center of the shaded picnic area in time to see her brother-in-law dive to keep the ball going for his team.

She winced. "That's going to hurt."

"This trip has been so good for him. I think he needed it as much as I did."

Melinda giggled like a schoolgirl as her husband stood up and brushed the sand off his chest, grinning sheepishly at her. Alan might be a slightly balding, thirtyish accountant, but the way her sister looked at him at that moment, he could well be a cover model for a fashion magazine.

"Stop drooling in front of the children, Melinda," Sunny teased, forcing away the envy that pricked at her. She wanted love for her sister and brother-in-law. She was happy for them, even if it did remind her of what she didn't have.

No parents. No one special like Alan.

No Dan.

Sunny braked her thoughts. If she didn't, she'd launch a big-time pity party for herself.

"He's my hero, even if my cooking has thickened his waist a little…"

"And you've worried the hair away from his brow," Sunny pointed out, trying to shake the urge to just break down and cry.

Melinda made a face at her. "More like he's driven me to boxed color."

"No!" *Make 'em laugh,* she told herself sternly. *Make me laugh.*

"Just the rinse-in kind," her sister confided with a mischievous twinkle in her eye. "Besides, thinning hair on a man is a sign of too many manly hormones, you know. I read it in a women's magazine."

Struggling to hide the clouds gathering around her heart, Sunny cocked one brow skeptically above the plane of the other. "Oh, that makes it gospel."

"All I know, Miss Medical Journal, is that when he saw that silky number I bought in St. Maarten, you'd have thought he was King Kong."

Sunny groaned. "I don't think I want to hear this." For more reasons than Melinda could guess.

"No, it's funny. I promise. I don't kiss and tell."

"Not much."

Sunny endured Melinda's playful smack on the arm and listened, the dutiful sibling. But when her sister told how Alan coaxed her, clad in the flimsy affair she'd bought for him, out onto their balcony for a romance that was rudely interrupted by the spotlight of a passing freighter, Sunny nearly choked on her soda. Okay, she had to admit, it was funny...and a relief to know even princesses bent their tiaras sometimes. Laughter was good medicine, especially at her staid sister and brother-in-law's expense.

"I was mortified," Melinda exclaimed. "Picture me and King Kong crawling on our hands and knees back into the cabin and drawing the drapes."

"Don't ever tease me about the predicaments I get myself into again."

The game evidently over, Alan approached the table, Jason

hanging onto his back like a monkey. "What are you two giggling over?"

"How sore you are going to be tomorrow," Sunny quipped as he slid onto the bench beside his wife.

"Yuck," Melinda exclaimed, shoving him away. "You are hot and sticky."

"I was going to go for a swim. Want to join me?"

"No, but I'll sit on one of the beach chairs and watch."

Jason walked around and leaned on Sunny's shoulders. "Aunt Sunny, want to go on one of the paddleboats?"

"Only if you rinse off first." Did she want to paddle around with Jason? No. She wanted to go back to the cabin and have a good cry. It would be a novelty for her…but she wouldn't do it. She'd go and act crazy and amuse her nephew as well as distract herself. It was *Dan's* loss, not her parents', that was taking her down. Although as much struggle as she was having, maybe it was both. Sheesh, she'd only known the guy a week, not even a whole week at that. *Lord, please…I don't want to break down now, whatever the reason. Let me get home first. Please.*

At that moment, she spied the arriving tender that carried passengers back and forth from the anchored ship to the shore. "I see Mike and Gail Madison. Let me check with them about Charlie, and then we'll do the paddleboat." She smiled at him as she got up from the table.

Mike Madison helped his pregnant wife off the floating ramp of the tender and on to the beach.

As Sunny approached them, she waved. "Is everyone packed up?"

After the open seating breakfast that morning, the couple had gone to the Meyers's and then to Dan's cabins to pack their bags for the pickup later on that evening. Everyone was required to have all luggage ready and outside the cabin doors before two in the morning. That way the cruise personnel could get them off-loaded and through customs as soon as the ship arrived in Miami.

"Ready to go," Gail told her. "Took all of five minutes in Dan's room. His dirty clothes were folded, separated by color, and tucked in the laundry bag. I couldn't believe it. That boy has always made me feel like a slob."

"Speaking of which, he called and left a message at the desk since we weren't in our room," Mike spoke up. "He and Mom are checked into a hotel near the hospital. The flight to Miami was uneventful."

"Have they scheduled surgery?" Sunny asked, hopeful to hear more about Dan, in addition to Charlie's progress.

"They're running some more tests and maybe they'll do something late this afternoon or early evening. Dan's as free with words as he is with his packing," Gail complained. "Nothing extra."

"And your mom?"

"Mom's a trouper. Prognosis looks good.'" Gail quoted her brother with a grimace. "That's all we know."

Sunny nodded, disappointment weighing down her shoulders. What did she expect, that Dan would say he was sorry through his sister? More like, *"Drop dead, nosy."*

Jason emerged from the water, free of the sand and dirt from the volleyball court. "Hey, Aunt Sunny. You ready?"

Sunny stepped away from the couple. "Well, keep us informed if there's anything we can do."

"Oh, there was a message for you, too."

Sunny turned back to Gail, her heart taking an expectant leap.

"Mom sends her love and thanks for being there for Charlie."

She smiled, a bright facade for the dark dive of her hope. "Glad I could do it." Even a polite "thanks for everything" from Dan would have been nice. At least that's what she tried to tell herself.

"C'mon, Aunt Sunny. I bet we can beat Marshall and Allison out to the end of the jetty and back."

Braced with a muster of bravado, Sunny kicked off her flip-flops at the water's edge and waded in. "We'll at least give them a run for their money," she said, determined to redeem the day by basking in her blessings, rather than wallowing in the disappointing pool of what might have been.

Twenty-two

*D*AN DIDN'T REALIZE he'd fallen asleep until he felt the warmth of a hand on his arm. He stirred, blinking his eyes in the artificial light of the surgery waiting room as he focused on his mother's face.

"You okay?" he asked.

"Just counting my blessings."

She couldn't have had more than a couple of hours' sleep since Charlie had taken ill, yet her blue eyes sparkled with joy. She took her favorite hymn about counting blessings one by one to heart. It carried her through thick and thin, she'd remind Dan when he was in a funk over something that had gone wrong in his world. It carried her through his father's death—and now...

"I'm a lucky woman to have two men looking out for me at my age." She squeezed Dan's arm. "I'm so glad you and Charlie finally worked things out between you. He told me how you threatened him if he up and died without my permission."

"I'd have done that for anyone. You know that."

"But you did it for Charlie." A wistfulness settled on her lips.

"So do you still feel that love at first sight is foolish?"

Dan shifted uneasily. He wasn't awake enough for this conversation. "I guess it works for some people…"

Once Charlie had been settled in a room, the doctors decided to put his surgery off until first thing in the morning. Even that depended on how much the medicine they gave him relieved the buildup of fluid in his chest. What Charlie had dismissed as a life-long abnormality from childhood rheumatic fever had become a life-threatening problem, although the doctor's prognosis was upbeat. It was after midnight before Dan and his mom had left the hospital to grab a few hours' sleep. They would return to the hospital to see Charlie off for a 6 A.M. valve replacement.

"Charlie was just like you, you know," Dan's mother went on, obviously on some course he hadn't yet caught on to. "He didn't want to go on the cruise with his golfing buddies, but when one of them fell and broke his hip at the last minute, Charlie filled in for him. Bob McGrath introduced us."

"Things certainly worked out in Charlie's favor."

Dan had been surprised to find out that McGrath, Charlie's attorney, was also Charlie's best friend. McGrath had even come to the hospital the morning Dan and his mother arrived to wish Charlie well before the surgery and assure him there was nothing to worry about. He gave his assurances regarding Charlie's will in a double-talk meant to escape Dan's mother's attention, but Dan caught on.

McGrath was guarded at first when Dan called him, but the minute Dan delivered Charlie's message verbatim, all that changed. It was as if he'd received a stamp of approval. For all the attorney told Dan, however, there was nothing to feed Dan's suspicions regarding his stepfather. If anything, Dan felt more and more guilty for turning McGrath's name over to the agency, especially when everyone kept saying what a great stepson he was and how good he'd been to Charlie.

"And there you were, dead set against going on this trip, and look what fun you've had."

"Huh?" Dan sat up. What *was* she talking about?

"With Sunny and her family."

"Oh…yeah." He had enjoyed himself. Who wouldn't around Sunny? "She's a trip, all right…and the kids. They're great."

"The Lord works in mysterious ways, I always say. And sometimes we just have to go with the flow on trust, rather than logic."

Dan glanced at his watch. This trust issue was spinning him on a spit lately. "I was hoping the surgery would be over in time for me to pick up Gail and Mike at the dock."

"It will be right on schedule, and so will you."

Dan gave his mother a skeptical look.

"Trust," she explained simply.

For the first time in a long while, Dan knew exactly what she meant. And that just made him feel worse. *Lord, I'm only trying to be cautious, not mistrustful.* How could he just ignore some very real possibilities regarding Charlie's past?

Dan stewed quietly as his mother picked up a magazine and started thumbing through it, humming her favorite hymn. She might as well have been waiting for a hair appointment instead of the outcome of a loved one's surgery. He'd missed that spiritual grounding, living with his mother, Dan thought. Till now, he hadn't realized how much a part of his life that had been. She'd moved out, and he'd moved away from God. Not consciously, of course, but the distance was still there. No wonder his prayers had been more static, harder for him to feel he was getting through. Guess that relationship was a lot like one between a rider and a good cowpony—as long as it was worked faithfully, a rider could count on it to get him through.

*Lord, I've taken more care of my relationship with my horse than I
have with You. All I can say for myself is I'm sorry…I didn't even realize it.* He drew a deep breath, resolve growing inside him. *But I
promise, I'll do my utmost not to let it happen again.*

Exactly at the predicted time, the surgeon came into the waiting room and announced the operation was a success. Charlie was
in intensive care, which was par for the course for heart surgery, but
he'd come through with no complications and was as stable as conditions allowed.

Dan waited with his mom until she could go into the ICU to
see Charlie, only to marvel at her continued strength and cheer. To
him, Charlie looked like death, hooked by wires and tubes to beep-
ing and humming machines. Once the time allocated for the visit
was over, he took her back to the hotel to rest until the next visiting hour, then drove a rented car through traffic to the cruise line
terminal.

The hot, humid Miami air made his plaid shirt cling to the
small of his back as he walked from a designated parking area for
passenger pickups into a giant metal-encased warehouse. Tourists
of every description and size scrambled in, over, and around long
lines of luggage. Dan scanned the mass confusion, trying to pick
out someone he knew.

He saw familiar faces, but not one belonging to a member of
his family. Or to the one person he wanted most to see—

"Mr. Jarrett!"

Dan turned to see one of the cruise officers making his way
toward him. It was the man who'd acted as liaison between the
communications room and the ship's hospital, coordinating the
transport efforts.

"How are your stepfather and mother?"

Dan shook his hand. "Charlie came through the surgery fine. It was a heart valve problem, so your quick action saved the day."

"And your mother?"

"Hanging in like a trouper."

"Quite a lady, that one. Reminds me of my own mom. Indefatigable and dauntless."

"That's her," Dan agreed, staring at the milling crowd. "I don't suppose you'd know where to find my sister and her husband?"

"What deck were they on again?"

"Princess, I think."

"That would be pink tags." With a wave of his hand, the uniformed man motioned Dan to follow him.

They passed mounds of luggage with purple tags, blue tags, yellow, and gray before arriving at the pink line. At the far end, Dan spied Mike piggybacking smaller cases on a large Pullman.

"I'll fetch you a cart for you and your parents' luggage," the officer offered.

"Appreciate it," Dan called after him. He reached Mike, who was struggling to get a straw bag brimming with souvenirs on the pile. "Need help, pardner?"

His brother-in-law grinned from ear to ear. "Boy, you're a sight for sore eyes. Everything okay at the hospital?"

"Dandy." Dan picked up the straw bag as well as two other carry-ons Mike pointed out. "Charlie's fine, for all that he's been through, and Mom's at the hotel resting until the next visiting hour. Have you seen Sunny?"

"She should be with the gray tags. Your stuff, too." Mike nodded toward the large open sliding doors where the throng funneled out into the parking area. "Gail is waiting over there with Mom's and Charlie's stuff."

"All this is just Gail's?" Dan exclaimed in disbelief.

"She bought everyone she knew souvenirs," Mike grumbled in

a tell-me-about-it voice. "Even the baby has outfits from every island we visited, complete with matching drooling bibs. What's the difference between a drooling bib and a regular bib?"

Dan snorted. "Beats me. I'd strap one of those stick-on diapers under the kid's chin, like a feedbag. That way, it'd catch what the kid missed and spit out."

"Nope. They're for the other end. I do know that much."

"Hey, it works for horses," Dan pointed out in self-defense as Mike tugged the stacked luggage over to where his wife waited with even more.

Gail looked at him, forehead creased. "What works for horses?"

"You don't wanna know," Mike told her.

"How are Mom and Char—"

"Mike'll tell you." Dan turned to dive back into the quagmire of bags and guests. "I'll send the officer over with the cart and get my stuff."

"Tell Sunny we said bye and thanks," his sister hollered after him.

Dan let the good-natured taunt slide off his shoulders. Besides, Gail was right. He was looking for Sunny. He wanted to thank her…and more. Just what, he wasn't sure. He just knew thanks was not enough.

A kiss wouldn't hurt…

At the thought, Dan's pulse kicked into a higher gear as he wove his way through carts, bags, and people to where the lines with gray tags were being picked at like carcasses by carrion.

"Mr. Jarrett!" The ship's officer waved at him from a center aisle.

"My family is waiting over by the double doors," Dan shouted back. He pointed in the direction, though neither Gail nor Mike could be picked out of the departing hordes. "I'll catch up to you."

At that moment, Dan spied a familiar hat, bedecked with a giant sunflower. Beneath it was Sunny Elders, flanked on either side by her niece and nephew. All three were reading the luggage tags.

"Hey, Sunny!"

She looked up, blue eyes widening.

Dan felt his heart trip—and then his foot, as the strap of someone's carry-on caught the toe of his boot. He stumbled and caught himself. When he looked at Sunny again, her eyes were sparkling.

"Careful, pardner. You need a keeper." Then her wry humor switched to business before Dan could reply in kind. "How's Charlie?"

"He's fine. Mom's fine. We're all fine."

The urge to pick her up and swing her around like the doll she reminded him of was stalled by Jason's sharp tug on his arm.

"I just saw your bag back there. But we can't find Aunt Sunny's."

"Yeah, and if we don't find it soon, it might not make it to the airline truck," Allison chimed in, exasperated as only a teen can be.

Dan stepped up to take control of the situation. "Have you asked someone to help?"

Sunny shook her head. "I was going to check all the bags that looked like mine first. Next time, I'm buying neon orange luggage."

She grinned, and Dan scrunched his toes in the points of his boots. *Steady*, pardner, he told himself, then nodded to her. "Just hang on to my bag and I'll see if someone can give us a hint. I'm an expert on tracing missing bags by now."

He hailed one of the baggage clerks and discovered there were two places to check: the missing tag line and the line by the customs office where luggage had been pulled for random checks. He found Sunny's bag at the latter. Somehow, he'd known it would be there. After all, it was Sunny's bag.

The latch was open and the strap was curled up beside it when Dan reached it. As he tried to stuff the packages and miscellaneous clothing items that had been taken out and inspected back inside, he understood why it was left open for the owner to deal with. He grabbed a piece of knit that refused to stay inside the rim and tugged it out to find the grumpy kitten that didn't do mornings staring up at him. This time, instead of making him cross, it flushed a grin to his lips.

"Oh, man, I can't believe they opened it!" Sunny's wail came up on him. "We'll never get it closed now. It took all three of us sitting on it last night."

Dan shoved the wadded shirt back in the side and leaned on the case so hastily, he nearly caught his fingers in its closing jaws. Fortunately, a broken sandal that had slipped out unnoticed saved him the embarrassment.

Sunny fell in beside him, tucking and pressing down with a vengeance. "I should have known some drug sniffing dog would single out my stinky horseback riding clothes just for spite, double-bagged or not."

Dan held up his hand for her to stop. "Wait. Let's do this together. Start at the back and tuck and close until we get to the front. Ready?"

Peering out from under the brim of that ridiculous hat, Sunny nodded. Dan wanted to kiss her. It was all he could think about as he forced the suitcase shut. Aware that they were objects of the attention of the customs officials, he once again resisted and fastened the strap around the case.

"Aunt Sunny, Mom says hurry," Allison called out from the middle of the terminal, voice carrying as if she'd brandished a megaphone. "She and Dad are saving you a seat on the bus to the airport. Dan, Jason's got your bag over there. I'll see you on the bus. Bye, Dan."

Sunny started to take the bag from Dan, but he held on to it. "I'll carry it for you. You just hang on to those souvenirs."

"Guess they thought I was smuggling manure," she said, matching his step toward the sign pointing to the airline luggage trucks.

"More like jousting equipment." He'd hoped for smile, but Sunny's face remained uncharacteristically sober.

"So tell me about Charlie."

"Surgery went fine. Valve replacement."

"Thought so."

They walked a few more steps.

"And…?" She gazed up at him, brows arched.

Dan's thoughts stumbled. He'd rather kiss than talk any day, at least where Sunny was concerned. "And Mom's fine."

"And…?"

There was so much that had to be said…so much that he couldn't think of a word. Finally, a lightbulb flashed in his mind.

"And Charlie gave me his attorney's card to call to make sure his new will and affairs were straight before the surgery, so that's helped narrow down who we're investigating now."

He'd gone a few steps more before he realized Sunny wasn't with him. She stood in his wake, staring at him as if he'd grown a second head.

"You…you gave information passed on to you by a man possibly facing death to your cheesy P.I.?"

Cheesy? "You wouldn't say that if you knew what he was charging me." The second the defensive words were out, Dan wished he could reel them back. But it was too late.

"Aunt Sunny, the airline buses are leaving," Jason shouted. "Hurry."

Sunny glared at Dan. "Give me my bag."

She grabbed the bag out of Dan's hand and started toward the gate, but the weight nearly jerked her arm out of its socket.

Dan took it up again. "Yes, I gave the information to the P.I., but—"

"Jason, go tell your mom I'm on my way as soon as I check this in. Don't let the bus leave without me."

The boy nodded and launched into a full gallop toward the gate to the buses. "See ya, Dan," he called.

"See ya." Dan set the bag down next to his while Sunny produced her tickets. A handler came to Dan with a stick-on tag.

"Which one?"

As Dan singled out the bag, Sunny turned, tucking her tickets into her purse.

"Tell your mom and Charlie they are in my prayers."

The message came out with scissorslike precision. She hesitated a moment, as if her words jammed somewhere in her throat, then she rose on tiptoe and gave him a peck on the cheek.

"And so are you, Daniel Jarrett...that someday you'll learn the meaning of trust."

"Sunny..." Dan reached for her, but she pulled away, just beyond his grasp, and ran toward the bus terminal gate.

"Excuse me, sir, but are you checking in your bag?"

Instead of answering, Dan just shook his head and picked up the case, at a loss for words.

"Hey, Dan. Where's the car?"

Mike hailed him from across the warehouse, which was nearly empty now. Dan had lost track of his family in his excitement to see

Sunny, to tell her how he'd missed her, how she'd been right about God showing him the truth if he would just open up his mind and listen. Then, though he still wasn't sure why, he'd lost his chance to say anything.

And now? Now Dan felt lost himself…as though he were in a place where no one would ever look for him.

Twenty-three

$\mathcal{T}$HE AFTERNOON SUN poured through the balcony doors of Sunny's apartment as she opened the vertical blinds. Instantly the off-white walls and pastel furnishings came to life, cheery and bright in welcome. The clown print she'd once purchased at a local exhibition grinned at her from its frame, hanging over an overstuffed sofa, but this was one time she couldn't muster a smile back, even when she remembered how Allison, with the authority of her seven years of age, had dubbed it *fine art* and pleaded with Sunny to buy it.

She dragged the heaviest of her luggage in and shoved it against the wall. She'd unpack another day. She didn't feel up to spending the rest of the long day in the laundry room downstairs. Besides, everything of immediate need was in her carry-on. This was the downside of her vacation—no more being spoiled with staff eager to satisfy her every whim, no more exotic meals to die for or exciting places to see and people to meet. Like Melinda said when they left the airport to go their separate ways, it was back to reality.

Mechanically, Sunny checked her answering machine while

inventorying the various souvenirs she'd purchased. The "straw" shopping bag—which had turned out to be plastic—had frayed open at some point between the cruise bus and the plane in Miami, so she'd had to stuff the articles in smaller bags. With all the confusion, she wanted to make certain she had everything lined up to take to work on Monday, so that no one would be forgotten.

The answering machine rattled on in its gritty recital of the callers' voices. There were two messages from her supervisor, who'd obviously forgotten Sunny was out of town and wanted her to pick up an extra shift; a reminder from the dentist of her appointment the following week; and several hang-ups. While the messages were typical, this time they pulled her down even more than she already was. Not one had been masculine, much less with a toe-curling drawl. She couldn't even call her mom and dad to cry on their shoulders. Melinda certainly wasn't up to it. Bless her, she was just getting over what Sunny was starting to face.

Mom and Dad were gone.

"This is ridiculous," she sniffed, erasing the voice tracks. Her sniff gave way to a whimper, and the whimper to a sob. "Oh, Momma…it hurts," she cried, seizing at the past with desperation. Things she'd felt but never said poured out along with her tears. Oh, she'd told her parents how she loved them. At least she didn't have that regret. She shown it, too. But there had been things she couldn't say, not when they were here. Not until now.

I miss you. I wish you were here to hold me now. Momma, is there someone for me like Daddy? Where did you find him? Daddy, make me laugh. Let's go fishing. Let's…

Who was she kidding? They couldn't hear her…not ever again. But there was Someone who could.

Abba! It was all Sunny had left in her, but that was enough. Her message was heard. She only had to wait, to open her mind and spirit to an outpouring of comfort and strength, of reassurance that all would be well.

Grabbing at a tissue, she blew her nose.

Crying is good for the sinuses. Her dad's saying made her laugh. Maybe he'd heard her after all and had sent his message via the Holy Spirit. It comforted Sunny to think so—to *know* so.

"I know, Dad," she sighed. "And it's not like I'm used to men leaving messages for me anyway."

Sunny splashed some water on her face at the kitchen sink. *It's over.* She wiped her face and hands with a paper towel and tossed it away. *In more ways than one.*

After the way she'd walked out on Dan, he was the last person who'd want to speak to her, particularly in a romantic way.

She'd had a good excuse of course, besides the wound of disappointment. For just one shining moment, she'd thought the eagerness on his face had to do with being glad to see her rather than with reporting he was closer to making his family miserable. Worse, he'd betrayed a trust. He was more concerned over a man's past than his own integrity. Besides, if she'd lingered, she would have missed her flight home to Houston.

"Face it, Elders, you'd make a poor cop."

She'd want to find everyone innocent—*truly* innocent. Maybe Dan was right about Charlie and she was wrong, but somehow, Sunny couldn't accept that, not in her heart at least. Her training made her a good judge of character, but at the same time left no room for her to pass judgment on anyone. That sort of thing impaired one's ability to give her all. Preserving life—be it a saint's or an incorrigible sinner's—was all that was important in her world.

If only she hadn't fallen for that cockeyed cowpoke. She knew better, yet that was exactly what she'd done. Now the man and the family that needed her had moved on and she was back where she started—alone.

Lord, I asked You not to let me get close…

Even as she prayed, Sunny withdrew the words. She couldn't blame God. She'd made the choice. Her heart had a mind of its own where Dan Jarrett was concerned. It was time she started thinking with her brain. Today she would wallow, she decided, yanking open the door to her freezer. She deserved it. Tomorrow she'd put the whole thing behind her and get on with her life.

A pint of mint chocolate-chip ice cream was the perfect prescription for wallowing. The last thing she wanted to do was cook or do anything responsible. That would wait until tomorrow. Besides, her refrigerator was almost as empty as Mother Hubbard's cupboard…or as Sunny's heart.

Exactly when she fell asleep, Sunny couldn't tell. The classic movie channel had been playing a western that faded into a dreamless sleep until she stirred at the sound of knocking. Blinking at the screen, she made out Humphrey Bogart banging on a door with his fists. The time period had progressed to the gangster era. A beautiful girl opened the door, and in a single step she was in his arms, kissing him passionately. So why was he still knocking?

Especially at ten o'clock at night, she thought, taking in the time on the VCR. The electronic buzz of her doorbell shattered her confusion, grounding Sunny in the present. Someone was at her door. She jumped up from the sofa, kicking over the empty ice-cream container and sending the spoon flying under the coffee table.

"Coming!" she called out, as her visitor hammered out another trilogy of knocks.

Standing on tiptoe, she peered out the peephole and jerked

back at the sight of a large eye looking back at her.

"Can I help you?" she asked, caution prevailing over her sleep muddled senses. She'd seen too many crime shows to just open the door to a fish-eyed stranger.

"It's me, Dan."

Dan? Sunny took another look through the peephole. Standing back, Stetson slightly distorted by the round of the glass, stood Daniel Jarrett in the flesh. Sunny's pulse kicked into overdrive, jarring both thought and senses. Her fingers fumbled with the lock. "Wait a...hang on...I—"

She finally pulled the door open and stepped back, as if fitting all of Dan's six-foot-plus frame into her line of view might convince her of what her mind refused to believe.

"What are you doing here? You're supposed to be in Miami."

The corner of his mouth tipped upward as he took in her disheveled appearance. "There's a passel of people there who disagree with you."

"Is Charlie okay?" she asked, failing to grasp the meaning of his words.

"Charlie is stable and doing as well as can be expected after having his chest opened up."

"What people? Why aren't you with your mother?" Questions ran through her mind faster than Sunny could process them.

"My family, who else?" A full grin stretched at his lips. "And Gail is with Mom. Everyone is fine in Miami."

Her questions stopped with the last, the one she was afraid to ask, and yet had to. She swallowed. "Then...why are you here in Houston?"

Dan hesitated, searching. The smile thinned to a wince. "Because I'm not in Miami?" His tone was that of a contestant who ventured an answer, hoping it was the right one.

She knew exactly how he felt. Her heart thudded to a stop, as if its beating might have caused her to hear him wrong.

A door across the hall opened and Sunny's neighbor, a football coach at the local high school, poked his head out.

"Everything okay here, Sunny?"

She resisted the urge to give him the shush finger. Instead, color flushed her face. "Sure, Rob. I...I was just inviting Dan in. He's a friend."

"Sorry I bothered you," Dan said to the man, reaching down and picking up a large suitcase.

"No problem." Rob nodded to each of them, a sly smile easing across his features. "G'night, folks."

Flustered at the look on her neighbor's face, Sunny backed out of the way to let Dan in and called a thanks to Rob as he closed his door.

Dan placed his luggage next to the identical piece Sunny had brought in earlier. One glance at her unexpected guest told her she didn't have the market cornered on embarrassment. He was as red as she felt.

"What gives?" She looked at the two Pullmans that had caused so much confusion on their first meeting.

"There was a baggage mix-up."

"I've heard of history repeating itself, but this is absurd!" She leaned over to check the tags. On pulling back the flap of the one she'd brought in, she read Dan's name and address on it in disbelief. "How could that be? You gave the man my bag. You knew..."

Dan's cat-that-swallowed-the-goldfish expression cut her off. She waited, heart pounding. Now what?

"Well..." The repentant cat needed to clear his throat. "I needed a reason to look you up, and it was the first thing I thought of."

Somewhere inside, the young woman who'd been so down in

the dumps since Sunny walked away from Dan at the terminal warehouse started jumping up and down with glee, but Sunny was afraid to turn her loose just yet. Maybe she should pinch herself— just in case this was a dream.

"A reason…" she prompted, taking this one step at a time. It was the safest course to an accurate diagnosis of the situation.

Dan peeked around the jam of the foyer entrance at the living room. "Mind if I come the rest of the way in?"

"Oh!" Sunny smacked herself on the forehead. "Sorry, I just woke up. I'm a little fuzzy on manners." She stepped aside and motioned him in. "Have a seat. Can I get you something to drink?" Her thoughts raced to her empty refrigerator. There had been a couple of cans of soda.

"Actually, I was hoping you'd share a pizza. We could order one up—everything but dead fish on it, right?"

Sunny looked at him in surprise at the familiar words she always used. "Where did you hear that?"

"Jason shared it during one of our guys-only trips to the pizzeria, and I made a mental note."

He made a mental note of how she liked her pizza? Be still her heart! Shades of Dom Perignon, how suave and debonair could a man get?

"And after a steady diet of crow the last day or so, I figured it'd be a nice ch—"

"Crow?"

"Yeah, well—" Dan broke off, puzzlement striking out his crow-eating demeanor. He dropped down on one of the plump cushions and drew up his foot. Stuck on the toe of his boot was a pint ice-cream container. Her laugh bordering on a hysterical note, Sunny hastily pulled it off. The giggling idiot inside her was going to escape yet.

"Didn't feel like cooking," she mumbled, rubbing the ice-cream remnants off the polished leather with the tail of her T-shirt.

She must have been a little too enthusiastic. Dan put his hand on her wrist, stopping her.

"Hey, I'm the one who should be squirming like a worm on a hot brick, not you."

Stunned, she looked at him. "What?"

"I was an idiot. You were right all along." He drew her down on the sofa next to him, still holding her hand, as if he thought she might try to get away. "The problem was, you had to leave before I could figure out...before I could tell you."

"You got the report that Charlie was for real, not the bum you thought?" *Lord, please don't let us raise hatchets over that again.*

"No. I took your advice and stopped listening to myself and started listening for God. I wanted to tell you about it and, I admit, I was still kind of seesawing with it, but when you hit me with that betrayal of trust bullet, I stalled."

"I didn't mean—"

"No, you were right. I did something I'm not proud of. I betrayed a trust given to me by a man who needed help, not deceit. I practically ruined my family's holiday. I acted like a total jerk."

Sunny couldn't help it, she jumped to his defense. "You had *some* reason. And I should have been removing the plank from my eye before I tried to help you—"

Dan put his fingers to her lips. "Look, I started apologizing first. Stop interrupting." At Sunny's startled look, he laughed. "I know it's hard for you to be quiet and not try to *fix* me, but try, Nurse Elders. I've been a boil on the backside of my family and I need to drain."

Sunny made a face at the allegory. "That was pitiful."

"But you get my drift, so just sit tight and be quiet."

Drawing up her bare feet beneath her, Sunny leaned against the back of the sofa. "Okay, lance away."

"I was wrong about Charlie. He's a fine man."

"So you did hear from the agency."

"I called the investigation off."

Sunny couldn't believe she was hearing right. He'd been so determined to get those reports...

"You said God would show me if I asked. Well, I know now that even though I had asked, I wasn't paying attention to anything I didn't want to hear." He looked down and away. "Quite honestly, I wasn't so sure God was even speaking to me since I'd stopped thinking much about Him and started dwelling on poor pitiful me."

"Oh, Dan." She wanted to reassure him that God never stopped talking to His children, but he spoke again.

"Reverend Stuart started preaching on trust, and you turned and looked straight at me. When I saw Mom going through the same thing she'd suffered when Dad was on his last leg instead of relying on her past experience of losing Dad, she knew everything was going to be okay because God had assured her it would." Dan shook his head. "Let's say I got His message and more besides. It hit me that if she knew Charlie was going to be okay, she also knew that the man she married was decent. Heaven knows, her judgment and communication with the Man upstairs has certainly been better than mine of late. So, I started looking at Charlie with an open mind and he...well, he just seemed different."

He ran his fingers through his hair. "No, I was different. For the first time my eyes were open and not blinded by my own agenda." His broad shoulders rose and fell with his effort to explain. "I don't know if I'm making sense, but I felt like God was trying to tell me something with all this. I don't think I really trusted in anything or anyone since Dad died. And it just got worse when Mom moved out." He sighed. "I just let my horse go fickle on me."

Sunny threw on mental brakes. "Huh?"

"My prayer life, my spiritual life—" Dan explained with a sheepish grin—"I didn't work it every day. I stopped going to the ranch...you know, the spiritual one that rounds up souls."

Always the cowpoke, heart and soul, Sunny mused with a smile. "It's easy to do... lose faith or avoid the ranch when you're left alone, or at least when you feel like you have been." She'd come so close herself. God, however, had prepared her. He'd armed her with an unsinkable sense of humor that might go under for a while, but always managed to bob her spirits back up to the top. She picked up the empty ice-cream container on the coffee table. "It can drive you to eating whole pints of ice cream in one sitting."

A laugh shook Dan from deep inside, forcing the cloud of confusion and despair that she'd brought home from the tropics up and away. The way Dan looked at her made Sunny feel as if she held the Nobel Prize in her hand, not a battered ice-cream container.

"Lady, you are something else. My instinct was to run the other way after our first meeting, but I couldn't help myself. I just had to see what was going to happen next in the wacky world of Sunny Elders."

"But I didn't even wear any of it this time," she protested, basking in the warmth of his encompassing gaze. "Unless you count what I wiped off your boot."

"Now I know that my being drawn to you was just another message from above, and I was ignoring it because I was fixated on proving Charlie Meyers a fraud." He shook his head. "Like that would take the sting out of my miserable existence, instead of the dose of sunshine I really needed."

Sunny stared at him. Was Dan talking about a vacation...or

something more? Was he saying what she *hoped* he was saying? Her mouth went dry as he reached across the short distance between them and took her by the arms.

"I knew I couldn't let you walk out of my life, Sunny. It was no accident that you and I kept being thrown together, and you know what? It *is* possible for two people to meet on a cruise and fall in love, just like Mom and Charlie. Because that's what happened to me. I'd fooled myself into thinking that you needed me, when the truth was just the opposite. I needed you."

Dan's words bounced off the walls of her mind, stirring all semblance of sense and reason into a state of unparalleled giddiness.

"Fact is—" he leaned so close that she felt the warmth of his breath on her lips—"I've stooped to stealing luggage, and all because you stole my heart."

He kissed her, a tentative brush, as if waiting for a signal that she might feel the same way. The gleeful female within refused to be ignored any longer and threw Sunny into Dan's waiting embrace. There was no more room for doubt or hesitation, only overwhelming joy. She didn't know who kissed whom, nor did she care. Dan loved her. He needed her.

"It *had* to be you," he whispered raggedly a moment later against the beating pulse in her throat. "I think I knew it when I hauled you out of the water on that horseback ride like a half-drowned kitten who'd bitten off more than it could chew. I was just too hung up on my own problems to listen to my heart."

Short of breath herself, Sunny leaned away to look into his eyes where flecks of amber glowed, stoked by intimate reckoning. His embrace would allow no further distance between them. The silly man, she thought, balancing somewhere between delirium and ecstasy as he locked her to him. As if she would try to escape from heaven.

"Or maybe it started when you knocked my hat off on the plane and gave me that ear-to-ear smile." He gave her a peck on the nose. "I just couldn't get away from you fast enough, and the more I got to know you, the less I wanted to."

An ear- to-ear smile. At that moment, that was all Sunny could muster, given there didn't seem to be anything in between those ears. Thoughts and feelings were suspended somewhere near the ceiling, dancing in euphoria.

"It had to be a freckle-faced, pug-nosed pixie with a name to match her personality."

Eat your hearts out, beauty queens. I'm about to swoon in the arms of my own tall, dark, and handsome hero.

Any other time, Sunny might have smacked herself for her catty thoughts, but she didn't want to wake up, just in case she was dreaming. She wasn't, was she?

Dan saw the alarm settle on her face.

"What's the matter? Are you—*ouch!*"

He angled back, disconcerted by the tweak she gave his arm. "What was that for?"

Sunny smiled sheepishly. "I was afraid I might be dreaming."

"But you pinched *me*."

"Well, if it was a dream, *I* certainly didn't want to wake up."

Laughter kindled between them. Then another kiss, and another, and another. Somewhere in between, a promise was made—vow of commitment and trust and love. Sunny didn't hear it spoken, but many realities existed beyond the scope of the five senses, God among them. As He was with them.

And where God was, there was always commitment. And trust. And love.

Epilogue

One Year Later

DAN RUSHED INTO the kitchen to answer the ringing phone, leaving Sunny to finish unpacking the little Thanksgiving ornaments he and his sister Gail had made when they were little. Their mother had kept them carefully wrapped in the attic, bringing them out for each holiday until last year's Thanksgiving cruise.

"It's a tradition, hon," he explained to Sunny when he showed up in the bedroom with them first thing that morning, still uncombed and unshaven, his robe hanging off-kilter from his impulsive trek to the attic.

She took each one out, smiling as she read *Dan* scrawled in a grade school hand on the Crayola-colored tail of a pine cone turkey. There was still a lot of that boy in the man, the way he'd grinned sheepishly as she opened the box to look inside. She placed the turkey on the pine sideboard, then placed the stuffed pilgrims Gail had made on either side of it.

Dan's love of family and tradition was one of the first things Sunny fell in love with.

A year later, she was his wife and their families were celebrating as one with a cooperative Thanksgiving dinner, followed by a seven o'clock service at Sunny and Dan's church. They both were as excited as children at Christmas to be hosting their first official gathering of the clans.

"Sunny, it's Mom. Do we need any more pies?" Dan called, drawing her back to the present.

Sunny stuck the empty box in a drawer and rushed into the kitchen to share the phone with her husband. "Hi, Mom. We're good on desserts. Remember, you two are retired." She swatted away the soft breath Dan blew in her ear. "Besides, Melinda has been on a baking spree since the fall bazaar. She baked over twenty pies and cakes herself, so just bring your appetites."

Sunny had to admit that having Melinda, the homemaker extraordinaire, as a guest was a little intimidating, but she didn't care. Her sister was back to her old self and that was all that mattered. Last summer, when Melinda and Alan had spent a week with them up at the hunting cabin near the falls, they acted more like the newlyweds than Sunny and Dan.

"Yeah," Dan said, taking the phone back. "Tell Charlie we took care of your mail and that check he was looking for."

"You've come a long way, baby," Sunny remarked aside, poking her husband in the ribs. Dan grimaced. Who would have thought a year ago that after Charlie recovered from his surgery, Dan would agree to administrate his stepfather's affairs so that the retirees could travel all over the country in their deluxe motor home?

"Tell Charlie the dividends are better than last month. I never will see you two again if you use all that for travel."

Sunny would never forget Dan's face when he'd seen how much Charlie made each month on interest alone from his lifetime of investments. Being a man of few needs and no family, Charlie had had no one to spend his money on until Esther came into his life. Over the years his funds had accumulated to a considerable estate. Dan confided to Sunny that he tasted crow every time he made a deposit for his stepfather, still ashamed of how stubborn and judgmental he'd been.

It finally came out that another Charlie Meyers in Daytona was the fraud whose creditors, among them the IRS, had frozen Dan's stepfather's accounts. The records were further convoluted by the similarities in their social security numbers. Naturally, Charlie was reluctant to share this with his new family. It was bad enough for him to have to confide in his new wife, even though the problem was through no fault of his own.

His Florida attorney was still taking care of remnants of the mix-up, but Charlie asked Dan and Sunny to handle their mail in Texas when he and Esther were away.

"Gail, Mike, and little Hannah will be here around three, so you'll beat them by an hour," Dan assured his mom. Putting his hand over the mouthpiece, he asked Sunny, "What are they bringing?"

"Vegetables and enough baby paraphernalia to stock Babies 'R' Us."

Dan repeated Sunny's answer to his mother. "Which is another reason you needn't moan about grandchildren to Sunny and me...at least not anytime soon."

Hannah Lynn Madison was born on Charlie's birthday and would never want for anything in her life according to the proud grandfather. He still carried that ridiculous photocopy of her sonogram, along with her hospital picture, in his wallet.

"Sunny and I are happy to spoil Hannah until the ranch is paid off."

"It's only a three-year note, Mom," Sunny said, forcing her way to the phone again. "Gail and Mike can have the first shift of grand-kids. Once we're debt-free, we'll take the second."

She leaned against her husband, listening as Esther reminded her son that they didn't have to wait for anything. But Dan was proud and had refused his parents' offer to forgive the money he'd borrowed from her estate for some additional land that came on the market a few years earlier. He wanted to make it on his own, and Sunny was much of the same mind.

"No, just bring your appetites like Sunny said. She's doing the turkey and stuffing. Yeah, I know, I can hear the static. I'll see you in a few hours. Drive safely."

Dan hung the portable phone on its base and turned his full attention to Sunny, trapping her against the wall as he bent over and nuzzled her neck with a throaty growl.

"You *do* know how to cook a turkey, don't you?"

"I've helped my mom do it many times," she managed, dis-tracted by the playful nibble on her ear.

This close to her husband, she could roll that bird, patty-cake it, and throw it the pan with one hand tied behind her back. His arms were a refuge to come home to after dealing with other people's emergencies for eight to twelve hours at a stretch. His lips were anesthesia for every ache known to this woman, and his hands could drive the cares of the world from her mind until he and only he possessed her senses.

Dan gave her one last nip on the earlobe and stepped away with a reluctant sigh. "I guess I'd better feed the horses." The way he looked at her, horses were the last thing on his mind.

"I guess I'd better stuff that bird," she said, with an equal lack of enthusiasm.

He walked to the door and slapped his Stetson on his head. "I never had this much trouble gettin' out of the house in the mornings till you came along, Mrs. Jarrett."

Mrs. Jarrett. It had a definite ring to it.

Sunny turned back to the turkey. She hadn't lied about helping her mother prepare the centerpiece of the Thanksgiving table. Her mother deftly handled the carcass, while Sunny rubbed oil and seasonings on it. Of course, this was the first time Sunny had ever dealt with the bird on her own, one on one.

Then again, she'd prepared turkey breasts, and on occasion, one of those turkey loaves. The only difference here was weight.

Sunny squared her jaw. If petite Melinda could do it, so could her tomboy sister. With a grunt, she hauled the twenty-four pound bird from the refrigerator and plopped it on the counter.

A few minutes later, Sunny stood in a lather from extracting the bird from its net and vacuum-sealed package and wrestling its flopping wings behind its back as she dumped it into the porcelain roaster. She stared at the giant carcass with a trepidation that something, even in death, required that much restraint. If its legs hadn't been locked by those plastic handcuffs, it might have gotten the best of her. As it was, when she peered into the dark breast cavity to be certain she'd taken out all the miscellaneous parts stored inside, a wing broke loose from its bind with a rigor-mortis snap and narrowly missed her eye.

Sunny had an entirely new respect for her foremothers, who'd had to kill the feathered beast as well as strip it, gut it, and cook it.

The plastic binding around the legs had to come off. As a child, she'd seen her mom pop them out with no problem, one drumstick at a time. Piece of cake. With a determined set of her jaw, Sunny seized one joint between two fingers and tried to free it, but in one gristly slip, the clasp had both her thumbs as well. She frantically disengaged her trapped finger, but the thumbs belonged to the bird.

"Dan!" she yelped, dragging the demon-possessed fowl, roaster and all, across the table. She tried opening the door with her sneakered foot, but it just slid around the knob.

"Okay, Tom—" she glared at the cold bird cuffed to her like an escaped inmate—"We've got to get this thing off." She yanked it out of the pan and opened the door with elbow grease—literally.

"Dan!" she shouted at the top of her lungs from the porch. "Dan! Help! Da—"

Her husband burst through the opening of the barn door in a dead run for the house. At the sight of Sunny standing on the porch, giant turkey swinging in front of her, he stopped short.

"What *are* you doing?"

Sunny mustered a pained grin. "The turkey and I are stuck on each other." She held up the bird. At least now she was relieved of the bulk of the weight by grasping its legs with her free fingers. "It tried to dislocate my thumbs. Better get wire cutters."

Dan closed the distance between them and took a closer look. "Who took *who* prisoner?"

"Yeah, yeah. Just cut this thing. Amputate its leg, whatever…I'm losing circulation."

"Where's the camera?"

"Dan! I'm nervous enough with everyone coming without them knowing I was bested by a dead turkey. Wait. I've got surgical scissors in the bathroom."

"Aw, honey, they love you because you made me the happiest man in the world, not because of your cooking."

Sunny glared. "Look, Jarrett. This plastic is cutting my finger every time I try to pull on it. No wonder they started making handcuffs out of this stuff."

With the flair of a hero in a black-and-white movie, Dan brandished his penknife. "You'll cut me with that."

"Not if you stand still and stop waltzing with the bird. I'll have both you turkeys free in no time."

"Stick *your* finger in here and see if you can stand still while someone with a bramble-chewing grin waves that thing around at your fingers."

Dan put his hands on her shoulders. "Trust me." There was laughter dancing in his russet gaze, but there was also that I-love-you-and-it's-going-to-be-okay look. Sunny felt its warmth spread through her, enough to warm the cold bird as well.

Easing the blade of the knife into the thicket of thumbs, drumstick, and plastic, the dull side to her flesh, he pulled up with easy stroke. The blade, worn into a curve from constant sharpening, sliced through the band easily, freeing cook and the turkey.

As the bird dropped, they both reached to catch it. Dan was quicker, but Sunny was a head knock behind him. She straightened with a yelp, rubbing her forehead with the back of her arm.

"You okay, hon?" Dan was trying to be concerned, but it was obvious from the way his lips worked to stay straight that a good laugh was ready to pick him up and shake him at any moment.

Sunny glared at him until the humor of the situation was bigger than the both of them. They laughed, joined at the heart and the funny bone. As Sunny finally gained control of herself, she shook her head. "I'll never hear the end of this one."

Turning, she pulled open the door for Dan to take the turkey inside. Retrieving the pan from the floor, she held it while Dan dropped Tom Turkey into it.

"You just need to show it who's master," he proclaimed.

"Now I have to bathe it again."

"Just give it a shower."

To demonstrate, he took the pan to the sink and began to hose down the turkey, washing off a straw it had picked up from Dan's jacket in its escape attempt.

"Are you done in the barn?" Sunny asked as she began to rub on some olive oil, per instructions in her recipe book.

The dressing was a mix. Working extra shifts at the local hospital so that she could have off for the four-day weekend and family visit hadn't left room for much preparation, but the beds were freshly changed, all the towels were washed, and the house was clean.

"Yep. I'd just finished when you hollered. I thought the house was on fire. Why didn't you just leave that contraption in place till the turkey was cooked?"

Sunny looked blank. "I thought it would melt and give everything a plasticky taste."

Dan shrugged. "I think Mom cooked it bound and gagged. Besides, that pop-up thing that tells when it's done is plastic."

Sunny hadn't thought of that. She felt color creep to her cheeks. "Wait a minute, Mr. Galloping Gourmet. How'd she stuff it with its legs crossed?"

It was Dan's turn to look stupefied. "From the neck?" He lifted the flap of skin and both of them peered into the cavity.

"Nope," they declared in unison.

"I feel like I've worked a double-shift already." Sunny wiped her forehead with the back of her arm. "Face it, I'm not Julia Child in the kitchen."

"Who cares?" Dan walked up behind her and, slipping his arms around her waist, brushed the back of her neck with his lips. "You know, Mrs. Jarrett, rescuing a damsel in distress makes a man feel feisty."

Sunny giggled. "Everything makes you feisty, Mr. Jarrett." She sidestepped his groping reach. "Besides, that feistiness is going to have to wait until tonight. We've got to get this turkey in the oven. They take forever to cook, I think."

"Or we could just stand right here and kiss until it's done."

As if to prove his point, Dan turned her and claimed her mouth with his own. Sunny's toes drew up inside her sneakers, digging into the soft innersole. Given the warmth that flowed from his lips to the farthest reaches of her body, he might have a point. Her knees began to melt in the onslaught, going soft as the stick of butter she'd melted earlier for the dressing.

"The turkey," she mumbled against his lips, resisting the urge to weave her greasy fingers through the thick russet brown of his hair. Sticky with oil, she held them flared away from his head, but whether they signaled protest or surrender remained to be seen.

Dan pressed his forehead to hers. "I have a plan."

The devious quality of his tone caused a quiver in her tummy. "Oh?"

"Let's shove this bird into oven. Mom and Dad won't be here until noon. The others aren't due in till one or so. The house is clean. My chores are done—"

"But shouldn't we baste—"

"This bird can do without us for an hour." Dan's gaze was as mischievous as Sunny felt. "And we'll stick some foil on top. It can't burn with foil."

The idea was sounding better all the time. Sunny rinsed off her hands and grabbed up a pencil and piece of paper.

"What are you doing?"

"I have to figure the cooking time."

Dan snatched the pencil away and tossed it on the counter. "You just cook all day till suppertime."

He pulled her to him and kissed her again. Would she ever get over this heady sensation? Sunny hoped not. It was enough to make her forget the world, much less a cold, unruly bird. But she couldn't. The multitudes were coming.

"Okay, start grabbing these containers and sprinkle them over it," she said, gasping for breath.

Dan looked wary. "*All* of them?"

"Yeah, just a little of each."

In a few seconds, the turkey was coated with salt, pepper, and a myriad of other condiments from the spice cabinet. Dan grabbed the foil and tore off a large sheet.

"What about the proctoscopy?" Sunny asked.

"Huh?"

"The stuffing."

With the speed and grace of the hunter, Dan upended the bird, pulling its legs apart.

"Okay, nurse, the patient is prepped."

Heavenly Father, bless this poor bird, Sunny prayed, dumping the stuffing into the body cavity and packing it with a spoon.

While Dan tucked the fowl back into the pan and covered it with a foil blanket, Sunny yanked open the preheated oven and slid the roaster inside. They both closed it with a bang.

"I hope it's going to be okay," she said, peering through the oven door at the aluminum-encased blob that was to be their dinner.

"The patient is just fine," Dan assured her, snaking an arm about her waist and pulling her to him.

"What are you doing?" Sunny shrieked as he hefted her off the floor.

"Going to get a head start on Thanksgiving."

"Whoa, Dan," she hollered as her head narrowly missed the table. "I don't need a concussion."

He put her down, as if he'd come to his senses.

She pursed her lips primly. "And what about the mess?"

"It'll keep."

Before she knew it, Dan caught her midriff with his shoulder and heaved her up, fireman style.

"This caveman mentality is shameful." Sunny steadied herself by grasping his belt as he started up the steps. The interplay of his muscles filled her with a primitive response that thrilled her. When her husband was playful, there was little choice but to join him. He was irresistible at his most devious.

Inside their bedroom, he put her down and gave her a bone-melting grin. "After all, this is our anniversary."

Sunny gave him a quizzical glance. "But we got married on Valentine's Day."

He hooked his thumbs in the waist of her jeans and pulled her to him. "But it was Thanksgiving Day that I knew."

"Knew what?"

"I knew without a doubt that of all the women on the boat, or in the whole world for that matter, there was only one for me." He kissed her on the tip of the nose, which was an accomplishment, considering she was floating on air. "And, Mrs. Jarrett…"

Mrs. Jarrett. She loved it when he called her that.

"Yes, Mr. Jarrett?" She nuzzled his nose like a lovestruck Eskimo. It was truly a day for Thanksgiving. *Heavenly Father, thank You for putting this man in my life.*

"It *had* to be you," Dan told her huskily, first with words, and then with his lips, his touch, his heart, and his soul.

Dear Readers,

If you noted my dedication, you saw it was to my family and traveling companions. This was not a frivolous gesture. Indeed, many of the "disasters" that happened to Sunny and Dan have actually happened to me or my "dedicatees."

I have my daughter to thank for that horseback ride. I wanted to tour a plantation home like any self-respecting author incorporating research with leisure. (I changed the horse's name to protect the innocent.) My friends took that wild taxi ride across St. Maarten and back in an attempt to catch a plane. Yes, the driver actually took in his laundry. My mom, son, and I—it was Mom's idea—were caught in a revolving door on a family cruise while spying on my high-school graduate daughter and her admirer. Exploding balloons, breaking coolers, cabins the size of phone booths…been there, seen it, or done it.

My writing colleagues have long pleaded with me to incorporate some of my misadventures in a book, so this one is for them…and for you. With it comes a message that hangs on a plaque in my mom's kitchen: "When life gives you lemons, make lemonade."

We had a choice, dear hearts. We could have lamented ourselves sour over how our life and plans were ruined by lemonlike experiences, but we chose to stir them with laughter and share the brew.

May it refresh both heart and soul.

Lyda Windsor

SHE WAS A FUGITIVE IN SEARCH OF A HERO...
THEN, ALONG CAME JONES

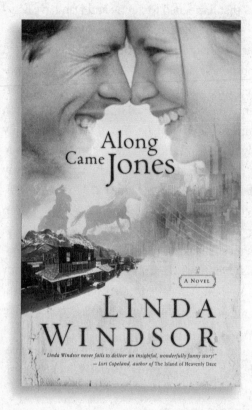

"If DEA agents, nasty bad guys, a sweet, vulnerable heroine, a wonderful, handsome hero, and a powerful message of faith and encouragement are to your liking, run out and buy a copy of Along Came Jones. You won't be disappointed."

—THE WORD ON ROMANCE

Framed for a crime she didn't commit, in flight from the law and a crime syndicate, New Yorker Deanna Manetti is so lost in the Montana wilderness that not even God can find her—or so she thinks. When trail outfitter Shepherd Jones runs Diana's car off the road, the ex–U.S. Marshal isn't sure what to make of his comely stray. Instinct says this duchess of disaster is on the run and needs help—a girl like her can't last long in the boondocks of Montana. But is Shep willing to risk his life and his heart to offer her the same refuge God once provided him? Love and laughter blossom at Buffalo Butte until the past catches up with the unlikely pair, placing their love, their faith...their very lives in jeopardy.

ISBN 1-59052-032-7

Along Came Jones by Linda Windsor

In spite of Deanna's confession, Shep had a niggling sense that he still didn't have the whole story. Or maybe his uneasiness was the result of the protective instinct she evoked in him. Taking in strays was a weakness of his, but this was a woman, not a cat or dog. Although, her spit and huff reminded him of a kitten, trying to intimidate for all it was worth out of fear. It was natural to want to coddle and reassure her.

And quite possibly dangerous. He must have taken leave of his senses to let her stay at his ranch, much less offer her a job. The more he thought about it through the meal and a second cup of coffee, the more convinced he became. Deanna Manetti was definitely on the run and afraid of whoever was after her. The physical threat didn't bother him nearly as much as the emotional risk.

Despite her appeal, she was like his ex-fiancée—city born and bred. And like Ellen, Deanna minced no words regarding her opinion of Big Sky country. As soon as she excused herself to go to the restroom, he slid out of his seat and headed for the old-fashioned wooden phone booth located between the restroom doors.

For all Shep knew, cultural and social differences could have been the issues that broke the proverbial camel's back between her and her estranged boss/boyfriend. She was here out of desperation, he decided as he dialed a familiar number.

"U.S. Marshal Service, Holloway speaking."

"Don't tell me you're still around, old-timer," Shep teased his longtime friend. "I thought you'd have hung up your six-guns by now."

Bob Holloway had run into the same sort of physical disability problem as Shep had, except his friend chose to take a desk job rather than leave the service altogether. Shep couldn't blame him for taking a sure thing rather than chasing a dream with a wife and five kids to support.

"Well, if it isn't the big game hunter. How are things in the high country?"

"Beautiful but troublesome." Shep glanced a few booths away where Deanna took her seat again. Maisy chatted with Deanna while she indulged in a slice of one of Town Diner's home-baked cream pies. The waitress insisted that it was on the house, a welcome to Buffalo Butte gift.

"Sounds more like a woman than an elk."

"It is. I need you to check out a Deanna Manetti—New York City, maybe Brooklyn with her accent…moved to Great Falls for a job with Image International. It's a marketing firm, I think."

"That it?"

"I have a license number and car to trace." Shep fumbled through his wallet for the note he'd made and gave his friend the data.

"Nice," Bob drawled. "A high-price city gal. You must have a weakness for the type."

"Once burned, twice shy. I just want to know what I might have to deal with," Shep explained, as much for himself as the man on the phone. "She's not been forthcoming with information. Claims she's running from a possessive boss/boyfriend."

"Don't tell me you've taken her in."

Wryness tugged one corner of Shep's mouth. "Didn't have much choice. It was *my* stallion that ran her off the road, even though she was on my property."

"And you felt obligated—"

"Yeah, yeah. Just call the sheriff's office in town and have him contact me when you get the info, okay, buddy?"

"Watch your back," Bob cautioned.

"I usually do."

The warning prompted a distracting rush of unwelcome memory. Shep hung up the phone, snatched back to a time he'd tried to forget. He'd been so busy watching his back, and that of the witness in his custody, that he'd failed to see what the DEA agent assigned to the joint operation was doing. Before Shep knew what was going down, he'd taken a bullet in the knee while protecting a female snitch.

A full-scale gunfight had broken out. The other agency hadn't bothered to tell the Marshals that the witness assigned to their transport and protection was being used as bait to draw out the big fish. His gung-ho partner got a promotion. Shep got an award and forced retirement from active duty.

He'd returned to the high country to reconcile the bad turns in his life. Psalm 18:33 became his mantra: *He makes my feet like the feet of deer, and sets me on my high places.* There Shep reevaluated his life, his love, and rediscovered the closeness he'd once known with God, before his busy life had come between them like a time-stealing, attention-grabbing predator.

Was Deanna Manetti a different kind of predator, either by design or by chance? Barely healed himself, Shep struggled with the inner voice that urged him to take her in. Why would God put another woman in his path after the last one had come between them?

Shep opened the folding door of the age-darkened phone booth and met Deanna's smile. It wasn't an invitation, but there was a part of him that wished it were. It was that part of him that scared him more than the possibility of some gun-wielding, jealous boyfriend.

Lord, lead me not into temptation, he prayed as he stepped up to the table and took the check. "Well, Slick, are you ready to hit the road?"

Nodding, Deanna gathered up the small purse from the vinyl seat beside her.

"Don't you forget the community hall meeting Friday night," Maisy reminded him. "Bring Deanna too. Maybe she can come up with a way to stir more interest in our Craft Days fund-raiser."

Even though he was committee chairman, Shep had forgotten. Deanna was disrupting his life in more ways than he could count.

"Better watch out for this one," Shep said to Deanna, with a sigh. "If the government had Maisy O'Donnall on their interrogation team, she'd unravel the secrets of the criminal world like a crocheted blanket."

Maisy snorted with indignation. "I'm just bein' friendly to this nice young woman. Not that she'd have a secret to her name."

Was that a check of alarm Shep detected in the deep pools of his guest's eyes or the shot of sunlight reflected on the diner's shiny door opening to admit a new customer? Reservation clouded over his playful humor as he followed Deanna to the checkout. He hoped he was mistaken.

The Fires of Gleannmara series

Maire ~ BOOK ONE

A fanciful, romantic tale of passion and faith that invites readers to the "God-graced mountains and plains" of Ireland. Maire, Gleannmara's warrior queen, finds her fierce heart is gentled when she takes a reformed mercenary—a Christian, no less—as hostage during a raid. At first she wonders what kind of God would make a fine warrior like Rowan of Emerys such a coward. But as she comes to know Rowan and witnesses the force of his beliefs, she learns that to the one true God meekness and humility are stronger than any blade of steel. And in the process, Maire discovers the transforming power of love and faith.

ISBN 1-57673-625-3

Riona ~ BOOK TWO

Riona, a gentlewoman of faith, discovers that her plan to help the disadvantaged includes not only the plague orphans in her charge, but the arrogant, handsome adventurer who feels honor-bound to save her and her lands by marrying her—with or without her consent. Lord Kieran of Gleannmara depends on nothing and no one save his wit and skill with steel, but soon a deadly twist of fate forces him to acknowledge his need not only for the lady Riona and her worrisome entourage, but for her Lord as well.

ISBN 1-57673-752-7

Deirdre ~ BOOK THREE

A Saxon pirate prince, loyal to neither God nor country, is skeptical of his Christian mother's predictions about his birthright...until he captures a devout princess with the key to both heavenly and earthly kingdoms. What his mother said about his true birthright seems possible after all, even when his new-found faith is battered by storms of betrayal that wash him and his half-drowned bride upon the seaswept shores of Gleannmara. Deirdre, the third heroine in the Fires of Gleannmara series, is an Irish princess wed to a heathen thief. Although she is a reluctant heroine, compassion becomes her shield, prayer her sword, and God's Word her direction.

ISBN 1-57673-891-4

MAIRE by Linda Windsor

"The Scots have landed! There's smoke rising over the ridge as we speak!"

Rowan ap Emrys assessed the chaos in and around the villa. Perhaps they could settle the outcome with shrewdness rather than by risking lives.

He turned to his bailiff, Dafydd. "Have the men form a line between me and the villa and hold it while I meet the raiders."

Rowan was glad Dafydd did not suspect the palm-wetting fear and dread threatening his cool demeanor at the prospect of taking up his sword again. The Scriptures said to trust in God, but they also said not to tempt Him.

"We will let God decide whether we have to use our swords or not."

Dafydd snorted. "This, from the man who singlehandedly turned away a Pictish attack—"

"My sword was my master then, Dafydd."

"And one to be feared, I'll swear by that."

Rowan glanced at the first of the painted warriors amassing on the hill. *Merciful Father, give me my sword to save lives, not take them.*

If saving his people meant bloodying his sword, then so be it. Thankfully, his words were free of the shared rage and anticipation of conflict infecting the men behind him. "Pray, good fellows. 'Tis a stronger weapon than swords."

Rowan believed this in his heart, but he could not feel the assurance of which he boasted. Indeed, the greatest challenge was not the hordes amassing in the distance, but to practice as he preached: to rely on God to make his plan work.

It was decided. The battle would be decided by a fight to the death between two champions: Rowan ap Emrys and Maire, warrior queen of Gleannmara.

The sun had reached its pinnacle at the start of the contest.

Now it dove like a phoenix of fire in the shadowed sea behind the western hills. Darkness was all but upon them, and still Maire had gained little more against her opponent than a few scratches. Time and again, Emrys's God managed to turn her opponent's flesh to air before her quickest thrust.

Not that the forces conjured by Brude's song had not done the same for her. Twice she'd felt the wind of Rowan's sword as it narrowly missed her neck. Her agility and speed were all that saved her. No, it was not the druid's gods Maire doubted, but herself.

She had used all her welltutored tactics...all but one. Maire gasped for air, her lungs screaming with the effort even as she did so.

"Give it up, little queen. Surrender your sword and return to your home."

"Never!" she managed through clenched teeth. The taste of surrender was too vile to consider.

"I'll not kill you, Maire."

"Then you'll die yourself."

Raising her sword, she lunged at Rowan. His defensive parry felt as though it shattered the bones in her arm.

"There must be a way to settle this without separating your head from that comely body."

Although Emrys offered words of reconciliation, his raised sword belied them. Maire fell back, escaping the deadly, whistling path of his weapon. Thrusting her blade upward as the man charged over her, she felt the engagement of flesh. Twist as he might, he could not avoid the hungry bite of her steel.

A scraping of metal collapsing against metal registered as his full weight dropped upon her. Maire struggled to gather her senses beneath the felled man. Something was wrong. Her sword lay sandwiched between them, instead of protruding from his back. Somehow its blade had been deflected! There was no room to move, much less use the weapon, pinned as she was by his weight.

Was she to die and leave her people to Morlach's dominion after they'd rallied so bravely to her side? At any moment, she'd feel Rowan's fingers about her neck, and she had no strength left to resist.

"I'll surrender my sword, little queen, if you give up the notion of taking my head as trophy."

What? Surely, he'd not offered his sword to her in surrender when victory was firmly in his grasp!

"I'll go myself as your hostage to prove my word true. My sword will be yours as long as you fight for what is right under my God's eye." His breath was hot against her ear, as ragged as her own.

"You'll swear loyalty to Gleannmara?" His sword would be an asset, especially if she were to battle Morlach for it—which she'd do or die trying.

"And to its queen, so long as she asks me to do nothing against my God's will."

If his God hated evil, He would see Morlach put in his place. And Maire would need the help of all the gods she could muster.

"As my husband?" Why hadn't she thought of it before? If she married another, Morlach would have no grounds to press her further in the king's eye.

Rowan's surprised laugh shook her from thought. "You ask too much! Why would I take to wife a painted vixen with sword as sharp as her tongue?"

Humiliation boiled in Maire's blood, fortifying her waning strength. She snaked her fingers between their bodies, and the long, thin blade of her stinger came loose.

"We marry, in name only, of course," she added as she pressed the razor sharp blade against Rowan's skin. His wince was barely perceptible, but it was enough.

"May I ask why this sudden proposal?" He grated the words out.

"I need a husband to be rid of a troublesome suitor. You need your head."

"Then I don't see where I have much choice."

"I'd have your word in your God's name," Maire added, somewhat offended by his decidedly reluctant concession. After all, it was *he* who'd admitted aloud she was comely.

"You have my word in the name of God, the Father Almighty, Creator of heaven and earth, that I will take you as my wife."

Maire shook her head. "That I will take you as my husband," she corrected, gaining satisfaction at his deepening scowl.

"However you wish to put it, milady."

"Then give me your sword...carefully." Her fingers closed about the hilt of Rowan's sword. It was still warm from his grasp. A surge of nearly lost triumph welled in her chest as if to explode like heaven's own thunder. Praise her mother's gods, she'd won!

The bards would sing of this in centuries to come, after all. She was just gone eighteen. She'd beaten a seasoned warrior in battle. She found the answer to Morlach's threat and secured the tribute with the same blow.

She held up Rowan's sword to the ecstatic approval of her clansmen. Floating on a cloud of triumph, Maire was unprepared when Rowan suddenly seized her in his arms and kissed her soundly on the lips.

As he released her, only the rising heat of embarrassment thawed her frozen state. Indignation grew to a roar in her veins, but before she could land a retaliatory blow on his smirking face, the Welshman caught her wrist and raised her arm along with his own as if they shared the victory.

"Mother and friends, I give you my bridetobe! God keep us all."